CASCADIA

AND

THE GREAT PANDEMIC

A NOVEL

by

ED STRUM

REMDUST PUBLISHING
Cascadia, Copyright © 2024 by Ed Strum
All Rights Reserved
ISBN 978-0-9913897-9-7

CASCADIA

AND

THE GREAT PANDEMIC

A NOVEL

Acknowledgements

I wish to extend my appreciation to Tom Steers for his technical consultation in the early stages of development of the radio play (The Burrow) and his subsequent comments and suggestions.

Many thanks also to Leslie Brown, Heather Couthaud, Jim Hooper, Jim Jacobs, Sandra Geist, and Brad Strum for their review, comments and suggestions about the plays and the novel.

I also wish to extend my appreciation to Ernest Pugh for his review, support and comments concerning the play, and to Eric Concord for his review and insightful and challenging comments as well.

I wish to acknowledge the influence of Becket, Camus and Kafka and to extend my admiration and respect to them for their creations in their unique genres in bygone eras. Their impact has been universal and lasting.

In writing the novel, my appreciation to Leslie Brown, Heather Couthaud, Sandra Geist, and Jim Jacobs for review and comments.

Books by Ed Strum

THE CONNOISSSEURS – A Play

MONTOBA: THE PRINCESS OF ÉLEVÉ – A Novel

THE BURROW – A Play

JOURNEY OF THE SCROLLS – A Novel

JOURNEY OF THE SCROLLS – SPECIAL EDITION

THE PRINCESS OF ÉLEVÉ – A Play

EVERY DAY IS A GOOD DAY – A Play

THE HOLLOW PENCIL – A Play

CASCADIA and THE GREAT PANDEMIC – A Novel

ADAM'S ARK and THE GREAT PANDEMIC– A Play

RICHIE – A Poetic Play in One Scene

A SENSORY FEAST – An Anthology of Prose Poetry

CONTENTS

Prelude
PART ONE – DEADLIEST VIRIONS
Prologue – 5 AP (After the Pandemic)
One: Sly – Early Winter, 5 AP
Two: Grace – Early Winter, 3-5 AP
Three: Adam – Early Winter, 2-5 AP
Four: Adam and the Virions – Winter, 6 AP
Five: Sly – Spring, 6 AP
Six: Grace – Spring, 6 AP
Seven: Adam and Grace – Late Spring, 6 AP
Eight: Che – Winter, 5 AP
Nine: Sly – Late Spring, 6 AP
PART TWO – THE BURROW
Ten: The Barn – Late Fall, 6 AP
Eleven: Danger Approaches – Early Winter, 6 AP
Twelve: Che – Early Winter, 6 AP
Thirteen: Che and Sly – Early Winter, 6 AP
Fourteen: Che's Mountain Trip – Early Winter, 6 AP
Fifteen: Searching – Winter, 6 AP
Sixteen: Finding the Outside World – Winter, 6 AP
Seventeen: Danger in the Blizzard – Late Winter, 7 AP
Eighteen: Moving – Late Winter, 7 AP
PART THREE – ADAM'S ARK
Nineteen: Executing the Plan – Early Spring, 7 AP
Twenty: Loading the Ark – Late Spring, 7 AP
Twenty One: The Open Sea – Summer, 7 AP
Twenty Two: Entering the Strait – Late Summer, 7 AP
Twenty Three: The Blizzard – Early Winter, 7 AP
Twenty Four: Reaping and Sowing – Early Spring, 8 AP
Twenty Five: New Life – Summer, 8 AP
Twenty Six: The Growing Community – Summer, 10 AP
Twenty Seven: Major Projects – Summer, 15 AP
PART FOUR – THE EXPANDING WORLD
Twenty Eight: The Great Sailing Adventure – Early Spring, 22 AP
Twenty Nine: Sailing Around the Horn – Spring, 22 AP
Thirty: Visiting Tristan – Late Fall, 22 AP
Thirty One: Returning Home – Late Summer, 23 AP
Thirty Two: Returning to Tristan – Spring, 32 AP
Thirty Three: Tristan and Home – Spring in North, 33 AP
Thirty Four: Visitors from the Sea – Spring, 42 AP
Thirty Five: The Castaways – Late Summer, 43 AP
Thirty Six: Cascadia Achieved – Spring, 57 AP
Epilogue: The Unknown – Spring, 107 AP

CASCADIA

And

THE GREAT PANDEMIC

And God saw that the wickedness of man was great in the earth. The earth also was corrupt before God, and the earth was filled with violence.

And the Lord said, I will destroy man whom I have created from the face of the earth; both man, and beast, and the creeping thing, and the fowls of the air; for it repenteth me that I have made them.

But Noah found grace in the eyes of the Lord. (The Lord said) But with thee will I establish my covenant; and thou shalt come into the ark, thou, and thy (family). And of every living thing of all flesh, two of every sort shalt thou bring into the ark, to keep them alive with thee; they shall be male and female. And take thou unto thee of all food that is eaten, and thou shalt gather it to thee; and it shall be for food for thee, and for them.

And God blessed Noah and his (family) and said unto them, Be fruitful, and multiply, and replenish the earth.

Genesis, Chapter VI, IX.

PRELUDE

It was the wettest of times. It was the coldest of times. An old black pickup truck followed the twists and turns and bumps of the dirt road for many miles, deep into an isolated canyon. It was in the dead of night and the only light came from the truck's headlights. The heavy rain, mixed with hail, came down in sheets and was turning to snow. The road was soon a quagmire of puddles and mudholes. It was bitter cold, and the wind rocked the truck back and forth as Ted tried to keep from veering off the road into the heavy brush. Rolling thunder shattered the silence of this isolated valley. As Ted approached a long low building with a metal roof and siding, a solitary figure darted out from the single door in the middle of the building, jumped on a motorcycle and sped past the truck and down the road. Ted parked the truck at the edge of the gravel parking lot, jumped out, and watched the tail lights of the cycle disappear into the distance. The darkness was complete. The rain mixed with hail and snow increased, and the strong wind blew the new snow across the gravel and into the brush. Ted turned on a flashlight and started walking toward the entrance.

Suddenly a flash of lightning lit up the sky and scored a direct hit on the metal roof. The lightning flickered and rolled across the roof and down the side. Ted stopped in his tracks for just a moment. From inside the building, a quick flash of light was followed by an explosion that blew off one end of the structure. The door opened and a man staggered out into the snow and wind. With his right arm, he was dragging a woman. He stumbled across the gravel lot toward two cars parked side by side, and then looked toward the flickering of the flashlight. He turned just when a huge explosion blew the metal roof into the sky. George let the lifeless body of the woman drop to the ground, pitched forward, and collapsed in the beam from Ted's flashlight. His face was bloody and his left arm dangled at his side.

"I think she's dead," George stated without emotion.

Ted dropped the flashlight and bent down to the woman.

"Angie. Angie!" He screamed and shook her. Then he dropped his gaze to the frozen ground. Ted turned to George.

"She was the reason I came all the way out here. What happened?"

"We had an accident, a break, a few days ago," George responded. "She breathed it in before she knew what was going on. It's a more virulent strain of pneumonic plague we developed. She didn't want to go to a hospital because that would cause questions about the lab. She's been getting weaker and weaker until she just couldn't breathe anymore."

Ted took a step closer to try and help the bleeding George get up.

"Don't touch me," George yelled, "get away from here quickly."

"What happened? What's wrong?"

"Necrotizing fasciitis."

"What are you talking about?"

"Flesh eating bacteria. I need a doctor."

"I'll get you to the hospital."

Ted lifted him up and helped him into the cab of the truck.

"That's not all," George said, "yersinia pestis as well, all three types."

"Jesus! What's that?"

"The plague. Septicemic, bubonic, and pneumonic plague. That's what got Angie. It's free to spread now."

"What on earth is this all about?"

Ted looked around as if he suspected eavesdroppers.

"Our lab way out here. We have experiments." George stopped talking and started coughing violently.

"I can't leave Angie lying out here." Ted picked Angie up and put her in the back of the truck. He scooped up the flashlight and jumped back into the driver's seat.

He then covered George with a blanket, and drove away. The snow was beginning to pile up in drifts on the dirt road. He hoped to drive the ten miles to the nearest hospital before the roads were completely covered with ice and snow. The glow of early dawn began to light up the sky.

"Tell me about that lab," asked Ted, "everything."

George stared out the window and spoke quietly.

"Our job has been to study all seven categories of viruses and virions and look for ways to increase their virulence, their power," he began slowly, "this is a very secret lab and activity." He coughed now and then while telling this story, got his breath back, and was able to continue. "You may not know about these categories of viruses but they have been established and studied for some time. We set up experiments for each category."

"Who knows about you? Who funds you?"

"Only a couple of people in the government actually know about us. When they set this lab up, no one knew what it was for. Then Angie and I were given the task of setting up experiments. A third scientist named Henry just joined us a couple of days ago."

"Where is Henry now? Was that him dashing away just now? On a motorcycle?"

George opened his eyes wide and stared at Ted.

"He did? I don't understand. I thought he was still in there, and was killed in the explosion."

"Why would he run away before the explosion? You say he just joined you? What do you know about him?"

George was silent and his mouth dropped open. His coughing returned and his breathing became very labored.

"Nothing actually." He became lost in thought.

Ted continued.

"We were afraid of this."

"What do you mean?"

Ted hesitated, then explained, "It was Angie that alerted us. I was sent to investigate her suspicions."

"What are you talking about?" Although weak from coughing, George's voice was strident. He was indignant.

Ted answered, "I think you have been sabotaged."

"Sabotaged? Who would do such a thing? That's terrible. We were making such good progress. All our work gone. And Angie's dead." George began to sob and then stopped. He was having trouble breathing.

There was silence for a moment, then Ted asked.

"These viruses you mention. Will they all just die now from the explosions?"

"Some will," George answered, "but many of the animals will survive and escape now, unfortunately."

"What animals?"

"Rats, mice, birds, bats, and of course, the fleas on them that carry the virions. They'll survive, along with the pathogenic bacteria and other viruses."

"And spread?"

"Yes. They are free now. And the viruses have become much more powerful. Lethal. And some form aerosols and travel on the wind."

Ted was silent for a moment. His gaze scanned the dark landscape. *So much lost,* he thought, *so much beauty, love, brilliance.* Tears came to his eyes as Angie's face swam into his mind's eye. *She was so beautiful.*

"Rest for a while until we get to the hospital. You'll need your strength then."

Ted continued to drive in silence as the snow grew heavier, and the going was very slow. As he came around a sharp curve, the truck nearly ran over a man lying in the middle of the road. It was Henry. His motorcycle was lying in the thick bushes by the side of the road, already partly covered with snow. Ted jumped out and ran to him. He was barely alive and unconscious. As Ted put Henry in the back of the truck and continued on, he realized the man had stopped breathing.

As he drove, Ted's gaze started to cloud over. After driving for fifteen minutes, he was gripped with a bout of shivering, then another more violent shaking. Ted lost control in the deep drifts and the truck slid into a ditch. His head hit the windshield and he began bleeding slightly from a wound to the head. His left arm smashed against the steering wheel and

4

was dangling down. The pain was excruciating. He got out to check the situation and realized that he would not get the truck out of the ditch. He climbed back into the seat and noticed George seemed to be sleeping. No, he wasn't breathing. He had succumbed to the disease. Whatever it was, it was powerful and lethal. Ted knew now he was in terrible danger.

He decided to walk the remaining couple of miles to get help, rather than stay there and die from exposure to the plague, or freeze to death. He plunged ahead in the growing blizzard, trying to follow the road as it was rapidly being blanketed with snow. The strong wind blew in his face, and as he struggled on, he realized it was becoming difficult to breathe and slowed his pace. He had covered much of the distance and saw a dim light far ahead. It was a small house. *Perhaps he could find shelter and tell his story,* he thought.

He approached a lighted doorway, gasped, and pitched forward, striking the door with his right hand as he fell. An elderly woman opened the door and looked down at the still form.

"John, come quickly, there's a man lying here!" she cried. "He's not breathing. Oh, John!"

The couple dragged the lifeless body inside.

"He's dead, Alice."

The couple keeping vigil did not know the horrible truth: that Ted's knowledge had died with him that night. Strong winds rattled the windows as the snow piled up. The electricity failed and Alice lit candles. The temperature dropped and the couple tried to keep warm with blankets. The snow and wind continued for two days and nights.

It would be many days before the truck and its occupants would be found, or the tragedy at the lab discovered, and by then the many animals carrying virulent diseases had scattered, and the fleas would have multiplied, the winds would have blown spores far and wide, and the plague would have spread to the vastness of the countryside.

Alice and John lived in isolation and near darkness for four days until they were able to report the death of Ted. The next day they were visited by three men, dressed alike in white Hazmat suits, who had found the abandoned truck and the bodies. They visited the lab, and then imposed a quarantine on the site, setting up a gate on the road far from the lab, and an armed guard. Days later, not by coincidence, similar labs in the Middle East and Far East, Europe and the Americas, received similar fates. A biological lab in western China, one in Siberia, another in Iran, and one in the Amazon jungle were all sabotaged and blown up, spreading similar pandemics throughout the world. This was the beginning of the Great Pandemic.

PART ONE

DEADLIEST VIRIONS

PROLOGUE – 5 AP (After the Pandemic)

The weather grew colder each year, and the rain seldom ceased. Lightning strikes hit many abandoned buildings, starting uncontrolled fires that spread rapidly by the winds that blew incessantly across the desolate land. The rivers were swollen and gradually eroded the banks, broke through dams, flooded fields, and toppled trees. Houses and other buildings along river banks broke apart and fell into the surging currents, changing the terrain forever.

There were few signs of living human life and yet life continued. Hungry dogs roamed freely, forming packs as they returned to the primitive behavior of their ancestor wolf, hunting small prey and deer. Cougars increased and came down from the mountains, spreading across the flat terrain, devouring sheep and goats that wandered freely. Horses became wild and cows suffered terribly. Wild animals survived and increased in numbers, and domestic ones diminished or became feral. The population of rabbits increased rapidly, providing food for foxes, eagles, harriers, and other predators. Mice, moles, shrews and voles, as well as rats, increased as well.

With few people alive to fix dams, and bridges, and roadways, the waterways returned to the way they had been hundreds and thousands of years before. The strong winds blew roofs off of houses and other buildings, smashed windows, and knocked many dwellings down. Other buildings just collapsed after months of incessant decline. Floods ravished river banks, toppling trees and collapsing houses. Fields became overgrown, roads were torn apart and covered over. It was the beginning of a new world, or some would say it was the return to an old world, a very old world. Along the ocean shoreline, the heavy seas pounded the cliffs and flooded the lowlands, taking back the land in huge chunks as coastline cliffs toppled into the surf taking with them house after house, no longer cared for by man.

Massive earthquakes along the Pacific rim created enormous tsunamis that raced across the surface to the shores, rising high above walls and dunes and even cliffs, devouring all in their paths, in some cases inundating land for miles inland. The combination of tsunamis surging into rivers and the heavy floods from incessant rain destroyed most of the buildings along the river banks, and the bridges broke apart and crashed into the raging waters. Inland, lightning strikes created massive fires that raged unchecked by man, reducing all in their paths to ashes.

In spite of all the destruction, the signs of man were still there. Many abandoned gas stations, super markets, houses and barns and shops, remained, but were dilapidated and often partially destroyed. In cities, office buildings and apartment complexes showed inevitable signs of decay, ugly, unpainted, with blown out windows and unkempt gardens. Warehouses and factories were much the same. Many had been looted, windows and doors smashed in. Most of the buildings were overgrown with vines and tall bushes and trees and scarcely visible. Highways and side roads and fields were all overgrown as well. Ships at dock were disintegrating and many were blown loose and drifted about and into the channels and rivers and seas. Train tracks were not attended and a long train carrying logs and various supplies had fallen off the rails, toppling onto its side, with ivy crawling through its wheels.

The winds knocked down trees and buildings and wires and soon there were massive power outages. Eventually all electricity failed, cars and houses and power plants ran out of fossil fuels and darkness gradually descended upon the land. Typhoons and hurricanes smashed against the coastlines bringing huge amounts of rain to the rivers and land.

Fires from lightning strikes raged out of control reducing entire cities to rubble, and huge forests to ashes. Huge storm surges from enormous ocean waves pushed into rivers and bays and inlets and inundated low-lying land, destroying every building and bridge created by man in their path. Nature was slowly taking back the land from the hands of man who had altered the world. It was five years from the first signs of the Great Pandemic that spread from town to town, from state to state, from country to country, bringing death at an increasing rate, skyrocketing into the millions each day.

The hospitals were initially overrun with cases, the various diseases spread rapidly, doctors and other medical staff perished, and governments spread misinformation to try and cover up the enormity of the Great Pandemic. It appeared any vaccines developed at the labs were also destroyed, by the saboteurs it was thought, or by inexperience, or by corruption, and could not be replicated quickly enough. In the first year more than thirty percent of the world's population expired, and by the end of the second year more than three-quarters of the population died. There were no longer any organized governments left and lawlessness took over the globe. After five years of the pandemic, civilization had vanished, and only pockets of humans existed. Most of them slowly starved to death.

Although signs of human life had receded or vanished in most places, there were also no corpses or cadavers, or even bones. As people perished, they rotted or were eaten, or their bones were chewed on. The cold winter snows covered the bodies for a time but the remains were soon reduced to bones, and then to dust.

Over the course of five years, the diseases spread rapidly and took many forms. Some immediately affected the brain or other internal organs and people died a quick death, or in some cases, a slow painful death. Some had rapid loss of muscle control or loss of control of the nervous system. Others had respiratory infections, loss of breath, coughing up blood and a speedy death. The few survivors gave various names to the diseases based on what they were similar to: Black Death, Spanish flu, smallpox, yellow fever, scarlet fever, pneumonia, ebola, the various flus that had names, and a variety of cancers. Those that could not point to a specific similar disease just called it the plague. But soon the survivors also became ill. Those that could help the sick dwindled and soon the sick and dying were left to die alone. Individuals fled families and communities to save themselves from the pestilence but it was generally for naught. They too became ill and soon perished. Others spread disease by fleeing to communities that were not yet sick and brought disease and death with them.

One of the last newspapers to be printed before the printing presses shut down told the story: a headline jumped out at two people stranded on the highway as they picked up the windblown front page.

"Look Alice," said the man, pointing at the headline.

It read "Last physician in San Francisco dies; people dying by the hour in the overcrowded wards."

"It's hopeless Ted," she replied, "we're out of gas and no one is on the roads anymore."

They got back into their car and awaited their destiny together, cold and exhausted. They fell asleep together as the wind blew incessantly across the lonely landscape.

The few other helpless and starving survivors agreed that these virions were much more virulent than those known previously but could not identify them. They also agreed that there were many different diseases or viruses and that most seemed to spread by contact with other humans, by wind, from vermin and flying insects, and from animals. Doctors tried desperately to save some and other doctors and scientists tried to identify the diseases, but they soon became ill and died, and the civilized world descended into chaos. Some people somehow survived but then succumbed to cold or starvation or exhaustion. Some fled from civilized contact and tried to avoid a similar fate to their brethren but often became weak or sick from lack of food or shelter and soon died a lonely silent death. It was the possible extinction of mankind at hand. But there were a few that survived against all odds.

On the west coast of the country, that had been called the United States, strong winds blew incessantly from the Pacific Ocean, the clouds rolled in continuously obscuring the sun, the temperature dropped, the tides were extraordinarily high, and the storm surges pushed water up the rivers and inundated the low coastlines. Giant waves surged in from the ocean into a great river located in the pacific northwest of a once-great nation. The wide mouth narrowed gradually going upstream as the river followed an easterly direction until it headed south for many miles, and then it resumed an easterly direction. At this point, approximately one hundred and fifty miles upstream, the growth along the banks was lush and thick.

One of those that survived was Sly. She had left her dying community hundreds of miles south of the big river five years before when the great pandemic began to decimate the population. She moved inland where population was sparse, traveling slowly on foot, and staying away from centers of population. Sly headed north away from evil and death and disease, or so she thought. She had befriended a few people along the way but soon found that they too were infected with disease and she fled in horror. She had become terrified of the possibility of contracting another disease. Shortly after beginning her journey, she had once been ill but somehow survived, then regained her strength, and continued on her journey. She was determined to find a safe haven.

Sly hoped to find others who were not ill and were not evil minded. But her first goal was to survive, and she needed to find food and shelter as she travelled north. She could not explain why she was travelling north but somehow felt it would be safer the further she went from the death she had seen in the south. Sly had ransacked a couple of stores to acquire what she felt she needed for a long journey. At an Outdoor World which had been left largely intact, she found a sturdy backpack, a sleeping bag, a warm jacket, shoes, a small portable camping stove, a large pot, matches, and dry food, which she felt was still nutritious and edible.

One day, Sly pushed into an abandoned supermarket for canned food and packaged pasta. She heard the rustle of mice and rats that had invaded before and shivered at the sounds. Armed with sufficient food, she marched north, following a small river. Every so often, a small stream flowed into the larger river, and it was this water source she felt was the safest to drink.

Before the pandemic, Sly had had no experience camping. But now, at twenty-one years old, she was learning new skills – survival skills. She'd had to – she had watched her friends give up, or fight with each other over food, and all had died, one by one. She finally fled in horror, determined not to succumb as all the others had done.

In this way, Sly slowly made her way north, covering several hundred miles, stopping often to rest, to eat, and to sleep. The journey was arduous as she covered rough terrain some distance away from a major highway now overgrown and littered with debris from winds and rain. She soon wore out her jacket and shoes, and her sleeping bag was in tatters. Her stove no longer worked and she was out of dry food. She needed new clothes, food, a sleeping bag, a stove, and even another backpack. She had endured several hot summers and very cold winters, never seeing another soul, never finding what she thought would be a safe place to stop, and was near to giving up. She wondered aloud why she was taking this direction, and began to doubt whether she would survive much longer. Yet another winter was approaching and Sly yearned for the company of others and a safe haven where she could stay for a while.

One night, as darkness approached, she spotted yet another dilapidated barn along the river. She checked it out to make sure it was abandoned and sufficiently safe, and decided to rest there for several days, to ponder her decision to travel north or to try a different direction.

The barn had a leaky roof where several roof slats had been ripped off by the wind, but she stayed away from the holes above as well as the opening. She also saw evidence of mice and rats, and also saw a barn owl in the rafters silently watching her. She smiled. She knew she had an ally. But she realized that her spirits were low, and she was becoming more and more despondent. She was physically and mentally exhausted.

She knew she did not want to continue the way she had been travelling much longer, and she knew she needed some rest and to think things over. She crouched between a couple of hay bales, ate some of her dry food, and drank some water before falling asleep. She left some of her dried meat and bread out for the owl as a token of friendship, and in case the owl had not found enough meat otherwise. The wind increased and the rain came through the opening in the roof and through some of the side slats but she ignored the noise and curled up in her sleeping bag for a sound sleep.

Sly woke up once to the sound of a meow, and a small kitten came close to her. She offered it a bit of meat and some water to drink but it kept its distance. Sly fell back asleep and woke up to the sounds of the kitten drinking water. She listened to the rattle of wind gusts against the loose boards on the sides of the barn and again fell asleep. She was exhausted and slept several hours.

Sly woke up in the dark and felt something next to her sleeping bag. It was the kitten curled up to keep warm. She named it Pandi. They both slept until the wind rattling the windows woke both of them. It was still dark and not yet daylight. Sly looked carefully at Pandi next to her. She was a multi-colored cat that seemed to be very affectionate. Sly patted her and she began to purr. Her spirits lifted and she knew that she and Pandi could carry on. Her strength returned and now she had another reason to survive. *Pandi's a Bengal,* thought Sly, *very smart. Feral. Just like me. A survivor.*

CHAPTER ONE

Sly - South of the Great River

Early Winter, 5 AP

Sly woke up shivering in the cold of the winter night. She had taken refuge in this abandoned barn that was still standing. It was a short walk from a small meandering stream she had been following. The wind whistled around the corners of the barn and rattled the windows. It was dark in the upper loft. The clicking of the wind driving the rain against the metal roof had a rhythm of its own. She pictured the wild countryside at night, the windswept pastures, the shrubs and bushes barely visible, and visualized the many pastures and corn fields and barns for miles around, bleak and barren in the dim light from the moon and the stars trying to break through the clouds. She heard the "hoo-h'HOO-hoo-hoo" of the great horned owl and pictured it hunkered down on a branch looking for a meal. There were many mice and voles in the fields so that owl would not go hungry. Whether that would also be true for herself and Pandi was another matter.

With winter approaching, Sly decided she needed to take time to replenish her food and clothes and supplies. She started to leave the barn and realized that Pandi followed in her footsteps, letting out a soft meow. Pandi did not want to be left alone so Sly put her into the top of her backpack. The truth was that Sly didn't want to be alone either. Sly wandered each day in a different direction from the barn to gather what she could. She dug up potatoes and carrots and onions, leeks and radishes and parsnips, turnips and even garlic, and stored them in a cool spot in the barn. She also collected apples and plums and pears from trees before they fell to the ground and rotted. She ransacked stores for food that was still likely to be viable for cooking on her stove. Her easiest and least favorite meals were dried packets that she could add water to, that would become soup or a meat dish or fish. She also found beef jerky in some stores, a treat for herself and Pandi. She intended to wait out the winter. She had been traveling for days wearing just ragged shorts and a tattered t-shirt, so she raided an abandoned clothing store for jeans and a warm shirt and jacket.

During another day she had visited an outdoor sport store in a small town and acquired a new sleeping bag, as well as another pot to boil water, a new portable camp stove, and fuel. She spied some dry camping food packets for later when she ran out of fresh food. On her third day, she found a sturdy backpack and heavy-duty shoes to replace her worn lightweight shoes.

Four days after discovering the barn, the skies cleared in the morning and the sun came out briefly. She had not had a bath for some days and wandered down to the edge of the stream with Pandi following her. She kicked off her shoes, dropped her ragged shorts and tattered t-shirt, rinsed them out, and hung them on the edge of a small bush. She kept on her belt, which held a long knife shaped like a dagger in a holder. She slid slowly into the cold water but it was refreshing nonetheless. She ducked under, washed her hair, and came up sputtering. She stayed under with the water up to her neck. It was wonderful. She was just about to come out when she heard distant voices. The ground offered nowhere to hide. It was open grassland and low scrub bushes from the river to the barn and she realized she would be seen if she dared to try and run.

The voices sounded closer. Two men were walking along the river bank. She tried to hide behind the small bush but one of the men saw her.

"Well, Joe, what do we have here? Lookee! Lookee!" The short heavyset man turned to the tall thin one and pointed at Sly. She stayed under the water as they approached.

"I think we should take a closer look, don't you?" The tall one moved toward her. He approached swiftly from one side of the bush and the short man from the other as Sly stayed under the water next to the bush. She reached for her knife in the holder.

The short man jumped into the water first.

"Don't worry, dearie. We won't hurt you. We just want to be friends." Then he lunged at her. She moved aside and stabbed him. He screamed and fell into the water. She pushed his body out into the moving stream. The tall man was moving toward when Pandi dashed out from the bush and bit his ankle. He yelled and lost his balance as he was reaching for Sly. He saw her holding a knife and tried to move back but his momentum carried him into her. Sly stabbed him as well.

She pushed him into the moving current. Shaking, she watched their bodies float away. They'd been the first ones she ever killed. Then she began to cry. She quickly climbed out, put on her clothes and ran back to the barn with Pandi behind her. She had no idea if the men were alone but took no chances. She made sure all of her food and clothes were hidden and then sat on a bale and wept. Pandi sensed her distress, nuzzled her and meowed. Sly held Pandi in her arms and they touched nose to nose. Pandi understood. This was the closest Sly had come to violent danger and she was shaken.

In the evening, she hooked up the camp stove and fuel canister and cooked a few root crops with dried meat. Sly curled up in her sleeping bag with Pandi beside her.

"Oh, Pandi," she said, "what have I done? I had no choice. I never want to do that again."

Pandi let out a soft meow as if she understood.

Sly thought to herself *I'm so afraid that this may not be the last time I have to defend myself.*

They slept soundly for several hours. She woke up in the middle of the night to the sound of rain pelting the roof and sides of the barn. Then she heard the heavy sound of hail pounding the roof. This lasted another hour and then it was silent. She slept fitfully for another couple of hours and then saw the dim light from early dawn streaming through cracks in the side. Pandi nudged her chin and rubbed her face with her nose. Sly peeked out to a winter wonderland. Snow had covered all the bushes and fields, and everything in sight. *It was beautiful*, she thought. Perhaps the world was not so bad after all.

It was snowing heavily and the wind began to pick up, catching the snow and blowing it into drifts. It snowed all day and through the next night. She was so glad she had stocked up on food. She decided not to go out since she would leave tracks and risk another discovery. She shuddered as she remembered the events of the day. She had had such a wonderful time in the water and it ended so terribly. She vowed not to be caught by surprise and let that happen again.

CHAPTER TWO

Grace - North of the Great River

Early Winter, 3-5 AP

Two years earlier, Grace believed the Great Pandemic, as it was already called, would soon reach her remote location. She finally decided to leave her island paradise and sail north with two of her women friends, Lucy and Marge, who urged her to come with them before it was too late.

"Grace," Lucy said, "Marge and I think that we have a better chance of avoiding this pandemic if we sail north. Come with us."

"She is right," said Marge, "I have heard that this thing spreads quickly."

Soon after Grace left with her friends on Lucy's sixty-foot sloop, the pandemic did reach the islands. It had first spread to her own island from a sloop which had sailed north along the shore of the pacific coast and into the wide strait. The sloop continued up through the wide waterway until it found the entrance to the harbor of her island, and pulled up to the dock. The five on board had contracted one version of a disease that affected the respiratory system. Three of them perished while sailing and were buried at sea. The other two lingered on and were able to sail into the strait and reached the island that Grace had lived on.

Sadly, they perished soon after docking. Some of the inhabitants came into contact with the coughing pair before they were aware of the deadly nature of the disease. It spread rapidly to the close-knit group of islanders. They did not realize how it was spread and soon each of them became ill and weak and soon died.

Grace, Marge, and Lucy took a year to sail slowly north up the inland passage and back, and when they returned, they discovered the tragedy. All on the island were dead or dying. She and her friends sailed slowly to nearby islands and discovered other signs of death and disease. Most of the inhabitants had fled and others had died.

The three of them returned to Grace's island, and docked Lucy's sloop. They gathered more food and supplies, and sailed Grace's forty-one-foot ketch throughout the many islands and discovered that the reports of the spreading pandemic were true. They returned to her isolated island in the north and sought to wait out the pandemic. It was so widespread that it affected all services. A series of storms battered the islands and knocked out all power at the same time. The last news they heard from the mainland was that doctors had identified several virulent diseases that spread very rapidly. With the loss of so much life so quickly, society was thrown into chaos. The feeling by the private isolated residents that everyone had a right to carry arms created a situation where an enormous number of firearms were easily available. With so many guns available, lawlessness became the norm. People were killing each other, looting all sorts of stores, and dying before they could even get to hospitals. Medical staff were diminishing either from death, fear or flight. With no electricity, a darkness settled over the land.

Grace knew her uninhabited island well and gathered what food she could find. The three of them prepared for a long dark cold winter. The island was exposed to winds and rain and snow but Grace and her friends were hearty folk and able to survive the winter. When spring arrived, her friends said they needed to return to Canada to see what had transpired there, so Grace decided to stay and prepare herself to travel south to find her sister, who had been living along the shore of the huge river that flowed into the Pacific Ocean. She pondered her decision as to whether she could sail the forty-one-foot ketch by herself into the ocean and down the coast and into the wide mouth of the river in search of her sister. She decided it was much too dangerous, and decided to travel inland.

She left in the summer on a small thirty-foot sloop that she could sail solo without too much trouble. It was now five years after the start of the Great Pandemic. Grace stowed what food and water and clothes she could fit on the sloop and sailed south through the hundreds of islands. She stopped at various harbors along the way and found no signs of life. She dared to venture on shore a couple of times to seek out either people or goods but left quickly and nervously, afraid in large part of what she might find. She continued sailing slowly through the islands for three months until she reached the southernmost bay of the Sound.

She pulled out a large map and calculated a route inland east of the road that had once been a major highway. She had reached the end of the water way that ran just where the overgrown highway turned inland. She crossed the highway and worked her way on foot away from the water. Grace determined that she had a little more than one hundred miles traveling by land to reach her sister who lived on the north side of the Great River, and more than one hundred miles inland.

This was new to Grace, having spent so much time on islands, and sailing to get around. She worried about finding some better transportation than walking alone on foot but felt she never would have made it sailing solo into the ocean and down the coast. *At least I can stop now and then and sleep and eat in peace*, she thought. She shuddered when she thought of the worst: that her sister had perished along with all the many others. But she felt she had to try. She had seen no one since leaving her island and hoped it would stay that way.

So many people had perished during the five years of the pandemic that the land appeared to be devoid of human life. Grace commandeered an abandoned motorcycle and several cans of gas and decided to see how far she could get. After loading what supplies she could into saddle bags, she travelled on a small side road back to the wide empty highway already somewhat overgrown, and headed south. She could still read some of the markers showing the mileage to the old southern border. That gave her peace of mind to count off the miles but that did not last long.

She ran out of gas about twenty-five miles short of her goal and sought refuge in a small hut a mile off the highway. It was open at one end but she thought she could avoid any rain if it came. And the rain did come down that night. It increased until it was a downpour. The wind picked up and pelted the side of the little hut. She huddled in a corner and tried to sleep but she found it difficult with the strong wind, which drowned out any other noises. Finally, the wind abated and she fell into a deep sleep.

She waited out the storm for several days. She found a bicycle and used that to go a few miles but a flat stopped her cold. Grace sought shelter once again from the wind in an abandoned hay barn. She was exhausted from traveling, climbed up into the loft, pulled the ladder up, and fell asleep, curled up in a corner covered with hay.

In the early morning, she heard a cry and saw a woman her age racing into the barn looking for a place to hide. Before the woman could get out of sight, two men came in after her. One was an unkempt man with wild hair and an overgrown beard and the other was bald and heavyset. They rushed in and cornered the woman. They lit a lantern to see. The woman screamed as the first man pushed her down and started to climb on top of her to restrain her. The second man tried to intervene.

"Not so fast, Hank. We are sharing."

The wild man turned on him with a growl. He pulled a knife.

"Back off, Butch. I saw her first."

There was a struggle and Hank stabbed Butch, who fell to the ground and lay still. Then he turned back to the woman who was still screaming and trying to escape. He hit her and she stopped screaming and stopped struggling. He was tearing at her clothes.

"That's better, dearie." Hank growled and tried to rip her clothes off.

Grace had reached unseen for a pitchfork while this was going on and flung it with deadly accuracy into the middle of Hank's back. He rose up and toppled over, knocking the lantern over. The hay caught fire and spread quickly. The woman sat up and saw the fire spreading quickly. She pulled her torn clothes together trying to fix them and started to run out. She saw the pitchfork, shuddered, and looked around. Then she looked up and saw Grace.

"You saved my life. I was sure he was going to kill me."

The fire created smoke and the woman began to cough. She ran out. Grace could not climb down in time so she kicked out two slats, threw out her backpack and jumped down. The woman helped her up.

"I'm sorry I could not help you down. I can't thank you enough."

"Do you know either of those men?" Grace asked.

"No. There are a few wild men on the loose. I've tried to avoid them but these two ambushed me. I ran but they caught up. You know the rest."

"What's your name?" Grace asked.

"Mary. What's your name?"

"Grace. Which way are you headed?"

"South."

"So am I. Join me if you want, Mary. Two can survive better than one." The woman nodded and they set off together.

CHAPTER THREE

Adam - At Sea

Early winter, 2-5 AP

Adam had been at sea for a couple of years, after he had joined the crew of four on a Nordland sailing trawler headed for the Antarctic. It was a large forty-four-foot trawler with a single square sail. The initial reason for the voyage was to fish, but when the news of the spreading pandemic reached them via another ship, they decided it was wise to stay clear of land. Fishing became a secondary reason to stay out to sea for longer stretches

Earlier, they had been fishing in the Sacramento River delta and met a crew on a ship docked next to them. The members of that crew had encountered signs of many people seriously ill and dying. The word spread that a Great Pandemic of many deadly virions was wiping out thousands of people and there seemed to be no way to prevent the rapid spreading, and the eventual death from the powerful plague.

They sailed down the coast of North America and then South America stopping periodically to fish and occasionally to sell fish and acquire supplies. Soon they realized that death had visited every port they stopped at and they began to stay at sea for longer periods. It seemed to be a worldwide pandemic. It was winter in the north when they left but it was summer in the southern hemisphere. They decided to take a chance under relatively mild conditions to sail around The Horn. They sailed into twenty-foot waves for a short distance but managed to reach the protection of the Falkland Islands.

Once again, they encountered terrible conditions. They stopped briefly to find water and some food but they found no one alive and left in a hurry. They headed for South Georgia and Grytviken and found two people living there, named Pam and Oliver. The couple were unaware of global danger and wondered why they hadn't seen any ships for months. Adam explained what they had seen and heard. It was a year from the time they'd left and winter had arrived in the South. When they first arrived, two of the trawler's crew, Jose and Kiran, showed signs of illness. They were quarantined in case it was one of the virulent viruses, but it was too late. The two faded rapidly, grew weaker and weaker, coughing blood, and finally just stopped breathing. They died in a month, within a few days of each other. They were buried in the cemetery near Shackleton's grave.

Adam and the others stayed for several months with the blessing of the inhabitants. They waited out the snowstorms and heavy winds until spring arrived in the southern hemisphere. The remaining three men, Al, Bart, and Adam, were now short-handed and decided to sail to Tristan da Cunha where Adam had visited before. He knew there were hardy sailors at Tristan. They thought that if the three of them could manage the trawler until then, they could augment the crew with a pair of adventuresome souls from Tristan. They encountered high seas and heavy winds, but after three weeks at sea, they entered the small harbor of Tristan. They were greeted with cheers.

One of the members of the Glass family named Herbert, who remembered Adam, told them that only one ship had arrived in the past year and the crew of the ship had told them harrowing stories of the pandemic in Africa and Europe. Thousands of people perished in an awful manner. Some gasped for breath and collapsed. Others lost control of all parts of the body until they stopped moving. The worst thing reported by the ship was the body being covered with a flesh-eating bacteria that caused the victim to scream in excruciating pain. Some people were put out of their misery. Adam found many of the tales to be too hard to believe. If he couldn't see such things for himself, such as the so-called flesh-eating bacteria, he reasoned that people were going crazy, or making up stories.

Adam described what he and his mates had seen. He asked if any of the Tristanians would like to join them on their return trip. They needed two able bodied seamen, to return the way they had come, fishing in the Southern Ocean on the way to the Pacific. They told the Chief Islander named James Glass that they would seek an island in the Pacific to wait out the end of the pandemic. The Tristanians declined and said they were sorry: everyone was needed to survive since they had lost all of their trading connections. It was as if they had gone back in time two hundred years.

Adam asked if they could trade some of their salt and spices for water and a small amount of meat to augment the fish they caught as they sailed. The Chief Islander said they could spare water since they had lots of it, and they could spare meat from their cattle herd.

The Tristanians wished them well, and watched them sail away and head for the Falklands.

"They have no way to sail away with only small boats. They might survive," Adam said quietly, and wished the islanders well.

"What about food?" asked Bart. "How will they survive without ships bringing in some types of food?"

"They are amazing people," explained Adam, "they have lots of water from the volcano mountain, they have cows on the other side of the mountain, they grow all sorts of vegetables, and they can fish in the sea. They might be short of spices but they will ration those. The one problem I see is that there is no way for them to go to other places in their long boats. They are isolated and have depended upon visiting ships. I wish them well. They are a hardy, healthy multi-ethnic community."

The three of them set sail for the return journey. Adam was the navigator, Al took the helm, and Bart and Adam managed the sails. They had hoisted a topsail to speed them on their way. It was now summer in the southern hemisphere. They stopped briefly at Grytviken and found no one alive. They shuddered and sailed on as fast as they could.

As they approached the Horn, they realized they were being followed by a flotilla of ships numbering in excess of twenty ships. They put up full sails and entered the gale force winds of the Horn. In the poor visibility from the storm, Adam decided to head directly south to escape the pursuit of the ships, which could no longer see them. This strategy worked but the winds and waves were rocking them viciously and Adam turned back to the east until the seas were much calmer. Adam believed the flotilla had continued and sailed around the Horn. They checked all the rigging of the trawler and once again tempted the Horn.

This time they rounded the Horn successfully in strong winds and managed to make it into the Pacific. They decided to sail directly up the coast of Chile and northward, fishing now and then. They covered only a few nautical miles before they saw a lone ship ahead floundering from the battering of the weather at the Horn. They approached cautiously, and realized the main mast had toppled.

Two men stood on the deck of what looked like a yacht, men waving and yelling. They readied their guns and sailed slowly to within shouting distance of the helpless ship.

"Who are you?" yelled Hank.

"We were separated in the storm from the others," shouted one of them, "we could not find them and then our mast snapped. We lost our crew overboard except for two of us. We think the others sailed ahead."

"We are helpless now. Will you help us?" yelled the other in a weak voice they could barely hear. Then he appeared to fall to the deck out of sight.

"What is your mission? Where are you headed?" called Adam.

"North," was the short reply from the one man standing, "are you going that way?"

"What is your mission?" Adam repeated. There was silence and then the first man replied.

"Will you take us on board? We can explain then."

"Do you have the pandemic on board?" asked Hank. Again, there was silence, a long silence.

"It is possible," spoke the first man, "Yanik is very sick."

Adam came alongside the ship with a gun near at hand. There was no sign of others except the two.

"Leave everything there and come aboard."

"I'm afraid Yanik cannot make it. He is fading fast. In fact, he is lying here hardly breathing. I need to attend to him. Please don't leave."

"We won't," stated Adam simply.

They stood by for an hour and then the first man called.

"I need to bury him at sea."

He did so, and then he lowered a small dinghy to row over and come aboard. He identified himself as Noah and confessed that the purpose of the large group of ships was to invade some place, where they could be safe from the pandemic. Adam and the others kept an eye on Noah as they continued north but could not see themselves abandoning him to the sea.

They were forced now and then to stop for water and a few basic items, including any spices and first-aid supplies they could find on abandoned islands. They set anchor in the Galapagos Islands and stayed for a few days. They saw no other ships. They need not have worried about Noah because he soon showed signs of illness. He coughed and began to shake uncontrollably, and had a fever.

At this time, all of the others were also aware of being sick. Adam found an uninhabited island, and docked the trawler in an inlet. They camped ashore for many weeks. Adam and Bart survived and recovered but Al and Noah grew weaker and weaker. They could no longer keep food in themselves and soon died of starvation. Adam realized that these illnesses might not all be contagious since the four of them had different symptoms. This was ominous to Adam since he knew not the source of them. It occurred to Adam that it must be from a certain type of fish that they caught.

Adam began to construct a theory of the worldwide pandemic, or plague, as it was called. It was not one or two or three types of virions but many, that all seemed to have been unleashed upon the world simultaneously. Furthermore, he reasoned, there was at least one type of poison that was aimed at food sources such as fish. And not all the diseases were contagious in the normal sense of the meaning. And not all were lethal, or at least to some people. He felt he had to solve this mystery if he was to survive and find others that had also survived so that they could form a small group to stay alive. He waited several months until he and Bart were strong enough. In the meantime, he rigged the trawler so that it could be sailed solo, with various connections to the helm to manage sails from there. He also set the helm to stay on a given course once set. After all, he reasoned, he might just have to sail solo one day. However, they could never leave the cockpit for long in case they spotted the armada of ships ahead, or for that matter, behind them. Before he died, Noah had only been able to tell them that the purpose of the flotilla was to find a place they could invade with little resistance, a place that was decimated from the pandemic. The group of sailors were fleeing their own widespread plague, and in particular, they wanted to find land they could farm. But he died before he could explain much more about the group of ships and their occupants.

As they sailed slowly north, Adam took the helm and was the navigator while Bart handled the sails. It was more than four years since the trawler had left the Sacramento Delta and Adam wanted to take his time sailing north. He planned to sail even further north in the hope that the northern islands were less impacted from the pandemic. He tried to show a brave front and appear hopeful in front of Bart, who seemed to have suffered a mental breakdown after Al's death, but privately had his doubts about finding any safe haven, and was constantly on the alert for foreign ships. His only hope was that the pandemic had run its course on land and that the flotilla had gone another way such as up one of the rivers flowing into the Pacific. They cruised north along the Baja Peninsula waiting for spring in the northern hemisphere to arrive. They stayed away from all areas that might still be inhabited and put in only in remote areas along the course.

Adam found it strange that they encountered no other ships at all. *The population must be decimated almost completely*, he thought. Millions must have perished. Every so often they turned on the radio for news, but static was their constant friend. They reached what had once been one of the most populous regions in the world: the Los Angeles area. They suddenly saw one ship sailing out toward them.

"Adam, look," yelled Bart, "there's a ship with two masts heading our way."

"It's a ketch," responded Adam, "maybe thirty-five-feet. It's much slower than we are."

Adam did not want to take any chance of disease or evil deranged people and headed out to sea with the wind astern. A shot rang out.

"I just heard a gunshot," cried Bart, "they're shooting at us."

"I heard it too," said Adam, "they're too far away."

Adam knew he had done the correct thing. They soon outdistanced the ketch and then set a northwestern course.

Adam wanted to sail near to the Golden Gate Bridge to see if there were any ships at sea. He had learned from his experience, though; from now on, his exploration would be limited to night, and he would douse his boat's lights first. It was dark when they sailed past the entrance of the river and there were no lights and no sign of life. He kept his course until dawn and found a small cove on the east side of an island to anchor in for the day. The area was overgrown and remote. Tall trees grew along the shore. In the morning Bart complained of being out of breath and wanted to rest a few days until he felt better.

But he did not get better. Adam tried to get him to eat and drink but all he wanted to do was lie down and sleep. Adam covered him and kept watch but he too dozed off. He woke up suddenly and looked at Bart. He was not moving. He checked Bart's pulse. The Great Pandemic had claimed another victim and Adam was all alone.

CHAPTER FOUR

Adam and the Virions

Winter, 6 AP

Adam took stock of his situation after burying Bart at sea. He had enough food and water for a week or more but he wanted to find fresh water just in case the last water they had obtained was contaminated. He also wanted to discover the complete set of virions that had been undoubtedly unleashed from one or more labs, or that had possibly escaped in some horrible accident. What were they? How many were there? What were all the symptoms to look for? What could be done about them other than trying to avoid them? Would they burn themselves out after finding no more "hosts"? Last of all, he wanted to know if any vaccines had survived the worldwide destruction caused by the pandemic and the weather that ravaged the globe, unchecked. There were so many mysteries surrounding this Great Pandemic. His own survival depended on figuring this out.

Another important task Adam had was to begin collecting seeds and bulbs and to start growing food once he found a safe place. And the biggest question of all: how many people still lived? Were most of them evil or were there enough good sane souls left to salvage humanity?

Adam had studied plants and botany and diseases of plants. Viruses, fungi, and insects caused various attacks on plants, but his knowledge of human illnesses was peripheral. Nonetheless, he was familiar with the seven classes of virions and the possible impacts on humans. He also had researched the Black Death, which was truly a worldwide pandemic. What concerned Adam the most was the suspicion that man (certain people) had increased the virulence of many viruses in laboratory experiments, and that some seemed to become more powerful through variants. He noticed how rapidly some people had perished from certain illnesses. He knew that some diseases were spread by human contact, some by mosquitoes, some by birds or bats, some by vermin or their fleas as in the Black Death, some via food or water, and some by air. Furthermore, cancer was caused by various viruses and yet the cause of some of the cancers was still a mystery to man. He pondered the challenge: how to avoid becoming sick when the pandemic had so many causes.

His immediate challenges were how to find safe food and water, how to reach a safe haven for shelter, and then how to grow food. His experiments of sailing solo helped with the second challenge. He sailed north along the coast until he saw the mouth of a huge river. He waited until night to attempt entry and then waited for high tide. He managed to overcome the surge of water from the river as it crossed the bar, and sailed along the south bank of the river until dawn. Adam pulled into an abandoned marina and, as he dropped the sails and set the ropes, he noticed his trawler was leaking. He thought it a wise choice to seek a smaller, safer boat to continue up the river and commandeered a twenty-foot sailboat.

Adam transferred his supplies and continued sailing upstream for several more nights. He encountered a small tributary and sailed up it for half a mile. He spotted a dilapidated barn near shore and decided to wait out the winter. After moving most of his food and cooking equipment into the barn, he wandered into the nearby fields collecting root crops for replanting, and also collected seeds whenever he found them.

Then the rain and wind began. It rained heavily for two days, then the temperature dropped and it began to snow. The wind whistled through the rafters. He noticed a small owl in the rafters and smiled. He felt that was a good sign. Adam hunkered down to wait for spring. Now and then the weather let up and he foraged for more roots to plant in the spring. On one trip outside he noticed the remains of a burned-out farmhouse and a large barn. There was no sign of life anywhere.

But in the fields around the barn, a bounty of food existed: potatoes, carrots (some still with seeds), onions, parsnips, beets, leeks, radishes, even turnips and rutabagas, were all available in abundance.

Adam went out one day when the snow was light. Through the mist some distance away he saw a figure struggling through the deep drifts. He could see it was a woman with long straggly hair. She staggered and plunged forward into a deep depression and disappeared from sight. He moved as quickly as he could through the deep snow and finally reached the spot where he had last seen her. He looked around and saw her lying at the bottom of an embankment leading to a ravine. She was covered with snow, except for her dark face peering through. She was not moving.

He waded down and picked her up. She murmured so he knew she was still alive. He put her arm around his neck and slowly carried her back to the barn. The snow had increased and was almost blinding. He managed to get her into the barn and wrapped whatever clothes he could find around her. She was obviously exhausted and almost frozen. He warmed water while he was trying to warm her up, then gave her a sip of tea and honey. She gulped it down.

"Easy. Easy. It's hot. You will burn your mouth." He watched her drink then asked. "What is your name?"

"Grace,' she mumbled.

CHAPTER FIVE

Sly – South of the Great River

Spring, 6 AP

Sly waited out the winter weather for several weeks, only venturing out at night to survey the landscape. It seemed to her to be desolate, devoid of life, other than a few rabbits, and wandering horses and sheep, now loose. She thought the horses would survive but doubted the sheep would, once wild dogs or cougars found them. The snow stopped and the wind blew it into drifts. It grew warm and the snow melted leaving moist ground. She did not want to travel when she would leave tracks so she waited. One night she decided it was clear enough on the ground and it was time to try to move north, staying away from any drifted snow. Her pack was heavy, laden with some dried food, her sleeping bag, spare clothes, a pot, and Pandi.

Before she resumed her march north, she and Pandi took a short scouting trip in several directions and found no sign of life. As she was returning to the barn, she spotted a figure staggering along the river bank. It was a young man about her age, and he was clearly struggling to stand. He pitched forward and rolled down to the water's edge. Sly approached cautiously and looked down. He was not moving and was so close to the river that one arm dangled in the water. She moved down and lifted his head. He looked up at her.

"Help me," he said.

Sly struggled to lift him up and put one arm around his waist and his arm over her shoulders. Somehow, she managed to haul him up the small embankment and across the open field to the barn. She settled him inside and gave him water to drink.

"Are you hurt?" she asked, "what's wrong?"

"Nothing unless you count starvation." He managed a weak smile. She smiled back and knew he would be alright with that show of a bit of humor. She quietly produced some of her dried food, heated a pot of water and concocted a pot of soup with various dried ingredients and a few potatoes and carrots she saved. He devoured the entire pot of soup and drank more water.

"My name is Shu, but I go by Sly. What's yours?"

"Norman, but call me Norm," was his simple reply.

"Norm, now you need to sleep and get your strength back. You'll be safe here."

"Do you live here?" he asked.

"No, I just stopped here for the winter. I was just about to move on when I saw you fall."

"Where are you headed?"

"North. I hope to get away from the plague."

"I was trying to do the same but I doubt one can avoid it. The death seems to be everywhere."

They talked a few minutes more and he gradually grew drowsy and fell asleep. Sly let him sleep, through the day and the next night. He awoke at dawn and they shared a simple meal. He asked if he could travel with her for a while and she agreed. While he was sleeping, she had quietly done another search for any root crops or fruit but found very little. However, she did enter the camping store she'd found earlier and fetched another backpack and sleeping bag. Sly divided her heavy pack and filled a load for Norm. They were both still pretty heavy since Sly added a few vegetables and some clothes she found in the store. As always, Pandi curled up in the top of her pack.

Norm rested one more day and at dusk on the following night they started out. The sky was overcast so the stars and moon were obscured. The going was slow, and hard work for both of them, but they made steady progress, traveling only at night. Sly could see like a cat in the dark, much better than most people, she realized, so she felt she had an advantage.

One night they came upon a campsite with several wild looking men with scraggly hair huddled around a fire. She would have loved to sit by a warm fire but knew she was lucky to have seen them first. They skirted the campfire and carried on until morning. They found a small shed and stayed the day. The weather still held so they carried on for three more nights until they came to the upper stream of a river. They followed it for several miles and it grew wider. Norm saw a moss-covered sign lying on the ground and overgrown with vines that said Hood River. Sly and Norm had no idea where they were but knew there was a mighty river to the north, so they followed the Hood until Sly spotted a wide river in the distance.

And then it began to snow again. They hurried along the Hood going north and saw a barn close to the intersection of the smaller Hood River with the Great River. They approached and found it to be full of hay but otherwise abandoned. They were out of water so filled up in the Hood River, then entered the safety of the barn. This time they curled up together with Pandi between them, and slept for several hours as daylight arrived. The snow continued and the wind picked up. Norm took the chance of building a small fire to heat the water, then Sly cooked a few of the root vegetables with some dried meat and they enjoyed their first real meal in several days. They were both starved and exhausted from traveling and realized the snow was a blessing in disguise. It would curtail the travel of others if there were any roving bandits or wild men around.

Sly noticed there were no signs of mice or rats. One night when it was virtually silent, she thought she heard a tiny noise and saw some hay moving. Slowly emerging covered with hay was a tabby cat. It took one look at her and dashed back through a hole in the hay. It was silent again. *Now I know why there are no mice or rats*, she said to herself.

Sly and Norm, and Pandi, stayed in and around the barn for several more weeks. One night they decided to explore the south shore of the Great River. A few miles below their barn they encountered a small marina and a sign that read "Columbia River". Sly knew this was the great river she was seeking, and the gateway to the sea. Norm went ahead of Sly and approached the entrance to the marina. When he was within twenty meters of the first group of boats, a man in a red parka, holding a knife, suddenly jumped out from the deck of a small sloop. Norm was unarmed and backed up as the man charged. Norm grabbed a branch to fend off the man. They faced each other while the man tried to figure out how to attack Norm. Sly raced forward to help Norm. She pulled her own knife just as two other men, one short and fat and the other tall and skinny, came out to join the first attacker.

"Norm," yelled Sly, "there are too many. Let's get out of here."

But it was too late to escape. Norm knew they had to fight and charged the first man, knocking the knife away. The other two men held knives as well, and charged, one on either side of their friend, who reached down for his knife. Sly took on the skinny one while Norm backed up, trying to defend against the other two. Sly feinted and stabbed the tall man who staggered away and fell to the ground, then turned to help Norm. He was outflanked and surrounded. Sly raced to intercept the fat man, who turned to attack her. As Sly ducked her attacker, Norm was wounded in the chest and arm by the man in the red parka. Sly charged the fat man, stabbed him, and turned to the man in the red parka The man realized he was alone, and that Sly was a formidable fighter. He charged recklessly but she sidestepped him and dispatched him quickly with a short stab. All three of the men lay dead on the ground. She sheathed her knife and knelt down to Norm.

"I'm done for, Sly," he moaned quietly, "I'm sorry."

"Oh, Norm," she cried, "don't be. I've got to get some bandages and try to patch you up."

"Don't bother," he whispered, "I only wish I could go with you wherever that leads."

"You will, Norm, you will always be with me."

Norm let out a gasp and stopped breathing. Sly was alone once again, except for Pandi. She buried Norm and the three men, and then trudged back to her barn, crying softly as she walked. When she had gone inside, she sat on a hay bale and began sobbing uncontrollably. Recollections of the death of her parents and her sister, to the pandemic, flooded her memory and Sly wept and sobbed in great gulps. Pandi jumped into her lap and nuzzled her neck and chin, her nose touched Sly's, until finally her sobbing subsided.

"You seem to understand Pandi," Sly said between sobs, "you seem to know everything."

She patted Pandi, and then fell asleep with Pandi curled up next to her neck. When she awoke, she ate a good meal, and decided to continue on before she ran into other roving bandits in that area. She had to find a safe place to stay and most importantly, she wanted to reach the sea.

The weather had warmed up a bit, so she hoisted her pack, and headed back down to the marina. She did not know much about sailing but thought she could handle a small rowboat to go downstream. Her plan was to travel down the river to the sea where she thought it would be warmer and she could find fish and mussels and clams and oysters. She imagined she could gather them and have a feast.

It was dusk with a slight moon. Sly loaded a twenty-foot rowboat with her gear, food, and miscellaneous supplies she found around the marina, and pushed off. She drifted downstream and periodically rowed in the direction of the north shore of the Columbia. Four hours later and ten miles downstream she approached the north shore. She rowed silently toward a rocky beach area with overgrown bushes and small trees. She beached the boat, unloaded her gear, and drew the boat up under some bushes to hide it. She loaded her backpack and moved cautiously inland until she reached an open field. To the north and south she could see nothing in the dim light, and gradually made out a house in the distance. Near it was a small shed. She walked slowly to the shed and entered. It was full of tools and a bit musty. She left the shed and moved slowly under cover of darkness to the house and found it deserted. She heard the scurrying of rats and cringed. She decided to avoid the house altogether and returned to the shed. By dawn it was overcast and the wind picked up. Rain pattered on the roof, which was comforting to her.

Sly relaxed enough to make a meal of dried meat (beef this time instead of chicken) and vegetables. She liked potatoes and carrots and onions and usually added parsnips if she had any, for flavor. She had found some tea bags in an abandoned store and made a cup of jasmine tea. She was content for now. She fell asleep to the pitter-patter of rain. She woke at dawn and heard the wind whistling past the shed. Rain no longer clattered on the roof, so she peeked out and saw snow. *It must be the last snow of winter*, she thought. She longed for the warmth of spring. It will be here soon, she thought, as she fell back asleep.

She woke at midday, and felt Pandi sleeping between her feet. She looked outside and saw that the snow had accumulated to a foot, the wind had stopped, and the sun had come out. "It will be a glorious day," she said out loud.

CHAPTER SIX

Grace – North Bank of the River

Spring, 6 AP

As the last beams smoldered in the fire that had consumed her barn hideout, Grace walked south, supporting Mary, the woman she had saved from the marauding bandits. They walked slowly, looking for abandoned stores for food, and clothes for Mary. They came to a small village which showed no signs of human life. A bedraggled scrawny dog came out from hiding, limped across the street, and disappeared between two buildings with broken windows. The wind blew trash down the long empty street.

"I remember seeing the movie High Noon," laughed Grace, "it looks like that here, doesn't it?"

"Yes, but even more like Gunfight at the O.K. Corral," smiled Mary, "with Burt Lancaster against the gang, and Kirk Douglas to the rescue."

"I guess it's my name," said Grace, "but I expect Grace Kelly to stick her head out from one of those broken windows any moment." She stopped laughing and lowered her head in thought.

"I think it looks more like Tombstone." Mary spoke softly.

Grace nodded in agreement. It was like a scene from any number of old western movies they had seen. It was a situation they had become accustomed to finding in town after town.

However, they pushed into a camping store and were able to find dried camping food, and a pair of jeans and a jacket for Mary. They carried on quickly, never sure if they would encounter anyone. The thought of finding another good soul never occurred to them; so many people had turned into feral versions of themselves. They stopped for the night in an outbuilding of a farm that was apparently used to hold hay when the barn was filled. It was empty now but was sufficient shelter for the two of them. They found this shelter just in time as the winter wind picked up. If necessary, they could stay there a couple of days.

Mary told Grace her story of leaving the dead and dying in the small town to the east where she lived. Her old mother encouraged her to leave before it was too late. Her mother was wise enough to see the makings of a pandemic and wanted Mary to have a chance at survival. Mary was her only child, and Mary had no children of her own.

"Go find a nice man in a safe place," said her old-fashioned mother. "Perhaps you can have someone to look after you, to have children, and to make a home. This plague will pass. Go."

Mary did. She traveled west for several weeks with a small backpack. She avoided several wandering wild men and found food in small grocery stores. She decided it was safer to travel at night and find a barn or other safe building to sleep during the day.

"I was surviving well enough until those two men saw me and trapped me."

"I only hope we don't run into any more of them," replied Grace.

"Sometimes I feel guilty," Mary said, "I often wonder how I managed to live for nearly three years with the plague all around. I ask how is it that I was spared surrounded by all that death and agony while others didn't."

Mary coughed now and then and Grace wondered if Mary had indeed survived all of the virions.

"I have also just wanted a home, a safe haven," Grace said, "I have been on the run for several years. I am hoping my sister just south of here is alright."

They waited three days until the weather grew warmer and the snow stopped. Mary coughed much more often and became weaker.

"I wish I could get you to a hospital but I don't think they are operating anymore. We're on our own," said Grace, as she boiled water for rosemary tea. She also used the hot water for eucalyptus inhalation.

Grace kept Mary warm and tried to get her to eat, but Mary was unable to take in any food, and grew weaker and weaker. The weather grew warm enough to travel but Mary could no longer do so. Grace watched helplessly as Mary declined and finally succumbed. Grace wept for Mary and all the lost lives. She found a secluded spot to bury her travel companion, and prepared to move south.

Grace felt she was only a few miles from the banks of the Great River, and once she found it, she could travel along the shore to the north to find the small town where her sister lived. Carrying her heavy pack, she set out at night. It began with a full moon but soon it was overcast, and her visibility dropped nearly to zero. After traveling several miles in the dark, she felt the rain coming down. It grew colder and her light rain cape was no longer enough to keep her warm.

Her heart beat faster with fear as she began to wonder if she would freeze to death in this sudden storm, and pushed on faster until she could find shelter. The wind grew stronger and it became much colder. The rain turned to snow and she found herself in a blizzard. It was late for such weather and it caught her by surprise. She was in the midst of a whiteout. In the very dim light, she saw a building in the distance. She struggled in the snow and became weaker. She lost her balance and toppled into a ravine. She laid there, too weak to get up.

A few moments later she saw a man looming over her. He scrambled down the embankment and lifted her up. She was frightened but her mind swam, and her muscles refused to help in her struggle. He helped her up the embankment and they slowly moved to the dilapidated barn. Once inside, he wrapped her in jackets to warm her up and made some tea to drink. She knew now that she would not die. Thanks to this kind man she would survive and carry on. Her confidence in mankind grew and her courage and strength returned.

After he cautioned her about the hot tea, he asked her name.

"Grace," she replied, "what's your name?"

"Adam."

"I'm pleased to meet you." Grace smiled.

"Likewise."

"Thank you for saving my life." They both grinned.

CHAPTER SEVEN

Adam and Grace – North Side of River

Late Spring, 6 AP

After Grace recovered, and Adam made a nice warm stew, they huddled through the night as the wind whistled around the barn. They spent a fitful night worried about the storm damaging the barn but the wind subsided and they managed a little coffee and a granola breakfast that Adam had acquired.

"I'm not sure this barn will last much longer," Adam said. "As soon as the weather allows, I want to find a stronger barn. Do you want to join me?"

Grace explained her plan to find her sister first. She thought she was east of where they were.

"I want to go east as well. I'll help you look for her. But first let's see if we can find a small boat. We should be able to travel up river a bit faster since this terrain along the shore is pretty rough."

They walked slowly along the banks of the Great River until they spotted a small marina inside of an inlet where some of the boats were apparently intact. Adam checked out several small craft but all seemed to have leaks in the hull or were severely damaged. They finally found a twenty-foot rowboat that he said he could handle. Adam rowed back to the shore of the river near the barn.

They each packed up as much as they could carry in their backpacks, and stowed as much as they could in the boat as well. They rowed slowly east along the north shore of the Great River. On their way, they came to a small river going northwest from the big river. Adam spied a two-level barn close to the river. There was also a small stream nearby. The barn was filled with hay. The soil was rich along the banks of the river. There were tall reeds growing along the bank for several hundred meters, where he hid the rowboat.

"This is a perfect spot," said Adam, "I could plant most of my seeds and bulbs and we could have a crop in a couple of months. I'll dig out the hay to form a room below. It should work for this year until next winter. Would it be alright if I do the planting while you look for your sister? You'll know where to find me if I can help."

Grace agreed. "If I don't come back, you'll understand, I hope. If she is alive, I'll stay with her."

Adam nodded. He would take his chances and hope for her safe return. Adam pressed a flashlight into her hands along with a small knife, which could be used as a weapon if necessary. Grace gave him a hug and Adam responded with a shy smile.

"I hope your sister is alright but I also hope you come back one day."

Grace set off alone at night with a small backpack that included some food, and water. Adam immediately started carving out a small room at the lower level of the hay barn, and then began planting. He picked a protected area along the shore surrounded by bushes and reeds but exposed to sun. Several weeks went by and he continued to expand the room so that it had a large area and a place to build a fire near the side of the barn so smoke would go out through the slats. He made sure all hay was far removed from the stove area. He pulled the hay from two other areas to create small side rooms. Entrance was from above with a sliding tunnel down to the room. He blocked the opening to the tunnel with a large bale and felt his efforts would create a safe concealed habitation for the rest of the summer and fall. It was as permanent as he could manage at this time.

Many weeks went by and one day he heard Grace calling his name as he was continuing his planting efforts. She appeared with tears in her eyes and her shoulders slumped. He suspected the worst and he was correct.

"There was no one alive. My sister died two months ago. I saw her grave. The last ones alive apparently left for the south. There was a sign posted. It was grim."

"I'm sorry." Adam replied.

"I will take up your offer to stay here. I have no place to go now."

Adam gave her a big hug and she held him for a moment. At least they had each other. He showed her his "garden" and explained that the first crops would come in within a few weeks. Then he showed her the tunnel and they slid down to the rooms below. She clapped her hands and grinned in surprise.

"You're marvelous. I never imagined you'd be able to create such a spacious home, a safe haven. Do you think we're alone here in this spot?"

"I think so but it'd be wise to do a frequent search of the area. I've planted crops for the fall and winter, so I hope we can stay here for a time until we come up with another plan."

Adam and Grace went out at night together and searched a broad area around the barn for any root crops or berry bushes or anything they could add to their diet. They spied some apple trees north of their barn and also some plum trees, and gathered what they could carry back. While it was still dark, Adam showed her a house he had found a mile southwest along the shore that appeared to have been inhabited in the recent past.

"I don't want to touch anything here in case the occupants return and get suspicious."

He also took her to another house about half a mile north of the river and another barn a mile north of their location. Both were unoccupied and dilapidated.

"One never knows if they will be useful in the future."

He looked at her solemnly. "If this barn has some problems or we are found, we'll have to move quickly."

Before they left, Grace found some spices and salt and pepper and even some flour kept in a cannister away from vermin. They walked back to their barn before dawn arrived. All the buildings they had seen were overgrown with blackberry bushes and ivy and other vines as nature was slowly taking back its land and reclaiming its wilderness. The cold wind began to sweep across the fields and it began to rain.

Adam was glad that he had created two side rooms. Grace took one and he took the other. He could hardly wait until his first crops came in. He expected radishes and carrots and leeks to mature first. Meanwhile he searched the house thoroughly that was southwest along the river, but did not touch anything. He even traveled several miles north away from the river and barn to find additional dry food until his crops came in.

One night, Grace asked if he thought there were many others still alive.

"Not many I should think, but there must be some. Someone must have filled this barn with hay not too long ago. And I'm sure there are still wild men roaming the countryside and even some groups trying to stay alive. I just hope we don't find any of them. We have to concentrate on ourselves."

"I agree. We should focus on our own survival."

A few days later Grace moved into Adam's room.

CHAPTER EIGHT

Che – Mouth of Great River

Winter, 5 AP

Che stood on the top of the dunes looking out to sea. He was part of a group of twenty-one men that had broken away from a peaceful community that objected to the militant goals of Che and his men. The peace had been shattered as Che talked increasingly of fighting the intruders that had invaded the rivers far into the land. The idea of war and fighting and bloodshed and conquering others was not appealing to the main body of peaceful people who believed they were safe from any dangers. The rest of the group shared Che's beliefs that they had to mobilize a guerrilla band to fight off the invasion of others from foreign lands.

Che and his group had left two years after the start of the pandemic when members of the larger community began to die from the mysterious viruses. Che and his twenty men marched north up the coast. After several weeks they encountered a small river and found a couple of small rowboats to cross to the north shore. They wanted to reach the mouth of a Great River, which they had heard about.

They rested on the north shore of this small river. Che realized some of the men were becoming ill. They stopped at an old abandoned fort overlooking the sea to recover their strength during the cold third winter of the pandemic. They built fires in the fort to stay warm and foraged for food, but many men became weaker and weaker and showed various signs of disease. Some lost control of their muscles and slowly deteriorated while others coughed blood and could not take food. Some died quickly and some lingered on until there were only three of them left: Che, Slinger and Bubba. Slinger and Bubba were weak but survived the pandemic.

One morning, Che woke with a feeling of despair. He felt fettered, alone, and.. *(what was the word?)* incapable of action. Shackled was the word he sought. He needed to <u>DO</u> something. Gulping down some blueberries and blackberries, he left the two others to search out the route he thought they should follow. As he stood looking out to sea Che saw a large group of ships sailing from the south. He counted a dozen ships. Each had some sort of gatling gun or a small turret gun mounted on the bow. They chased a large barge and began to fire on it. The barge tried to fight back with their lone gun but were outnumbered and sank quickly. The lead ship in the convoy suddenly changed course and headed inland via the small river. All of the others soon followed except for one ship, a ketch, that continued north. Che thought this was some sort of invasion fleet arriving from the south. They each carried a strange flag he could not recognize. They disappeared from sight and he hurried back to tell the others.

After he described what he saw, he said he would scout a bit to the north in the direction of the ketch. Che was the strongest of the three and took some days to march north to find the mouth of the Great River. As he marched, staying on the highest points he could find and still be close to the sea, he felt the ground shake and realized that must be an earthquake. He was not in a mountainous area but high enough to see a large body of water to the east of him and the wide river several miles to the north. Che decided he had to reach the point where the river actually entered the sea and covered the several miles quickly. He was on a low sandy spit that narrowed the opening to a few miles across. The current was very swift and he realized that if he and the other two tried to cross there in a small boat they would be swept out to sea. He turned back and headed south to give Bubba and Slinger the news. They would have to go around the large bay and the wide part of the river he saw in the distance to the east before they would cross to the north side.

He soon reached the area where he had looked out to sea high on a dune. There was a road heading east from a gap in the dunes that was already covered with sand for a couple of kilometers inland. Behind him was a concrete rest area with the roof blown off but the walls still stood. As he looked out to sea, he realized how disappointed and even despondent he was, but he vowed that they would continue their quest. He felt the ground shake again, this time so strongly that it knocked him to the ground. He stood up and looked out to sea.

He saw an enormous wave headed in his direction. He looked around and ran to the safest spot he could find. It was the concrete rest area behind a very high dune covered with tall grass. He looked back and saw the wave racing toward him and growing in height as it reached shore. Che guessed it was at least thirty feet high and continuing to grow. He ducked inside the concrete walls and hoped that they would withstand the impact of the water. He watched the water pour through the low gap and rush along the road. The high dune slowed the wave slightly and lessened the impact of the wave but it pushed over the dune and hit the concrete wall protecting Che. The wall held. He gripped a sink alongside one wall as the wave washed over him and headed inland. Other parts of the shore were much lower and the wave formed huge rivers moving relentlessly across the land, knocking down trees as it went.

Che had seen enough. He headed back south to find his two companions, and saw the devastation all along the coast from the tsunami. When he returned, he found Slinger and Bubba hiding in the remains of an old fort that had withstood the tsunami. They were shaken but still alive. He reported his grim news to them. It would be nearly impossible to cross the mouth of the Great River to the north, and besides that, he had heard about the ketch that had broken from the armada. This group of men had joined a very large group of men who had set up camp previously at the mouth of the river on the north shore. They were a hostile group, and preyed on other travelers.

Che said he had come upon a man and a woman on his return journey, who told him about the ketch and how it had attacked two other ships sailing past. The man named Carl also said there were reports of another larger group that had followed the river into the mountains some months earlier. They wanted to form a safe community where they planned to avoid the spreading pandemic.

"Why don't you join them?" suggested the woman named Eileen. "It's not safe down here. We're thinking about heading into the mountains ourselves."

"Keep your distance from us," Carl said, "we think we have one of the viruses." He coughed suddenly.

"We both have a fever, a sore throat," responded Eileen, "and we have trouble breathing. We have seen that in others before they died."

"I'm sorry to hear that," Che said, "I have seen plenty of death myself. I wish there was something I could do to help you. I have watched helplessly while others died. I hope you recover." He paused. "Have you heard of any cures, or remedy, anything to stop these viruses?"

"No," replied Carl, "I wish we had."

As Che rested in the fort, he suggested to Slinger and Bubba that the three of them try to reach that community in the north and join them. Che did not tell them one other thing the man had mentioned: that there was also a small group near that community in the mountains trying to build an army to fight roving bandit groups. The group on the north bank was just one of those bandit groups preying on travelers. It was indeed a lawless land.

Che was a revolutionary at heart and longed to fight against these predatory groups. He felt they were returning to the dark ages when such tribes attacked all across Europe.

They stayed in the fort throughout the fourth winter from the start of the pandemic. They spent time collecting food for the journey. When the two men were strong enough, Che suggested that they save time and head directly east until they encountered the Great River further inland. He said they would cross some small mountains but felt they would save much time that way. The men agreed and loaded up their meager supplies. They each had a backpack with water, some food, and a sleeping bag. They counted on finding sheds and barns along the way.

"I know an old overgrown road near here that goes east over the mountains," Slinger said, "Why don't we follow that? It would be much easier and there should be some small farms and villages along the way."

Che and Bubba agreed. They found the route and followed it through forests and valleys, now and then passing neglected farms and a couple of towns, all of which seemed to be abandoned. They always approached carefully just in case they encountered a place that was inhabited. This area was remote to start with and became even more desolate when the people fled. It was not clear where the people went but they were gone. They left behind dry food which had not yet perished or been eaten by rats and mice. There was one small store that had warm clothes that they acquired and a small pot they could carry.

After several days of hiking, they realized they seemed to be following an ancient trail. The forest became quite dense but they also crossed small roads that were heavily overgrown. The trail came to an end when they encountered a small river. It began to rain heavily and they searched for shelter of any kind. Bubba wandered away a short distance and let out a yell.

"Che. Slinger. Come here. Look at this," he called, "we can stay here until the rain stops."

They ran to see what he was talking about. It was an enclosure with gates and walls made of roughly cut logs and two long buildings with an open area between them. Forest fires had come close to the area but had not touched the fort itself which showed little signs of destruction. The gates and walls had kept out large animals and there was no smell of food. Other buildings around the compound had not survived

"I think this is Fort Clatsop," Che said. "I mean it's the place that Lewis and Clark and their group stayed in for the winter of 1805."

"Do you mean this is still the same fort?" asked Slinger.

"No, of course not," answered Che, "this is a replica but much like the original. It must have been used as a tourist attraction." He pointed to the ruins of the other buildings. "If it was good enough for those guys, it's good enough for us. Let's get out of this rain."

They pushed open the gate, went inside to the open area, and secured the gate again. There were several "rooms" in each of the two long buildings, with makeshift beds, two on each side, with a simple fireplace in between. opposite the entrance. They picked the first one on the left and moved in out of the rain. They built a fire and settled in.

The rain continued steadily for two weeks. When it finally ended, they started out by going south a mile or two until they reached the end of the river. They resumed walking in an easterly direction. After a couple of weeks of hard walking they encountered a much larger river. They headed south again until they made their way around its source and resumed hiking east.

And then it began to rain again, and did not stop for ten days. Che found a barn next to a big house that seemed intact. They stayed there until the rain stopped and the three of them recovered from the arduous walking. Slinger and Bubba were strong but not used to carrying a pack so the going was slow. They only managed a couple of miles a day. With the rain delays and stopping for a night or two now and then, they took three months to reach the area of the big city, now abandoned. Using the overgrown roads and bridges helped them cross small and big rivers. Slinger remembered the big drawbridge that covered the mighty river. They made their way slowly along the road, passing abandoned autos and trucks, until they walked across the drawbridge to the north side of the wide river. The bridge was so badly damaged from neglect and storms that it appeared about ready to fall completely into the river. As they hustled rapidly across Che pointed out the sign which said "Columbia River".

They followed the shore of the river for several miles and camped in an abandoned warehouse. Bubba was becoming weak and not able to keep food down. Che and Slinger feared the worst but they vowed to make him feel as comfortable as possible. After a week, much to their surprise, Bubba began to rally and grew stronger. He was able to take liquids, and then solids, and gradually grew stronger as the days grew shorter. They stayed there for several weeks, spending much of their time foraging for food and water. And then the heavy rain began again.

CHAPTER NINE

Sly – North Shore Columbia

Late Spring, 6 AP

Sly waited until the snow melted so she would not leave tracks. She was terrified of being found by one or more of those wild roving men. She kept her knife sharpened and on her belt at all times. She decided she would now attempt to reach the goal, a longtime goal of hers, of reaching the ocean. She waited until night, then loaded her backpack, and with a dim moon to guide her, walked carefully down to the site of the boat. She loaded the twenty-foot rowboat with her gear and pushed off. Under cover of darkness, she hugged the north shore for about five miles.

All of a sudden, looming out of the dark she saw a major problem. The river had a set of locks blocking her path. They were unmanned and partially damaged, probably from one of the boats floating freely. She decided she had to move on so she unloaded the boat and laboriously and slowly dragged the boat up the embankment and past the locks. She hid the boat under bushes along the shore and swiftly and silently went back for her gear and backpack, and the frightened Pandi. It was becoming daylight so she left much of her gear in the boat except for the food. She found a small office space near the locks and broke in. As daylight arrived, she ate a small amount of dried food and slept fitfully for several hours. She heard more rain during the day and found it to be soothing. She again fell asleep and woke at dusk to the sound of Pandi purring. The rain had stopped. She returned to the boat, pushed it down to the river and loaded it up.

Sly drifted slowly through the night along the shore for more than twenty miles. Pandi kept her amused by sitting quietly on the bow watching the water go by. Sly called her a "watchcat" since she seemed to be keeping lookout for any danger. Finally, they came to a small river entering the big river from the north. It was daylight and she felt she needed to stay away from the big river. She rowed up the small river for half a mile and found thick reeds along the western shore. She pulled the boat into the reeds and sat and listened for sounds. It began again to rain so she sought shelter. She saw a barn a short distance away.

Sly approached the barn and realized it was filled with hay. She decided it was a warm enough spot to rest for the day so she could carry on at night downstream. She curled up in her sleeping bag and fell asleep quickly with Pandi next to her head. She was awakened by Pandi's meow and a sudden movement of a hay bale next to her. She froze and reached for her knife. She wondered what sort of huge animal would be hiding there. The bale was pushed aside easily and a woman slowly emerged. When she saw Sly holding a knife, she shrank back.

"Who are you?" said the woman. "What are you doing here?" She reached for a nearby pitchfork and held her ground.

"I could ask the same of you," replied Sly.

"I live here. My name is Grace."

"Oh, I'm Sly." Sly put her knife away and the woman dropped the pitchfork. "I'm sorry. I was just stopping for the night. I won't bother you." She started to get up and pack her sleeping bag.

"Wait. You look starved. Would you like something to eat before you go your way?"

"Well, I haven't had a warm meal for several days while I traveled." Sly hesitated. "Where do you live? Not under that hay bale?"

"As a matter of fact, we do. My friend is away searching the area around to see what he could find. Follow me."

Grace pointed to the tunnel. "Just slide down."

Sly did, and after sliding down twenty feet or more came into the cavernous room. Grace covered the entrance with the hay bale and followed her.

"This is amazing." Sly shook her head in wonder. "Just like Alice in the rabbit hole. How did you do this?"

"Adam did it all. He only finished it a few weeks ago. Have some soup."

Grace ladled out a bowl of soup into a homemade cup. Sly sipped it slowly. It was heavenly.

"Where did you plan on going?" asked Grace.

"I'm headed for the ocean. Always wanted to go there."

"I'd think twice about that. Adam came from there some months ago. There are reports of groups of bandits robbing and killing people down near the mouth of the river and along the coast." Grace warned. "Why don't you stay with us for a while? We've got room." She pointed to the spare room. "Adam and I share this one now." She pointed to the other side and smiled.

"I'd like that, at least for a bit. But how can I help?"

"You can help harvest crops. And look for fresh water. Lots of things to do. Get your gear. I'll show you our secret garden on the way. Things just starting to come in. Carrots and radishes and such."

PART TWO

THE BURROW

Like the womb, The Burrow is a place of shelter, safety, sustenance and survival, and a focus of fertility. A group gathers in the confines of The Burrow, each with their own diverse goals and roles, and desires. They coexist with a feeling of isolation, hopelessness and helplessness, yet they are drawn together as they face common enemies. As they realize their inevitable launching into the outside world approaches, they prepare to leave as a team with common goals and plans, and with joy, hope, love and humor.

CHAPTER TEN

The Barn

Late Fall, 6 AP

Several months have passed by and summer has come and gone. Crops have come in from the "garden" created by Adam, and the results have been very successful. Sly kept putting off leaving for the ocean, since she found it to be wonderful to be part of a family for the first time in many years. She felt Grace was like an older sister and Adam like an older brother. Sly enjoyed the night, and felt at home out in the dark. She often felt like a feral being, a fox or vixen searching for a nest, her own home, her own space, but was content to live in peace for the time being.

Grace made the hay barn into a home as well as she could. Their home was the lower section of the back of a hay barn, which had two levels in the back half. Normally this barn contained hay as well as equipment, but in this case, it was completely filled with hay bales during the recent summer and fall. The real entrance to the barn was above. The room was created in a corner of this lower section, against the back of the barn, with hay on all sides stacked to the floor above separating the upper section from the lower. Entrance to this hay room was via a step tunnel that came from high in the barn. The inhabitants slid down the tunnel and then crawled into the room.

Adam and Grace had occupied the lower corner of the barn while the barn continued to be filled with hay and Adam had to keep changing and fixing their entry to the tunnel until it was filled. When the process was reversed and the farmers started taking out bales of hay, he then created the entry in a place which was out of the way and would not be discovered immediately. It was a never-ending exercise although removal of hay bales occurred only periodically, generally every couple of weeks, but he had to monitor removal very carefully so as not to be discovered.

One side of the room faced the back of the barn and was about one bale thick so that a bale could be removed to allow smoke out, air in, and to listen. In the center of the room against the back of the barn the floor boards were removed to create a deep dirt pit for a fire. The fire pit was circular and surrounded by large boulders to protect the barn and hay from fire. A large old grate spanned the top of the pit. This fire pit was only used at night when the smoke could not be seen. There were two old rough logs to sit on, one on each side of the fire pit. An escape hatch existed in the floor, covered by a bale of hay. The overall feeling was of a claustrophobic burrow.

A small side room was carved out on each side of the main room, which contained backpacks with attached bedrolls, and camping equipment. Everything was very old. It was late in the day, and nearly dark. The dim light, coming through the slats in the back of the barn, was augmented by one or more candles sitting near the fire pit. It felt like an underground burrow or bunker.

Grace entered from one of the side rooms. She shuffled in on the straw covering the wooden floor. She took a large pot from behind a hay bale, picked up a gallon wineskin which held water, poured some into the pot and put the pot on the grate. She took onions and leeks from a burlap sack, and put them near the pot for use in making a stew.

She wore very old, worn clothes, shirt and pants, as a transient hobo might wear. These clothes were once of very high quality, expensive when purchased. She reached into her backpack and pulled out a rolled-up set of old papers and a pencil. She unrolled the paper, thought for a moment, sat near the candle, and began writing on one of the sheets of paper.

There was the soft muffled sound of rushing water nearby as the river rushed downstream, mixed with the sound of the wind racing across the open grassland, rustling reeds near the river. There was a loud thump from above, then silence. Grace grabbed a shotgun from behind a hay bale and cocked it.

"Who's there?" She paused. "That you, Adam? Who's coming down? Speak!"

Adam slid down and entered. He wore overalls and a checkered jacket. He dragged a large burlap bag.

"Don't point that thing at me. It might be loaded."

"It is," she said, "Two shells."

"My God, you coulda killed me."

"Why didn't you answer?"

"Didn't hear anything." He was distracted. "That tunnel's getting smaller. Too many twists and turns."

"Did you cover the entrance? With a hay bale?"

"Course I did," he replied.

"See anyone out there? Still some light."

"Not a soul. Wild and desolate. Nature's taking back the land."

"What about her? Did you see her?"

"Nope."

Adam continued on with his tasks. He took out a few potatoes and parsnips, and put them near the other vegetables. He looked at her and back to the pot. He dropped the sack and went into the side room. She stopped writing.

"What're you doing?" Grace asked.

He didn't respond. She looked at the pot then returned to her writing. He returned without the jacket, looked at the pot and then at her. She finally stopped writing for a moment.

"Why didn't you start the fire?" he asked sharply, "it'll take a long time for this stew."

"Someone'll see the smoke," she replied and looked at him. "What do you have in the sack? Potatoes? What are those?"

"Parsnips. Beets and turnips too." He took them from the sack and laid them out. "Harvested most of the potatoes. I'll hide the extra."

"Where?" He didn't answer. She continued. "If you leave them behind, they'll find them."

"I found a small shed up along the river. Overgrown with reeds and grass."

"I hope you can use the leeks and onions next to the pot," she stared at him. "How long 'til we'll have to move on?"

"Couple of weeks. Not much more. Winter's here. They're starting to use lots of hay. They'll discover the tunnel soon."

"Can't say I'll mind too much. It's stuffy here. I feel claustrophobic. Can hardly breathe."

"Thought you liked it here. It's like a home now. It's spacious."

"Hay all round us. Hay above us. Sleeping in that little room all surrounded with hay. Like animals in a burrow, underground, waiting to be dug out. Like rats in a hay barn. I feel as if I'm breathing hay. I even find hay in our food. I want a home with fresh air and a view."

The light got gradually dimmer as they talked. Night approached.

"Think I'll try the radio. It'll be dark soon."

The radio crackled and whistled as he ran through frequencies.

Grace spoke. "It's no use. They're never any transmissions."

"There could be someone left, trying to transmit on some frequency."

"It's a waste of time."

"Must be someone out there besides the farmers."

There was silence for a moment. "Where'd you learn about this radio stuff?" Grace asked.

"I'd left my farm to join a group of four others on a forty-four-foot Nordland sailing trawler to fish. I was the navigator and operated the ship's radio too. When some of us saw that this monstrous pandemic was deadly and spreading fast, we tried to go far from it, out to sea."

"That was a good idea. Where'd you go?"

"Headed for the southern oceans. Antarctica. It was summer. Stopped at ports for food and water but saw the pandemic was everywhere. Only a few people here and there, all very sick. We left quickly."

"I'm not surprised." Grace hesitated for a moment. "What'd you do?

"We tried to stay at sea. We rounded the Horn, and stopped at the Falkland Islands."

"That's a long journey. Any signs of life there?" Grace asked.

"None. We went ashore to find food and water but left in a hurry."

"And then what did you do?"

"Went to South Georgia, and stopped at Grytviken."

"Does anyone live there?" asked Grace.

Adam replied, "Yes, and they were still alive. A couple named Pam and Oliver. They were unaware of global danger and wondered why they hadn't seen any ships for months. We explained what we had seen and heard. It was a year from the time we'd left and winter had arrived in the South. When we first arrived, Jose and Kiran showed signs of illness. We quarantined them in case it was one of the virulent viruses. It was too late. They faded quickly, grew weaker, and died within a few days of each other. We buried them in the cemetery near Shackleton's grave."

"Must have been sad. What did you do then?"

"We stayed several months with Pam's blessing. We waited out the snowstorms and heavy winds until spring arrived in the southern hemisphere."

"Where'd you go then?"

"Headed for Tristan. I've been there before. We had high seas and heavy winds and it took three weeks but we made it into their small harbor. They greeted us with cheers, and a member of the Glass family, Herbert, recognized me. However, we couldn't go ashore. They were turning away all ships and people to be safe."

"Now, that's smart. Then what?"

"Herbert told me that only one ship had arrived in the past year and the crew of the ship had told them harrowing stories of the pandemic in Africa and Europe. Thousands of people perished in an awful manner. Some just gasped for breath and collapsed. Others lost control of all parts of the body until they just stopped moving. The worst thing reported by the ship was the body being covered with a flesh-eating bacteria that caused them to scream in excruciating pain. Some were just put out of their misery."

"My Heavens. That's horrible. No wonder they don't want anyone to come ashore."

"I told them what I'd seen on our journey and then asked if any of them would like to join us on our return trip. We needed two able bodied seamen, and would return the way we'd come, fishing in the Southern Ocean on the way to the Pacific. We told the Chief Islander named James Glass we'd seek a place in the Pacific to wait out the end of the pandemic, and would return the two Tristanians when it was safe."

"I'll bet they didn't go for it."

Adam smiled.

"The Tristanians declined and said they were sorry: everyone was needed to survive since they'd lost all of their trading connections. It was as if they had gone back in time two hundred years."

"You can't blame them." Grace said. "So, what did you do then?"

"I asked if we could trade some of our salt and spices for water and a small amount of meat to augment the fish we caught as we sailed. The Chief Islander said they could spare water since they had lots of it, and they could also spare meat from their cattle."

"That was kind of them. Then you left?"

"The Tristanians wished us well, and we headed for the Falklands."

"What will they do? The Tristanians have no way to sail away."

"They'll survive."

"What about food? How will they survive without ships arriving?"

"They're amazing people. They have lots of water from the volcano mountain, lots of cows on the other side of the mountain, they grow all sorts of vegetables, and they fish in the sea. They ration salt and spices. It's true they can't go far in their long boats. They're isolated and have depended upon visiting ships. I wish them well. They are a hardy, healthy multi-ethnic community."

They stopped talking for some time and then Grace continued.

"Then you left the Falklands and made it back around the Horn?"

"It was tough but we made it all the way to the Galapagos with Al, Bart and me. Then Al and Bart died. I sailed solo back to the river."

The radio continued crackling as he kept trying frequencies.

"You're wasting your time. Nobody's gonna answer."

Adam turned the radio off, then stirred the fire, and chopped kindling on a log.

"I'll get the fire ready to go. It'll be dark soon."

He moved logs around in the fire pit, then chopped more kindling on a log with an axe. There was silence.

"Before they discover the entrance," she said, "can't we fill it in? Move the entrance lower?"

"They'll see the bales were broken. Gotta be gone before they do."

Grace shuffled sheets of paper around.

"What're you doing?" Adam said with irritation in his voice.

"Writing!" She looked at him. "My journal, can't you see?"

Adam spoke with an edge in his voice. "You making the stew?"

She snapped back at him. "I started it! You can finish. I'm busy now."

Adam spoke sharply. "I grow all the food – why can't you make the stew?"

"You think this isn't important?" She shuffled her papers.

"More important than eatin'?"

"This is my job, to record what happened."

"What're you talking about?"

"Herodotus, Tacitus, Plutarch and Pliny."

"Who are they?"

"Ancient Greek and Roman historians."

"Well? So what? They're not gonna help us eat."

"If it weren't for them, we wouldn't know much about their history, would we?"

Adam was somewhat defeated. "Someone's gotta make the stew."

He turned to the pot, stymied, then began cutting up the vegetables and putting them in the pot.

Grace waited for a moment and then continued in a quiet voice.

"I'm up to the pandemic now. You can help. When did it start?"

"It's been going on for five years, but it started long before that."

"What do you mean?"

"This world was filled with corruption, violence, greed, and racism back then. It was growing, sanctioned, and applauded from highest levels. Mobs were growing, bigotry was rampant, guns were carried everywhere. Honesty and decency were under siege."

"I know all about racism," she said, "it's part of a much bigger issue."

"What do you mean by that? What issue?"

"It's called discrimination. If it isn't about black people like me, it will be about Chinese or Japanese or gays or another tribe."

"Or Jews. I understand. Many people will always find a way."

Grace nodded and resumed her questions in a soft voice.

"Back to the pandemic. Who started it?"

"Them, not it."

"What?" Grace was confused.

"There's more than one deadly virus. Everywhere we went, stopped for food or fuel, they described it differently. Spread by touching, sneezing, wind-blown. Some caught it from food, or animals."

"How do you know there was more than one type of flu?"

"Symptoms were different but all lethal. Coughing, spitting blood, in the brain. Just went crazy. For some, they couldn't keep food down, like a deadly stomach flu. Starved to death. There were even signs of the flesh-eating bacteria. Sometimes people just stopped breathing."

"That's what the Tristanians heard. How could all these flu types spread so quickly?"

"They were designed to. Most of the time people got some type of virus before they even had symptoms, after it had already spread."

"Who started all these virus types? All at the same time? Crazy."

"This was planned on a massive scale, not an accident."

"Are you sure? But who? Who could it be that did it?"

"Could've been anyone." He paused for a moment. "Even us. But many countries have such labs."

"All these countries couldn't work together. They hate each other."

"Sabotage. That could be coordinated. Why're you asking me all these questions?"

She snapped at him. "You're old enough to remember how it began!"

"You were old enough." He stopped for a moment. "We survived. That's what matters."

She spoke sharply. "We never talk about it. We hardly talk about anything!"

He snapped back. "When I work from dawn to dusk, trying to survive, what's to talk about?"

He chopped up more vegetables and put them in the water heating in the pot. She shuffled her paper as she wrote.

"Wonder if anyone's out there." He continued to behave in an agitated fashion.

"Pull the hay away and look."

He went forward to the back wall, pulled a hay bale from the wall and looked out. It was quite dim at this time.

"It's getting dark. I better start the fire."

The wind began to pick up and was whistling around corners of the barn. He went to the fire, used the flame from the candle and a scrap of paper to start it. There was a long silence, and then a faint scratching noise coming from the back wall.

"Why're you so nervous?" Grace asked.

"I thought I heard something." Adam replied.

"Who'd be around here? It's nighttime."

"I wish I could see outside." He peered out. "I'm sure they can hear us."

"They're far from here. Don't worry." She leaned down and continued writing. The scratching noise became louder and shook several boards.

"I heard it again. I'm sure of it. It's coming from the back." Adam peered through the slats in the back of the barn and shrank back.

"It's a cougar trying to get in. She must smell the stew."

He grabbed the shotgun, ran over to the tunnel, and scrambled up it to the outside.

"Leave her alone. She's just hungry" Grace called out.

There was the sound of the shotgun. He returned quickly.

"You didn't shoot her, did you? She did no harm."

"No, she ran away," Adam said, "but then I saw someone far away down river. Looked like a couple of people."

"How could you see them that far away?"

"I have very good eyesight." Adam said.

"They must have heard the shotgun."

"The wind muffles the sound. But we'd better keep it down just in case."

"Not much we can do about them – if it was anyone."

"Maybe you're right. My imagination."

She started to write while he paced back and forth across the straw on the wood floor.

"Tell me how it began." Grace persisted.

"I don't know, but when this started five years ago, the rumors said there were explosions in secret biological labs all around the world."

"Explosions? In more than one lab?"

"All about the same time. Fires or explosions. Strange."

"How could that happen? It doesn't make sense."

"Sabotage. I told you before." He turned to the radio. "Think I'll try the radio again."

The radio crackled and whistled as he ran through the frequencies. "Nothing."

"Those old batteries won't last if you keep trying."

"I only try at night, and I have backup batteries."

"Who are you trying to reach?"

"Must be someone out there besides these farmers. Some good people"

"Maybe there is and they'd be worried about batteries too. Why only at night?"

"Signals travel better then. Ionosphere's lower."

The radio noises continued and then he turned it off.

"What's that?" she asked. There was no answer. She continued writing. He moved toward the tunnel.

"Where're you going?" she spoke sharply.

"Up through the tunnel. I hear something." He listened. "Hear that? Someone's out there."

"It's your imagination."

"This time, I'm sure. Where're the night binoculars?"

"Over there." Grace pointed to the area where tools were stored. He grabbed the binoculars.

"I'll be right back." Adam left via the tunnel.

"Be careful!" She yelled after him, then checked the stew, added vegetables, and continued writing. He rushed back in.

"Someone on horseback's coming toward the barn. Douse the light."

She put out the candle. They listened to the sound of hoof beats coming closer, circling the barn, and leaving.

"They didn't stop. Must just be a patrol."

"We've got to be more careful. I think they're getting suspicious."

"He didn't stop so he wasn't too suspicious."

"I also saw another one in the distance. At least a mile away."

"It's dark. How could you see that far? Must be a tree."

"Wasn't a tree. Not with four feet."

"Think there's more?"

"Maybe. I think they're gone." He stopped for a moment. "No sign of her out there. Don't think he saw her."

"She'll be back. She's a night animal." She turned to write. "Must be a few survivors. Somewhere."

Adam chopped up more vegetables as he talked. "Yeh, but mosta them starved to death."

"There were millions starving to death even before the plague."

He didn't feel the need to answer her. "I doubt there's more than a handful now. Scattered."

She talked, almost to herself, thinking. "I remember reading studies of mitochondrial DNA. Man was close to extinction 75000 years ago. There may've been only a few dozen women to reproduce. All living in Africa."

"Yeah, so all mankind's descended from a few women then?"

"That's right. And studies show they spread all over the world from there. To Asia, all over Europe, across the land bridge to North America from Siberia, down to South America."

"And that took thousands of years, right? So, how come we had all this racist stuff when everyone was related by DNA? The people on Tristan are all shades and colors. They don't seem to have racism."

Grace thought about this for a moment. "I guess it took a long time to develop this race thing. And I think the environment had something to do with it. All I know is, when they asked people in an exercise to stand next to each other on a big map based on DNA, there were all colors and shades together."

"That must have been a big surprise when they looked at each other."

Grace laughed. "I told you before race was just part of a bigger thing called discrimination. Some people need to look down on others. Someone to hate, someone to make themselves feel superior."

"Well, that might be solved now. Not too many people left to hate."

They smiled at each other and worked together in silence. Grace broke the silence. "Maybe we should help repopulate the world."

"It'd take more than us."

"We could do our part. I'm still young."

"We have enough trouble feeding ourselves."

"Maybe we could fix up our hay filled bedroom. Make it more romantic."

There was silence. He did not want to go there. He chopped up the last of the vegetables, replaced the lid, and stoked the fire. He continued. "Where're the spices, salt and pepper?"

"Over there. In my 'cupboard', that hole in the hay." She quietly returned to the subject. "It's my job."

"What?"

"To help repopulate the world."

"I thought you're a writer. That's your job!"

She laughed. "That's my other job." He also laughed. She had gotten his humor back.

"Pretty good at your job. Both of 'em."

"I've got a few good years left." She became coy. "We could have lots of kids, don't you think?"

There was silence as he removed the lid and checked the stew, then stoked the fire. There was more silence.

"When the pandemic struck, you said you were a teacher. What made you want to write?"

"I always wanted to write but I needed to do something to live."

"What did you do?"

"Got a job on an island up north. I was starving."

"Good reason."

"It was a small school. I taught all grades, all subjects. Lived in a little wreck of a place."

"At least it was home!"

"Some home! That didn't last long. I had to go inland."

"Because of the pandemic?"

"Yes. I was the only one left that hadn't died. I was the last to leave.

"And then you headed south?"

"Yep. That was the end of my dream of being a writer or a journalist."

"You still can be! But now we've got to get on with living."

"Surviving, you mean. Haven't written a thing in a long time."

"You're writin' now, aren't you?"

"Yeh, sure! I don't even have paper to write on. I have a few old scraps and some pencils."

"Reminds me of Rodin. He used scraps of paper and charcoal from the fire."

"When'll you get me some scrap paper?"

He lashed out at her, angrily and impatiently. "You think it grows on trees?" Then he calmed down. "Look, don't worry, next time I go to one of the dumps, I'll find you something to write on."

"Any kind of paper will do as long as it isn't rotten."

"I'll find some wrapped in plastic."

"Maybe there's some in a wrecked store I saw coming here."

"Strange, isn't it? The greatest legacy of civilization will be all those dumps, those mounds spread across the wasteland."

"Nature will cover them up." Grace mused. "Never know they were there. Like the Mayan ruins."

She went back to writing and shuffled the paper trying to organize it. He stoked the fire and checked the stew. He went to the radio again and heard crackling and whistling as he tried to find a transmission. There was none.

"I don't understand it. Must be someone out there on the waves. Somewhere."

"Maybe there is and you're not picking it up."

"If there was, I'd hear a different sound."

There were more sounds from the radio but no contact so he turned it off.

Grace returned to her favorite subject. "It's been such a long time since I had a safe secure home."

"Don't blame me for that!"

"I'm not!"

"When I found you in the blizzard, along the trail, in the ditch, you were ragged and homeless, and almost dead. I've done my best."

"I know. I was desperate! I was exhausted!" She began to sob. "I was hungry! I was lonely!"

"If you had a white face, I wouldn't have seen you. You'd be dead."

Her sobs turn to laughs. "If we didn't have a blizzard and I fell, then I'd still be in that ditch?"

"I would have seen you and picked you up."

"That's reassuring!"

Adam went over to her, put his arms around her, and hugged her.

"This is home! Longest I've been in any one place in years!"

"When are we going to find a place that we can stay in and not have to run from?"

"We will, we will. Be patient!" Adam tried to sooth her.

"I want to settle down, have a nice home, and raise a family."

He interrupted her. He threw the poker against the grate with a clang.

"Stop complaining! We're lucky to be alive! I've been on the move ever since this pandemic started. You think I like this any more than you do?"

As suddenly as he started, Adam calmed down and acted as if nothing was said. He lifted the lid, stirred the stew, and put the lid back. Then he continued talking

"Wish we had some meat for this stew." He moved around in nervous agitation. "Where is she?"

"She went to get carrots."

"I'm worried they'll catch her. No telling what they'd do to her."

"Don't worry. No one's caught her in all those years she's been on the run."

"There's always a first time."

"She's clever, very cunning like a fox. She knows how to take care of herself."

"Smells trouble miles away, like a wild animal. Still, I worry."

Adam paced back and forth, stopping to listen, then looked up as if he could see out. Grace tried to reassure him.

"Don't worry. She's learned what she needs to know – to survive."

"She was so young when it started. Never had a chance."

"What do you mean?"

"I mean like us – to be educated, to learn about history, and art and science."

"Why does she need to know that? It's no use anymore."

"You could teach her some of that," Adam argued, "besides, it might be useful one day. If we ever had children, wouldn't you want them to be educated? To know about art and music and history and science, and many other things?"

"Yes, but how? With what? We don't have books." Grace's dripping sarcasm was ignored by Adam. "But I could use all the paper and pens and pencils you got me."

"We still have museums some places. There must still be paintings and sculptures not destroyed that we could go find one day when it becomes safe. And there must still be books in abandoned libraries that haven't been burned down or destroyed."

"You are a dreamer." Grace's voice was just a little bit softer. "Just a little while ago, you were talking about working from dawn to dusk, trying to survive, and now you're running a school for the children we don't have yet."

"I know surviving comes first but we all have to dream. I could teach science things and you could teach art and history. Couldn't you teach her some of that now?"

"Wish I had one of those computers we used to have."

"What good would that do? There's no electricity anymore." He pondered her request. "I'll get you that paper."

He paced back and forth as if he were a caged animal.

"Why are you so jumpy? You're nervous as a cat."

"Thought I heard something out there again."

"It's just her coming back. Or maybe the cougar again."

He tended the fire and stew, and then continued his frantic pacing. She tried to stay focused on her writing. Suddenly they heard the distant sound of a single rifle shot to the west, down the river.

"That was a shot! Far away!" He rushed across the floor and entered the tunnel. "I'm going up!"

She yelled, "Be careful! We don't need you shot up!"

He left. She wrote for a while and then checked the pot and returned to write. He slid back down.

"Nothing! I was sure I heard it! Down river!" He did the same as Grace, checked the fire and the stew.

"I'm glad it was nothing!" She softened her tone and became a little more sensitive and sympathetic. "Why are you so worried?"

"They've been looking for me."

"What're you talking about?"

"My knowledge, my skills. I can grow food anywhere! They know little about farming."

"You don't know that," she was vehement in her response. "They don't belong here. Brought in the plague."

"We don't know that."

She was filled with hatred. "Well, I do."

"The pandemic was already here. They looked for an isolated place."

Grace continued in a tone of hatred that Adam had not seen before.

"Maybe it was a different virus but they brought it in by ship."

"We don't know that either."

"They killed our people with those high-powered rifles. They took our land. Those invaders destroyed my life!"

"The pandemic spread and killed people. The land was empty. They survived somehow and just wanted to farm. What's wrong with that?

She calmed down a bit. "All they know is how to harvest hay and that's not farming. What a joke! Farmers! One old cow. Horses." There was a long pause.

Adam continued. "If she's not back in a minute, I'm going to search for her." He paced back and forth. "I'm really worried."

"Don't be. She went the other way, remember? Up river!"

"She might have gone back down river. Maybe they saw her."

Grace changed the subject to what was really on her mind.

"We're too close to the farmers. Let's get far away from here."

"I agree. We'll have to move soon, but that's not so easy to do."

She heard sounds from the radio as Adam fiddled with the knobs.

"Why do you keep fiddling with that? No one's there."

"There has to be someone out there."

He kept fiddling for a moment then turned it off. She continued.

"Think she'll stay with us?"

"I'll ask her. Maybe."

"She's ready to settle down with her own nest."

"I agree. Pretty soon." Adam replied.

"But she needs another bird before she builds that nest."

"There aren't many other birds around."

There was noise from above.

"Someone's coming," Grace whispered. She grabbed the shotgun and cocked it. Adam doused the lights.

CHAPTER ELEVEN

Danger Approaches

Early Winter, 6 AP

Sly slid down the tunnel and Grace put away the shotgun.

"There you are."

Sly said, "did you see the cougar? He was beautiful."

"We heard him, or her," Adam replied, "we chased it away."

"Got the carrots," Sly said, "brought radishes as well. Want anything else?"

"Well, if you find any wine out there…!" Adam asked with a smile.

"Listen to the man, will you?" Grace laughed. "A real connoisseur! For the stew, of course! It's been so long since anyone made wine."

"I could make wine," replied Adam, "if I could find an old vineyard, maybe I could get the grapevines back in shape."

"I remember some vineyards on some of the islands where we're going," Grace said. "Those were the days! Wine and cheese and bread!"

"All gone!" Adam responded. "When we find a safe refuge, I could grow wheat. I'd have to learn a bit about making cheese."

Grace replied, "I'll help you make bread. Let me think about cheese."

"Oh, I'd love some bread," said Sly, "milk and bread. I'd be so happy with that."

"I'll look for some grain," Grace said, "maybe there's some left."

"I haven't seen any. Just hay." Adam noticed Grace moving away toward the tunnel. "You goin' somewhere?"

"Need to take a nature break. Bet that old silo up river has some grain. Be right back."

"Be careful. You never know what's out there."

"Don't worry. I'm pretty clever too."

"And bring some cheese back with you."

"Sure, why not! To go with the bread and wine?" Grace disappeared into the tunnel.

Sly became quiet. "Don't remember ever drinking wine. My special treat's milk, when I can find it. I've been on the run so much I hardly get much of that either."

"If I had wine, I could toast your anniversary properly, but here's something even better!"

Adam walked across the hay covered wooden floor and got some milk from behind a bale of hay.

"Fresh this morning, chilled in the stream!"

"Oh, you're wonderful! You remembered about the milk!"

"I made three cups for us. We'll have a toast when she comes back."

She ran to him and hugged him.

"Take it easy." Adam moved away from her embrace. "Hard to believe you've been with us only one month."

"It seems like more. This is the longest I've stayed anywhere."

"You think you want to go with us? Stay with us? We'll have to move soon."

"I'd like to. Where will we go?"

"Good question. Wish I knew. Away from danger."

She sat on a log watching Adam as he was lost in thought.

"What's wrong?"

"It's a wasteland out there! As if millions of swarms of tiny locusts had…"

She moved close to him. She spoke gently. As she talked, she touched him.

"Don't, Adam. It'll be alright."

His voice wavered. As he talked, she moved in closer, lightly caressing him.

"Corruption, lawlessness, then so many died, from the pandemics, starvation. Then war…" He drifted off.

"That turned things upside down."

"After you were born, even before, we treated others like animals."

"So, we lost our right to feel superior?"

"Our moral imperative. Corruption, even then from the highest level."

"That's what I meant."

"And now we're the animals! They're the hunters."

"I feel like a wild animal. You've seen those wild cats? I feel like them."

"Feral cats! They're savage! They live in a burrow, a hole in the ground."

"That's what I want. My own hole in the ground, my nest."

They heard a noise.

"Someone's coming. Must be Grace." said Adam.

They heard someone sliding down the tunnel. Sly moved away from Adam. Grace slid down the tunnel onto the floor with a thump.

"No grain in the silo! Just rats. And I didn't see any people out there!"

"What about a cat?" Sly spoke up. "Pandi seems lonely. Cats always need another cat to play with and keep them company."

Grace shook her head no.

"Nope. But I agree," she said, "I often think I hear mice scurrying around. But what about that cougar? Nice kitty! Here, kitty, kitty."

"Funny," said Sly, "but if we had a male cat, we'd soon have many mouths to feed."

"That can wait. We've been waiting for you, Grace. Take this cup." Adam poured milk into three cups as talk continued.

"What's this for?"

"Sly A little celebration. One month. Let's toast! To many more." They raised their cups in a toast, then he turned to Grace. "And soon, it'll be three months in this burrow."

"And even longer in that first barn after you found me in a ditch."

"You were on your way to see your sister. Sorry about that."

"You didn't find her?" asked Sly.

"I found her," Grace replied, "she died. Then I returned to the barn."

"Well, anyway, you've been with me many months."

"Seems as if we've been together forever," said Grace.

"I'm very happy here." Sly said. "I feel as if I have a family, a home."

"We feel the same way. We hope you stay with us."

"You said there were rats in the silo?" said Sly, "after the grain?"

"Just one." Grace answered. "He left. Why?"

"Ever notice why there are no rats or mice in this barn?" Sly went on.

"An owl I suppose." Adam said.

"Not down here. See that hole between those two bales? Pandi has been earning her keep. She's a great mouser." Sly put her milk there.

Adam returned to the business of the stew. "This stew could use something. Any parsnips or turnips left out there?"

"Just a few. I'll get 'em." Sly got up. "Everything else's gone except potatoes."

"Anything'll help this pot." Sly headed for the tunnel. "Be careful out there! It's dark."

"Don't worry. I'm a night animal. I can see in the dark." Sly disappeared into the tunnel.

They sat quietly for a moment.

"Oh, look Adam," Grace pointed to the hole in the bales. "It's Pandi. She's still very shy with us. Don't move."

A small, multi-colored, somewhat thin cat slid out and began to drink the milk. Adam turned his head and then moved. The cat disappeared.

"I think Sly is right," Adam said, "Pandi must be keeping us mouse free."

Grace got up, lifted the lid on the pot, and then put it back.

"The stew's nice, but we need protein. Wish we had meat or fish for it."

"I could look for fish in the river."

"That river's been polluted for years. Try the streams where we get our fresh water."

"Should be a few fish there. Next time I fill up I'll get one for the dinner!"

They heard a rifle shot coming from the west, followed quickly by another. There was silence. They froze.

Grace spoke softly. "He didn't leave. You were right about seeing that other one."

"They must've seen 'er."

"She's on the other side of the barn. She's too smart to be seen."

"She's in trouble. I've got to go out." He ran to the tunnel entrance.

"Wait! Someone's coming!"

They froze. They killed any lights. They heard people approaching above, moving slowly, as if searching. The voices had a gruff sound. One voice was deep and the other high pitched.

"He headed this way but I lost track of 'im."

"It's getting pretty dark. Be hard to find him."

The sounds of voices receded. Then they heard sounds of them running, then shouting.

"There he goes!"

Grace heard the sound of a rifle shot to the south west side of the barn.

"Think I got him. Where'd he go?"

"Down near the river. Into the reeds."

"We'll never find 'im in the dark. He can't go far! Let's come back when it's light."

"Hold on a minute! He was heading for this barn. Shine your light in there."

Adam and Grace heard the sound of them in the barn entrance above.

"Nothing but hay here. Let's check the other sides."

They heard them encircling the barn on horseback to the north side, then back to the east, and then around. As they turned to the back of the barn, they heard the sound of the cougar snarling.

"Watch out. It's a cougar."

Adam and Grace heard the sound of horses neighing. Then they heard the cougar snarling, and the horses galloping away to the west. The sounds diminished and finally stopped.

"A close call!" said Adam, "glad that cougar was still hanging around."

Grace and Adam relaxed and moved around again

"They were talking about a man, not a woman." Grace said.

"Maybe they thought she was a man. Sounds as if they might've got her."

"I was wrong. Go find her!" Grace pushed Adam toward the tunnel. "Wait! I hear someone."

Grace grabbed the shotgun.

CHAPTER TWELVE

Che

Early Winter, 6 AP

The heavy rain continued for three days and then stopped. The sun peeked through the clouds early on the fourth day. While they waited, Che and Slinger made sure Bubba was really healthy before they started the trek east along the south shore of the Columbia River. Following the river, they thought, would eventually allow them to reach the mountains. They wanted to cover as much ground as possible before they would have to wait out the winter.

They each carried a large backpack loaded with food, a few warm clothes, some cooking gear, and each carried a long knife. Che had taken some time to find an arms store. He did find one eventually. It was abandoned. It was also empty. He shuddered and realized that the few men that might have survived along with themselves would be armed, heavily armed.

The heavy rain began again just as they were about to start marching. After a few days, it finally stopped, and Che decided it was time to start out. They marched slowly east, keeping the Great River in sight. There were abandoned roads going east as well as north and south. They were all deserted and overgrown. They saw no one but decided to stay clear of roads just in case they were spotted by roving bandits. Che wanted to travel at night but Bubba objected.

"I can't see in the dark," he whined, so Che took a chance on walking during daytime. The first few days they were fortunate but then they ran into a pair of roving wild men. He could see their ragged looks and unkempt hair and decided to avoid them. Just before Che and the others disappeared into the woods, they were seen by the men. Two shots were fired at them but they missed. Che and the two others hid in a thick stand of juniper and stood motionless. The men did not find them.

"That was a close call, Che," Slinger stated, "I think we should travel at night from now on. You can go ahead and scout for us and I'll lead Bubba. We can't take any more chances."

"Agreed. But let's look for a place for the night now."

They saw a small cabin nestled in the woods. Che approached stealthily with his knife in his hand. He found it empty. There was dry food on shelves, and even old beer in cases. He took a chance that it was all still good, especially the beer. They set out their gear and put together a meal using the dried camping style food in heated water. Che had one pot that served the three of them. They each enjoyed the beer which had the test of time but was still drinkable. Bubba was feeling much better albeit tired from carrying the pack.

In the morning Che was stunned to find that Slinger was throwing up. It was similar to the sickness that Bubba had, except that he also had some kind of skin rash that spread rapidly. His temperature was very high and Che determined his sickness was in the same virus classification as measles or something like that. He hoped it was not a more virulent disease such as smallpox. They did their best to get him to drink to try to get the fever under control. After two days, the fever subsided. Bubba suggested it might be food poisoning. Slinger had eaten some canned fish from the shelf and they had not, so they guessed it was something like that.

At any rate, it took another week for Slinger to recover sufficiently to start out again. They gave him a lighter pack which made the going even slower, for Bubba especially.

It became very cold and the rain began again. This time it was accompanied by strong winds which gave them even colder conditions. Che was forced again to find shelter. They had only covered two miles. He found a small shed just big enough for the three of them, although they had to avoid one end where the roof had been ripped off and the rain dripped in. The wind blew all day and all night and the rain pelted their tiny shelter.

Finally, the rain and wind abated. Once again, the three of them started out at a slow pace. They covered ten miles over the next two nights and were feeling better about their progress. Then they encountered another difficult situation: they were skirting the edge of a stand of spruce and juniper when they saw two men ahead on horseback. Other than the two wild men with rifles, these two men were the only ones that Che had encountered in many weeks.

They waited until the two horses were out of sight, and then in the dim light, Che and the two others tried to reach a small shack before they were discovered. Just as they were approaching the cover of the shack they were spotted. Two shots rang out and Slinger and Bubba fell to the ground. Che dashed into the nearby woods. The men approached the fallen two men, looked, and began to search for Che. They could not find him in the thick brush and gave up.

After they had left Che went to each of the men on the ground and saw the hits were mortal. Che saw the men in the distance west of him and decided to reach a barn in the opposite direction. He had almost reached it when two things happened: he saw a slight figure dash away from the barn into the reeds alongside the river; also, one shot was fired and grazed his leg. He had just a moment to dash into those same nearby reeds, fell to the ground, and crawled into the thickest of them. He listened for a few minutes as the men approached the outskirts of the reeds. It was quiet and then one spoke in a deep voice.

"We'll never find 'im in those thick bushes." They walked away.

Che heard a rustle and looked up into the eyes of a young woman. She was not afraid.

CHAPTER THIRTEEN

Che and Sly

Early Winter. 6 AP

Adam held a heavy knife and Grace held the shotgun as Che slid down the tunnel and landed heavily on the floor.

"Who're you? Don't move!" Adam raised the knife above his head.

Che did not move as Sly slid down the tunnel and landed lightly on the floor.

"Put that gun and knife away. They were after him. The cougar ran away."

"That's what the shooting was all about? After him?" Grace asked.

"When I came outta the barn, I saw him running this way, so I ducked into the reeds." Sly explained.

"Think they saw you?" asked Adam.

"Don't think so, but I didn't want to give away the barn." Sly responded.

"What's your name?" Adam asked him.

"My name is Che," he responded quietly.

He moaned in slight pain.

"What's wrong with him?" Grace asked.

"They shot him. He's hit in the leg." Sly answered.

"How bad is it?" asked Adam.

Che answered. "I don't know. I can still walk. I think it's just a flesh wound, but it hurts like hell."

"We'd better look at it. Sit on that bale. Roll up your pants leg," Adam ordered. "What happened?"

"They saw me a mile from here. They had horses but I forgot about those powerful guns."

"You took off, you say?" Grace asked. "Headed this way?"

"When I saw her, I thought I'd be safer in the reeds. They saw me."

"They'll be back early." Adam said. "We only have a few hours."

"Let me do that, Adam." Grace pushed Adam out of the way and stooped down.

"Is there anything I can do to help?" asked Sly.

She got very close to Che and hovered over him.

"Sure, Sly. Help me fix him up. Get that rag over there. And that kit." Sly got a rag and the health kit from the supplies.

"Sorry we don't have much first aid stuff." Grace apologized. "Just this camping kit from years ago."

Sly opened the First Aid kit and rummaged around in it.

"There's a bandage left. I'll use it."

"This's what's left of our National Health Care System!" Adam mumbled under his breath.

"Grace, I'll take care of him." Sly pushed Grace gently toward the stew pot. "You have to look after the stew."

Sly spoke softly in a very low voice, seductive in tone. "I'll take care of you. Sit still. You hurt anywhere else?"

She touched him and checked him out.

"I'm alright."

"Where'd you come from?" asked Adam.

"From the coast."

"You see anyone on the way here?"

"No. It was strange. I think everyone's dead. Saw lots of different graves."

"No people? No bodies?" Grace asked.

"Saw lots of cougars. Wild dogs. Vultures. Everything's empty, rundown, overgrown."

It was silent for a moment. Sly broke the silence. "You can get up and test your leg."

He got up and walked slowly around as talk continued.

"Where're you headed?" Adam asked Che.

"Before I left the coast, two older folks told me about a group camped way up in the mountains. They were telling me how to get there but died together before my eyes. I couldn't help. Just stayed a distance away."

"Sad. It gets old people faster. What do you know about this group?"

"An abandoned village. Old houses. Lots of barns. A large group. Hope they're still alive."

"And if not? We might be the only ones still left." Sly stated.

"Except for the farmers." Grace put in. "Don't forget them."

"I'll try that radio again." Adam said. "Must be someone out there."

"Hurry." Grace urged. "We need to get moving and get outta here."

Adam turned the dial of the radio and they heard the sound of the crackling and whistling of the radio.

"Nothing?" Che said. "I'm not surprised." Adam turned the radio off with a click.

"Che, if they're alive, tell me more about this group. What you learned."

"Good spring water, not polluted. They feel safe there. Food's a big problem. They fish, but don't know a thing about growing food. They gather nuts, berries, and fruit, anything to eat."

Grace spoke up. "Just like the native peoples did, before the European invasion."

Adam continued intensely. "What about grains? Wheat, corn, other grains? The group know about those?"

"Not that I know of. They must be fighting starvation."

Adam turned to Grace in an excited voice. "I could help them. Teach them farming!"

"You do that!" Che said. "But I'm going to start a small guerrilla group there."

"What kind of talk is all this?" Grace spoke out. "We don't even know if anyone's alive."

"It's our best bet. Our only bet. We've got to leave."

Sly changed the subject. "You still want the parsnips and turnips? Might even be a rutabaga or two."

"Alright," Grace said, "but hurry! We'll eat, then leave. No telling when we'll eat again. How far do we go?"

"Two weeks hiking." Che answered. "We follow the river upstream." He turned to Sly. "Wait. I'll go with you." He and Sly left through the tunnel.

"Maybe she's found that bird for her nest." Grace mused.

"That's good. I'm worried. Sooner we leave the better. Let's start packing."

"You're right. Shouldn't take chances. I'll save this stew for later."

"Stew tastes better with age anyway."

"I couldn't enjoy it now. I'd rather eat on the road, when it's safer."

"Better check the radio one last time."

The radio crackled as Adam fiddled with the dial then he stopped turning it. A light static sound emanated from the radio since it was left on.

They packed up, drained the water from the pot, put the vegetables in a bag and stowed the pot.

"I'm putting the bag of vegetables in my pack," Grace said, "and the pot with yours."

"I'll find fresh water later. We have less than eight hours. I doubt they'll follow."

"Not even when they discover this burrow of ours?"

"We'll have too much of a start. They won't know which way to go."

"I hope this new place is really safe. I want a home, to settle down and raise children, lots of them. And educate them."

"And have a real farm, a vegetable garden, a wheat field! Lots of animals, of all kinds and shapes and sizes."

"A real community! Of all shapes and sizes," Grace pauses, "and shades of color. Finally, something to hope for! We'll call it Cascadia."

Sly and Che rushed back in to the barn and slid down the hay tunnel.

"You're wrong!" Che yelled. "They didn't wait 'til morning. They're headed for us!"

"You sure?" Adam spoke with a sense of urgency. "They're away from the river? You're positive?

"Yes. We saw a light to the west, down river. They're heading toward our entrance above."

Adam moved a hay bale from a spot in the floor.

"I thought this might come in handy someday. My escape hatch!"

He pried up a couple of boards from the floor.

"Where's it go?" Che asked.

"Away from them! Quickly! Take everything you can and head into the reeds."

"Won't they see us out there?"

"Keep in the shadow of the barn so they can't see you with the light. I'll be right behind."

"What'll we do in the reeds?" Sly asked Adam. "They'll find us there!"

"I'll be right behind you. I have a small boat hidden nearby."

"What then?" asked Che, "Are we going to row it up river? Dangerous."

"We'll get across the river while they're busy here. Let's go!"

Everyone grabbed a pack and various loose things and ran to the exit on the floor of the hay barn.

"Follow me, Sly." Grace stepped down through the escape hatch onto the steps below.

"I'll pass your pack down, Sly," Adam yelled, "Quickly. Grab the radio, will you Che?"

Sly stepped down through the escape hatch onto the steps.

"Alright," Che said, "Give me that shotgun. You go ahead. I'll be right behind you."

"What're you going to do?"

"Delay them a bit. Go. Quickly."

"And torch the barn. That'll keep them busy." Adam went down the steps.

"I can play the game too," Che mumbled to himself.

He cocked the shotgun and shuffled to the tunnel. He heard footsteps approaching and then the voices of two people. They gradually became audible to him and he heard one speaking with a deep voice and the other with a high-pitched voice.

"See that loose bale of hay!" the deep voice spoke, "Help me move it."

As Che reached the top of the tunnel, he heard the sound of a bale of hay being moved, and being flung onto the nearby floor. The deep voice continued.

"It's a tunnel! Let's go down! Shoot if you see anything move!"

"I don't know. It's so narrow. Wait! I thought I heard a noise."

"It's nothing. Get in there. I'll be right behind." He saw Che emerge quickly from the tunnel. "Watch out! He's got a gun!"

In rapid succession, Che fired the shotgun at the big person with the deep voice, who yelled in pain and fell to the floor. The other person fired the rifle and a bullet grazed Che but he fired the other barrel of the shotgun and it killed the remaining person. He slid down the tunnel, holding the two high-powered rifles the two men had possessed.

"That should delay those bastards. Permanently!"

He admired the rifles, and still had the empty shotgun.

"These could come in handy," he mumbled.

He moaned in pain. Sly came up through the escape hatch.

"Che! I heard shots. What happened?"

"I had some business to take care of." He gave out an involuntary moan.

"You're hurt. You've been shot."

"I'll be alright. Go get Adam. Tell him it's alright now to come back."

"Don't move. I'll be right back to take care of you." Sly went down the hatch to get Adam.

The radio crackled loudly. The sounds became clear. Che heard Morse code on the radio. (Dash dot dash dot, dash dash dot dash.) CQ – Calling anyone, over and over, followed by the Station ID.

CQ CQ CQ DE ABC ABC AR.

"Adam, come quickly," he yelled, "it's the radio, the call signal. There's someone out there!"

CHAPTER FOURTEEN

Che's Mountain Trip

Winter, 6 AP

Sly was glad they still had the barn refuge. She knew if it had burned down there would be no turning back. As it was, she and Che could take an exploratory trip into the mountains to see if it was worthwhile for Grace and Adam and the two of them to move out of their safe haven.

"Would you look after Pandi while I'm gone?" Sly asked Grace.

"Of course. No need to worry. She'll keep us company."

Adam suggested they use the two horses to save some time and ride as far as they could before traveling on foot. They made good time the first day but the terrain soon became very rough along the river and Che thought it better to hike from there. They had stayed in a barn filled with hay the first night and Che decided that was a good place to keep the horses until they returned to Adam and Grace.

"It's getting colder, Che," asked Sly. "do you think we'll have snow?"

"I don't think it's that cold yet," he answered.

Che took the lead and picked his way along the north shore of the river as it gradually narrowed. They carried two packs with enough dry food for a month, and found water in small streams as they travelled. They also carried a small portable stove, a pot, and fuel to heat water for a warm meal now and then. The terrain was devoid of human life but they saw packs of dogs in the distance now and then, and a cougar one time. Che had packed a gun in case it was needed, but they tried to avoid any of the packs that could be a problem. They were able to find barns of one size or another to stay the night. Most of the barns they saw were falling down but now and then they came across a sturdy one with minimal damage to the roof and sides.

"Che," Sly asked one day, "if it takes two weeks to reach this place, and we only have food for a month, aren't we cutting it kind of close?"

He smiled. "Don't worry, we can always find a bit of food here and there. This way we are travelling as light as we can."

They did indeed make good time for the first several days, marching through the desolate land, keeping the river in sight. They saw only the one cougar on the way, far in the distance, and watched until it wandered in the opposite direction. They stopped briefly at two unoccupied homes and saw two corpses at the first, picked clean by predators. They shied away, fearful of some form of plague, but found a safe room in the second house far from the dead, and they stayed part of the night.

They began walking in the middle of the night under a full moon, but before they saw any sign of daybreak, the sky became overcast, blocking the light from the moon, the winds picked up, and soon a light rain began to fall. They took refuge in another house which showed severe damage from high winds over the years, with leaks in the roof, windows broken, and rain coming in one side of the house from the driving winds. On the other side, they found a dry room and slept until late morning, awakened by heavy rain and very strong winds. They peered out and saw the rain mixed with hail and then snow. They decided to wait out the storm and ate some dried packaged food mixed with water.

"Che," Sly spoke softly, "this was a good decision. I'm afraid we're in for a delay from snow. It seems to be increasing."

"You're right," he answered, "I'm going to have to look for more food in case this turns out to be a few days longer than I planned."

"I'll help," she replied, "I saw an overgrown garden on the other side of the house. Let's take a look."

They bundled up from the cold and snow and wind and Sly led the way. They foraged in the high growth and found potatoes, carrots, onions, leeks, parsnips, and turnips. They hustled back inside and searched through the house for any sort of cooking pot larger than the small pot they carried. They were in luck when they searched a cupboard filled with an assortment of pots.

In less than an hour they had a simmering pot of chopped up vegetables, augmented with some of their dry meat. The snow storm lasted all day and all night and they managed two full meals of their warm stew. Once they looked out a window and saw a small bedraggled cougar prowling around the outside, drawn by smells emanating from the house. Che was about to shoot it when Sly stopped him.

"Don't, Che," she put her hand on his arm, "it's just starved. It'll go away after a while, when it senses us."

"Maybe," Che mumbled, "but it may lurk around, knowing we have food, trying to get some. We don't have any extra food."

When the sky cleared the next day, there was no sign of the cougar, but they kept an eye out behind for several days, in case they were followed, but saw no further signs of the cougar. They guessed it managed to get into the house and searched for any food it could find. Sly left behind a small amount from their stew for it to find.

After more than a week of clear, warmer weather, and hard walking, they approached the outskirts of a rambling settlement. There were three small outbuildings around a large house, and a large barn nearby, which they guessed were the original buildings. Scattered around were five other small buildings which seemed to have been built hastily.

"Che, put on this mask before we start poking around." She produced two facemasks to prevent them from breathing airborne viruses. "This will give us some protection. No telling what remains of any of the viruses around here."

They peeked inside one of these small buildings, and realized it was a building with a set of bunks inside, that served as sleeping quarters for many people. There was a graveyard off to the side with more than a hundred graves in it. There were no signs of life and no corpses in view. They ventured into the large home and found evidence of a dining hall and large kitchen designed to feed the many people that must have been living here.

Sly meandered into a small building next to the large house, and moved slowly through the house. She came to a room that seemed to be an office.

She saw a corpse stretched out on a bunk. It seemed to be a man with a long white beard. He was holding a piece of paper in his right hand. Sly grabbed the paper and dashed out to find Che. They read it silently together.

"Let's bury him and leave here quickly, Sly. This place gives me the creeps. That seems to be the end of my dream."

"Let's get back quickly to tell Adam and Grace," she responded, "they had such high hopes for finding such a utopia."

Suddenly they heard the sign of a horse neighing from the direction of the barn. They raced over, slowly looked inside a window and saw two horses, somewhat emaciated, but still alive.

"Get some water for the trough and I'll dump some hay for them." One was a stallion and one was a mare and both ate hungrily and drank water until they were satiated.

"It must have been only a week or two since the last people perished or were not able to care for these two," Che said.

They searched all of the other buildings and found no other animals or corpses. They spent two more days huddled in one of the empty bunkhouses while the two horses gained strength, and saddled them both with the tack they found in the barn.

Che led the way back down the trail from the desolate mountain community, along the edge of the river. They made good time for a day but then the horses tired, and the rain began again. They saw a barn which still had lots of hay in it and brought the horses in to eat and rest. They went slowly into the house adjacent to the barn and found the place dilapidated and in disarray as if it had been ransacked. There was no sign of life. They put together their own warm meal and listened to the wind rattling the windows, one of which was broken. The rain turned to snow and blew in through the window. Che went out once to check on the two horses. After having their fill of hay, they had curled up awkwardly together, the stallion's head on the mare's neck.

Che looked into the distance through the driving snow and saw a lumbering light brown animal. He came racing back into the house.

"There's a grizzly bear coming this way, Sly. Shut the doors so he can't get inside."

"Relax, Che. He is not interested in us. He's probably hungry and picked up the smells from our meal. He'll go away soon."

She was right. He or she sauntered away slowly after sniffing the air.

Sly had explored the house while Che was gone, and on his return, quietly motioned him to follow her. She directed him into a small room with a single bed, where they curled up listening to the wind and snow pelting the sides of the house. They slept soundly.

In the morning they looked outside to a winter wonderland. Che thought they were only a day's ride to the barn where they had left the other two horses. They packed up, saddled the horses, and rode slowly through the snow, searching for windblown paths where the snow was not too deep for the horses. They reached the barn at night where they had left their other horses and were greeted with their neighing. The two on which they were riding responded. The snow resumed and they put all four horses together with lots of hay and water. They slept soundly once again.

In the morning, Sly woke up Che.

"Che, what are we going to do with four horses now?"

"I think we should let the two we found in the mountain go free. We don't know much about this pandemic and whether it can affect horses. They'll be better off running free. With two of them together they will be able to fend off any cougar they find. Let's just take the other two back to our barn."

The snow had turned to a light rain and they set off at a good pace. They reached the hay barn and Grace and Adam by nightfall.

CHAPTER FIFTEEN

Searching

Winter, 6 AP

More than a month passed by since Che and Sly had left and Grace was worried. It was the dead of winter and lighting was dim. Darkness approached. The wind was strong and whistled around the corners, thru the slats, and was rattling the boards of the outside of the barn. Adam tested the radio. He ran through the stations but could not find any activity.

"Nothing. Can't understand it. If Che heard a CQ why don't they keep trying?"

"Maybe their batteries are low." Grace responded. "What's a CQ?"

"Calling anyone. They want whoever hears to respond. I'll try again when it's darker."

"Where're Sly and Che? It's over a month. Maybe they stayed."

"Che said he'd come back no matter what."

"It's getting cold."

"Feels like snow."

Adam tried the radio again for any sounds of activity, hoping to receive something from anyone out there. He heard nothing. The outside world was silent. Grace was irritated by Adam's continuing attempts to locate someone.

"Adam, you told me you'd wait until later. Why can't you build a fire? It's freezing."

"I suppose it's dark enough."

He removed the grate and put logs in the fire then put the grate back.

"What'll you do if someone comes on the radio? Those batteries are almost dead."

"We found a generator downstream, and gas. In an abandoned store. Good for a few hours."

"Why don't you use solar panels? To charge batteries. Lots of it around."

"Someone will spot them. But I put a small aerial on the metal roof. Good for five hundred miles."

"Why don't you do it now? When it's night. You know the frequency they came in on."

"When I hear something. No telling who might receive a CQ. Better to wait."

"Suit yourself. But when you searched downstream for miles, you found no one."

"I hear something."

Grace and Adam heard faint sounds and gradually realized what they heard were the sounds of hoof beats coming closer, getting louder and louder. Grace recognized what they heard.

"Horses."

"Must be them. 'Bout time. Let's be careful. Douse the lights."

Grace did. "Wonder why it took them so long".

"Must've been some trouble. Don't move." He got the shotgun.

They heard the sound of horses neighing. Then they heard sounds above and then Che and Sly slid down on to the floor. Grace hugged both of them.

"Glad to see you. We were getting worried."

"She was. I wasn't. How's the community? You find it?" Adam asked as he casually worked on the fire.

"Yep," Che responded, "All dead. Graves everywhere. Some bones. Overgrown."

"You're right about the food," Sly added, "It looks as if most of them died from various forms of the pandemic viruses, and then the rest starved to death." She reached into a pocket and pulled out a paper. "We brought you back a note."

Che urged Adam. "Written by the last survivor." He pointed to the note. "Read it."

Adam read the note out loud. "Please tell our story. Everyone dead. I'll be gone soon. Tried to raise food. Weren't too successful. Lost our crops. Severe winter then drought. People have been starving to death, then new people brought types of deadly flus that spread fast. Horrible. First old folks, then children. Couldn't do a thing. Cows and cattle also died. Went mad. Water must've been polluted. Doc went early, said many diseases, all kinds, that spread before symptoms seen, we couldn't control. No food. God save our souls. Amen. Deacon."

Sly murmured. "Horrible. Really sad. If they didn't die from the plague, they starved to death."

"The pandemic," said Adam. "He said 'many diseases'. That's just what I thought. What kept you?" He turned to Che.

"Ran into heavy snow. 'Bout half way back. Holed up. We stayed in an old house."

"There was even an old bed still there." Sly smiled.

"I see why you were delayed." Grace grinned.

"If everyone's gone, isn't it our job to repopulate the planet?"

"With only two of us it'll take a long time. Adam, what do you think?" Grace turned to Adam. He turned to Che.

"You didn't see anyone up and back?"

"Not a soul. Just more graves and bones along the way. Dead animals too. Cows and horses and sheep. I think they starved to death also."

"Nothing living?"

"Cougar now and then, and coyotes and foxes. A lot of wild animals."

"Stands to reason," added Grace, "Without people around, wild animals should increase."

"Not all of them," put in Sly, "Didn't see many raccoons. But we saw some wild dog packs."

"And a hungry grizzly." Che rolled his eyes.

Sly had been showing increasing signs of exhaustion or sickness. Che was concerned.

"Sly, you need to get some sleep now. You're not too well."

"What's wrong with her?" Adam asked.

Grace touched her forehead. "No fever."

"I'm alright," Sly tried to reassure him. "Let's move to the old house over there. There's no one around."

Grace answered, "Adam's afraid someone might still come. Looking for those guys."

Che turned to Adam. "After all this? Adam, we didn't see a soul down river. We rode at least ten miles."

"We'll move there soon. Not yet." He stopped and asked, "Where're the horses?"

"Tied up. Where should I put them?"

"I found a shed off some distance away. Come, I'll show you. They'll keep the old cow company."

Sly asked Adam, "Any milk? I'm famished. I need to drink something."

"Drink some of this fresh spring water," said Grace. "Adam, do we have any milk?"

"A bit. I'll get more. But the cow's not long for the world though."

"We passed a goat and kid just before we got here. And a couple of lambs."

"We'll go get 'em in the morning," Che said.

"That'd be great. Maybe we can have that lamb stew after all." Adam looked at Sly for her reaction.

"Cute little lambs. How could you?"

Che rubbed it in. "Baaa! Baaa!"

"Let's go, Che. Look after that fire, will you?"

Che and Adam left them and Grace stoked the fire.

"It's really cold," Sly said, "The snow will reach here soon. I'm cold. Che was right. I'm sick."

"You're just chilled. I'll build up the fire. It's pitch black outside. No one'll see the smoke."

"Grace, I haven't seen Pandi. Is she alright?"

"She's fine. She's sleeping back there in the hay."

"I missed her."

"I think she missed you also. After you left, she wandered around for a couple of days looking for you.

"Pandi." Sly called. "Where are you?"

There was a plaintive mew from behind the hay. Pandi strolled out, stretched, and walked up to Sly, rubbing her leg and meowing. Sly gave her several pats, picked her up, and nuzzled her.

"You look well fed. Grace has taken good care of you."

Pandi touched noses with Sly.

"Is she hungry? I'll give her some milk."

"I'll take care of that."

Grace left to feed Pandi.

"Why is Adam still so worried?"

Grace returns. "He can't believe there's no one left. Expects someone to show up any moment."

"Che thinks we should just go out and find them and wipe them out."

"They'll just have to work that out. Both of 'em are stubborn. Really strong opinions."

"How're we fixed for food? I'm starved. We ran out a couple of days ago."

"Thought you could live on love."

"That just makes me hungrier."

"We have lots of milk from that cow. And lots of potatoes."

"And meat?"

"Not 'til you and Che bring back those lambs. Those cute little lambs. Baa!"

"I suppose if I don't think about it, and if I'm starved enough."

"And now we have another mouth to feed."

"You mean Pandi? She has a small mouth. And besides, she earns her keep. I haven't heard mice scratching around in the hay for some time."

"Better start up that stew again. Look behind that hay bale, will you?"

She poured water into the pot then chopped vegetables. Sly slowly moved a bale of hay.

"Wow! You have lots of food here. It's like a cupboard, and full of vegetables."

"I decided to make a little room and Adam searched for everything he could dig up."

"Enough for a couple of months?"

"At least until the new root crops come up."

"He plans to stay awhile?"

"He wasn't sure what you two would find up there."

"He must've guessed. Glad he did the planting."

Grace and Sly paused and listened to the sound of the very strong wind whistling around the corners of the barn, as it continued to increase in strength. Grace shuddered.

"Wind's starting to whip up. Gonna be a cold night."

"Wonder if it's snowing yet."

"Take a look. Move that bale aside."

Sly moved a bale which landed with a plunk on the floor and she looked out. The wind was even stronger.

"Wow! The snow's blowing through the slats."

"What's it look like?"

"Don't know. Too dark to see. Must be wild out there. Not fit for man nor beast."

Sly tried to lift the bale back in place but couldn't. Grace came over and helped her lift it back.

"You really are sick. You need food and plenty of rest."

"I'll be alright if I just get something to eat."

"Hope the guys get back soon."

"Could they get lost in the dark or snow blinded?"

"It's not very far away. But I'll feel better when they return."

They heard the sound of someone returning. They heard the feet of someone walking on the floor above.

"You got your wish. They're back."

"Someday the wrong person might come down. We're taking a chance."

"We need a signal. I'll work on it with Che."

"Good idea."

Che slid down and landed with a plunk. Sly gave him a hug.

"No need to worry. Here he is."

"Where's Adam?" asked Grace.

"Milking the cow. She perked up when the horses joined 'er. Doubt she'll last the winter."

"Good thing you're getting that goat. We'll need some milk."

The sound of the wind whistled again around the corners of the barn causing them to listen. The wind had a rhythm: it subsided for a moment and then increased as if a series of waves.

"I hope the goats and lambs survive," Che mused. "We saw 'em near an old shed next to the trail."

"I hope they stay put and don't wander." Grace tried to assure him.

They listened to the faint sound of footsteps growing louder, approaching the barn. They heard the crunch of snow and the stamping of feet.

"It's Adam," said Sly simply.

He slid down slowly and dropped a pail on the floor with a clank.

"Here's your milk. Didn't spill a drop."

"Thank heavens. I've dreamed of milk. Haven't had anything for a couple of days."

He poured milk into a cup and gave it to Sly. She gulped it down.

"Easy, now, easy."

She laughed. "I guess I'm a bit primitive. I'll be a little more civilized with the stew." Sly poured some of the milk into a dish, and put it near two hay bales. "Pandi. Pandi." She said in a soft voice. "Have you been catching mice while I was gone?"

Pandi shuffled out slowly from between the bales, looked warily around, saw Sly, then began to lap the milk. Sly patted her and she began to purr.

Pandi slurped the milk quickly and disappeared.

They heard the sudden sound of very strong wind gusts buffeting the barn, and whistling loudly.

"How's the dinner coming?" Adam came over to the stewpot and looked at Grace.

"Be done soon."

"Sly'll need to fill up. She's on empty."

Sly turned to Adam. "What's it like out there? Snow was coming through the slats."

"A full-blown blizzard's coming in."

There were more sounds of the wind continuing to increase in strength.

"Wind's already forming snowdrifts," Che said.

"We can't go get the lambs and goats now," Sly said.

"Don't worry." Adam responded with a laugh, "They won't go anywhere."

"Stew's about ready," Grace said to Sly, "Get a bowl from my cupboard."

Sly shuffled across the floor and picked up four wooden bowls.

"Where'd you get those? I didn't see 'em before."

"Made 'em while you were gone."

"You're turning into a regular pioneer woman."

"We're all becoming pioneers, like it or not."

"Adam and I've been talking," Che said quietly, "About going downstream."

"You went there already," Grace retorted.

"You went ten miles last time," Sly added, "Isn't that far enough?"

"No, we mean much further. Fifty, a hundred miles."

"This weather's terrible." Grace said. "It's dangerous. I don't like it."

"That's half way to the sea," said Sly.

"We know," Che replied simply.

"Why do you need to go?" Grace argued. "You'll run into more of those guys with guns."

"We're gonna need some livestock," Adam finally chimed in, "Another cow, maybe a couple more horses."

"Wish we could find a good Border Collie to help herd," Che added.

"Chickens? Laying hens?" Grace asked.

"That'd be nice." Sly piped up, "What about a rooster? Won't we need one of those?"

"Anything we can bring back, maybe even another lamb," Che said.

"I hope so," she said, "If those two lambs are boy/girl you're not touching the wool on their backs."

"Not even wool? Nice warm wool on a cold winter day?"

"Well, alright, maybe as long as it doesn't interfere with repopulating our animals."

Sly slowly went off to the side room. She touched her forehead. She stumbled. Che saw her go and followed.

"A nice wool blanket would be nice," he said as he left, "for you."

"I'm worried about Sly," Adam turned to Grace, "Do you think she's got one of the viruses?"

CHAPTER SIXTEEN

Finding The Outside World

Winter, 6 AP

"If Sly had the plague, they'd both have died on the way back," Grace dismissed Adam's thought, "Forget about it."

"Not necessarily. That note said it takes a while to get symptoms. Before that, you can infect others around you."

"So, we could all be infected with a form of pandemic virus?"

"Possibly. But the virus spreads quickly. So, you're right. No one else seems sick. I'll forget it."

"I don't think she has the pandemic virus." Grace stated.

"Alright. But she's definitely sick from something. Maybe just the flu. It's winter, after all."

"When do you think you'll leave?"

There were more sounds of the wind whistling around corners but with only a slight decrease in strength.

"Soon's there's a letup in the blizzard."

Che returned from sitting with Sly and gave a report to them.

"She just needs rest. This stew's good. Really tasty."

"Parsnips, leeks, rutabagas. That's the flavor," Grace answered.

"These look like beans here. What are they?"

"Lentils. Found some dried ones downstream. In a house with a pantry."

"Delicious!"

"Che, how long'll you be gone?"

"Couple of days, if the weather's not too bad."

"Will you two fetch the lambs and goats while we're gone?" Adam asked Grace.

"Sure thing."

"Che, Sly looks terrible," Adam stated, "You don't think she picked up something on the trip, do you?"

"Like the plague? Forget it. She's just exhausted. Not enough food. She'll be alright."

"She's just cold and hungry," said Grace, "We should take her some stew. She'll recover I'm sure, with a good night's sleep."

Grace filled a bowl with stew and disappeared to give it to Sly.

"Think I'll try the radio again," Adam said after a silence, "Wind's let up."

They listened to the sounds of the wind decreasing and becoming more like a slight breeze. At the same time, over the sound of the wind, they listened to the radio crackling and whistling as Adam tried all the frequencies to find something. Che turned away.

"I'll build up the fire. Gonna be a cold night."

Suddenly the sound on the radio stopped and the pattern of CQs came in slowly.

CQ CQ CQ DE ABC ABC AR. The transmission from Station ABC was the distinct pattern of a CQ.

"That's it!" Che yelled. "That's what I heard before, Adam."

"That's a CQ all right. Calling anyone."

Grace returned. "What're you gonna do?" she asked.

"Guess we'll take a chance. Help me with the generator, Che."

"Where is it?"

"Behind that bale."

Che shuffled and dragged the generator across the floor.

"Got it! And the gas."

"Fill it up and start it."

Che poured gas into the generator and tried several times before it started.

"There she goes. Transmitter hooked up."

The generator started up and idled quietly. They began to hear another CQ coming in but it sounded slow and weak as if the sender was getting weak or the machine was low on energy.

CQ (Pause) CQ (Pause) CQ.

"That's strange," Adam said, "He's altered the pattern. It's slower."

"He's faltering," said Che, "It's irregular."

Another CQ but even slower and weaker. CQ.

"He's running out of power, Che." Grace leaned forward to listen to the weak signal.

"Or getting weak from starvation."

"Adam, why doesn't he use his voice instead of these signals? It's faster."

"First of all, it takes much more energy to transmit voice than to use simple Morse code. They might not have that much energy from the generator. Or themselves. But I don't think that's the only reason."

"What do you mean?" Grace asked.

"They want to remain anonymous. With your voice you reveal too much."

"Maybe it's a she. Don't want to tell that." Che chimed in.

"Or maybe you don't speak English." Grace said. "Or you're lying. Here's another one."

Morse code came in from ABC.

CQ (Long Pause) DE ABC (Pause) AR.

"Respond Adam," Che yelled, "before they sign off."

"Here goes. Gotta take a chance. We are BBC." Adam sends his Morse code.

BBC: ABC DE BBC BBC KN.

ABC: QTH MTH WD RIV = OP IS SAM KN.

"It's faster now," Che said, "before you responded, it was as if he'd given up hope. Now he sounds excited."

BBC: QTH UP RIV = NAME IS ADAM = HW WD K.

ABC: SEV KM K.

Adam was busy and needed to be prompted to explain to Grace, who hovered over impatiently.

"What'd he say?"

"His name is Sam. He's located at the mouth of a wide river. It's our river, I'm sure."

BBC: WHT SIDE K.

ABC: N K.

BBC: RU OK K.

ABC: N FUD = WEAK K.

"And now?" asked Che, "What'd he say?"

"Our side of the river. You were right, Che. He's starving and weak."

BBC: HW MNY K.

ABC: 2 K.

"There're two of them."

"Must be a trap," Grace mumbled, "Probably a whole group."

"I don't think so," Che shook his head, "Ask about the weather there."

BBC: WX K.

ABC: LT SN K.

BBC: TK TRL NSIDE K.

ABC: K.

BBC: SK.

ABC: SN CL.

"What'd he say?" Grace wanted to know.

"Snowing. We can't wait for a letup in the blizzard. They won't survive."

There were periodic sounds of wind still whistling and snow blowing.

"What if Grace is right?" Che said. "What if it's a trap?"

"I've thought of that. Get one of those rifles."

"I've only found a dozen shells."

"Bring 'em all." He hesitated. "On second thought leave a few. Grace and Sly might need a few."

"The other rifle?"

"Grace, we're gonna leave one rifle and the pistol."

"Only six shots in the pistol."

"That'll be enough."

85

"What're we gonna need guns for?" asked Grace.

"I hope a mountain lion didn't get Sly's little lambies."

"He might be hungry but not as hungry as her."

"That's the attitude. This is survival."

"How long before you'll be back?"

"Couple of days. Depends on how weak they are."

"We're gonna carry them back?" Che was incredulous.

"How else? Got a better idea?"

"Drag 'em in the snow?" Grace tried her sense of humor.

"Funny. We're leaving before dawn. If Sly's better, you two better do the same. Leave early to get those lambs and goats."

"And when you get back could you start up the stew?" Che asked Grace.

"Two more mouths to feed."

"One last thing, Che," Adam ordered, "Fill up those wineskins with milk."

"All four?"

"Yep. And eat another bowl of stew before we leave."

"Sure thing!"

"And get some sleep. No telling when you'll have either."

"I'll see how Sly's doing."

"I'm fine," she yelled from her room. "Come on in." Che went to join her.

"Grace, you can handle it?" Adam asked.

"Are you kidding? Remember, I'm a pioneer woman."

CHAPTER SEVENTEEN

Danger in The Blizzard

Late Winter, 7 AP

It was two days later. The light coming through the slats in the side of the barn was gradually fading as dark descended upon them.

Grace chopped stew vegetables and stoked the fire with an iron poker.

The wind whistled around the corners of the barn blowing the snow into drifts against the sides of the barn. Grace heard the distant stamp of boots. She heard a Knock – dah-di-dah.

"That you Sly?"

Grace cocked the pistol. Sly slid slowly down the tunnel and dropped a pail on the floor with a clank.

"I did it! See, that wasn't so hard."

"What wasn't so hard? Not spilling a drop?"

"That, too. No, milking the cow. I'm getting to be a regular pioneer woman."

"You were almost a dead pioneer woman. You scared me. What was that knocking?"

"Didn't you know? That's our signal. Morse code. K for OK like the end of the messages."

"I see. Sly, you seemed to recover pretty quickly. I'm glad."

"You all thought I had the plague, didn't you?"

"It did cross my mind, but if you did, I doubt you and Che would've made it back."

"What would you have done if I did have the plague? Throw me out?"

"Of course not. We would've helped you recover."

"Well, you needn't have worried. I'm pretty sure you only get it from the living and dying."

"What do you think you had then?"

"Maybe a mild version of normal flu lingering around. Or I was just exhausted. Doesn't matter now."

They heard the sounds of the howling wind as the storm picked up intensity.

"Sly, I'm worried. The wind and snow are really picking up out there. Where are they?"

"Don't worry. They'll be back soon. They know what they're doing."

"It's two days. It's getting dark. I'll feel better when I hear those horses."

"The stew hot? Just in case. You know what Che said."

"Delicious. I added another parsnip and leek. Steaming."

"We were lucky we got those critters before the storm got worse."

They heard the sound of the soft faint baaing from lambs and goats inside the barn.

"Now we know the sex of the two lambs. She's pregnant already."

"They got a start on us. They start young."

"Wish we'd found a billygoat back there."

"Did you check out the sex of the kid? When he grows up…"

"That's incest!"

"Not in their minds. Besides, how do you expect to repopulate?"

"How long before we have baby lambs?"

"I don't know. Adam would know. Probably a few weeks."

"When I was milking the cow, she looked so forlorn."

"A bull would perk her up, get her juices flowing again."

"We're getting a Noah's Ark here, aren't we?"

"I know a remote island up north. There's a deep bay where the English defended the place against the Americans. That was around the time of the Civil War, but buildings were still standing a few years ago. Rich farm land nearby, barns, and a mountaintop lookout for our army."

"Let's load them all up and sail away. But that'd take a big boat. A really big boat."

"Must be one in an abandoned marina or shipyard somewhere. Adam could sail it."

"That'd be exciting. Always wanted to be near the ocean. This'd be even better."

The sound of the howling wind got even stronger. It was a very intense storm.

"Sly, I've been wanting to ask you. You said your real name is Shu. You have Asian heritage, is that correct? Asian-American?"

She smiles. "Yes, can't you tell. Mostly a mix of different Asian types, with a bit of other stuff thrown in, as far as I know. Why do you ask?"

"Just curious. Thinking about what Adam has said about Tristan."

"What about you?"

"Mostly African-American, with Indian and Native-American, and other stuff thrown in, as far as I know. Just like you."

They laugh together. "What about Adam?" Sly asked, "Scottish?"

"Yes, some, but mostly white meat for sure." They roar together. "And Che is Hispanic-American. I guess the main thing is American.

"You mean like the Tristanians? Mixed heritage but all Tristanians?"

"Yes, but soon we'll all be Cascadians. Just Cascadians."

"That's a wonderful thing to think about, Grace."

There was a sudden rattling of the barn from the howling wind that brought them back to the present situation.

"Wish they'd get here. Sounds really bad out there."

"They may have passengers, don't forget. It'll take them longer."

"Is one of those horses a stallion?"

"Don't think so."

"Well, let's take stock. We need a billygoat, a stallion and a bull."

"And a rooster and hen. That would be nice. And ducks and geese. And another cat to keep Pandi company."

"Don't like the cougar idea? What about pigs? A sow and a hog."

"I don't like pigs!"

"If we have pigs, we can leave the nice little lambs alone."

"I love pigs."

"Thought you might. We'll need a huge ship, our own Adam's Ark."

They heard the faint sound of horses plodding through the snowstorm, coming closer to the entrance to the barn.

"Listen!" Sly whispered.

There was a long silence and then they heard the stamping of feet on the floor above.

"They're back."

"No, wait. I didn't hear our signal."

"Maybe he forgot." Grace spoke in a sotto voce manner. Sly did the same.

"No, I don't think so. Something's wrong."

There was someone attempting to come down. They heard the movement of the hay bale above as someone entered the tunnel.

"Someone's coming." Grace spoke very softly.

"Uh, oh. Grab that shotgun. Outta sight. Kill the light." Grace put out the candle. It was pitch black.

They heard someone sliding down the tunnel and landing with an awkward thump. Sly could see in the dark very well but the stranger strained to see. He yelled loudly.

"Anyone here?"

"You bet!" Grace replied.

"Look out," Sly screamed, "He's got a rifle."

He fired a rifle shot wildly and Grace returned fire with her shotgun. He fell to the floor with a heavy thump.

"Good shot. You got 'im."

There was the sound of a big scuffle above, distant but not too far from the tunnel. They heard a shot being fired. Then there was more scuffling, the sound of a falling body, and then silence.

"Something's going on," yelled Grace.

They heard morse code: Knock dah-di-dah. K for OK.

"It's him. It's Che," Sly blurted out, "Our signal."

Sly returned the knock in Morse code: dah-di-dah.

Che slid down the hay tunnel and landed with a thump.

"Boy, are we glad to see you." Grace said.

"I hoped you'd be ready when you didn't hear our signal. Adam got the other one."

"Other one?" asked Sly.

"They ambushed us as we headed toward the barn. They were waiting."

"You're wounded."

"Just a slight one. He got off one shot before Adam got him with the hay fork."

"What are you smiling about?"

"I knew you'd be here to fix me up."

"Don't be so sure. Three strikes and you're out."

"Where'd these two come from?" Grace asked.

"They must be friends of those others. Adam was right. We're not alone here."

"Here she comes." Adam yelled from above.

"Hold on a second!" Che pushed Grace and Sly away from the tunnel.

A young woman came flying out of the tunnel and landed very hard on the floor.

"Let me help you up," Che said, "That was a hard landing."

He reached down and helped her up.

"Thank you," she spoke softly.

"It's a girl!" Grace yelped.

"Her name's Sarah," Che said, "She hasn't eaten for days. Milk's all gone. Do we have any more?"

"Just got some," Sly stepped in, "Let me help you, Sarah. Warm up near the fire while I get you more milk."

"There's one more," Che continued, "Let's not forget Sam. She operated the radio transmitter."

"Oh, yes!" Sly said, "She?"

Sam also slid down quickly but landed lightly on the floor.

"Samantha," Che said, "Grace, can you help her? I need to help Adam."

"Can you take this dead guy with you? I hate looking at him."

"He's not going anywhere. We'll get 'im in a minute."

Che crossed the room and went up the tunnel. Grace went over to Sam.

"I'm Grace. This is Sly. Sarah's having some warm milk. We'll get you some."

"Thank you. We're glad to meet you."

"Here's your milk. We have some warm stew as well. Get some bowls please, Sly."

"I'm starved." Sarah looked up a moment from her milk, "Thank you."

Sarah slurped her milk. Sly got bowls and put them on the logs. Grace filled two of them.

"You'll warm up with this. Eat slowly or you'll get sick."

There was a Morse code signal: K, then an answer K by Sly.

Che entered, and held three rifles, two of which were new ones that were also high powered. He held one up.

"We have four of the finest rifles ever made. Night scopes. I found lots of ammunition in their saddlebags. Even some exploding shells. We're set. These guys must be the army."

Che noticed Sam who held one of the rifles with reverence, as Adam entered.

"You hold it as if you knew all about it?"

"She does," Sarah responded, "Sam's been the champion sharpshooter for three years in a row."

"Pretty impressive," added Adam.

"She can knock an apple off your head at a thousand yards."

"And Sarah's been second every time," Sam interjected, "She's also the rapid-fire champion."

"What distance is that shot at?" asked Che.

"She's hit ten out of ten targets at a thousand yards."

"Bigger targets," Sarah added.

"Like the size of a man?" Che said. She nodded her head yes.

"We've brought something tasty for the stew." Adam held up the meat he was talking about.

Sam and Sarah continued slurping stew since they knew what he was holding.

"What's that you're holding in your hand?" Grace asked.

"Pork?" Sly answered, "You killed a pig?"

"Well, actually, a wild boar we saw in the brush. Che shot it and cleaned it."

"And we have something else," Che added, "We stopped at a barn. See these."

"What are those?" Sly asked. "Chicken eggs? They're huge."

"Turkey eggs," Adam answered, "Four of them. Didn't think they'd be missed."

"I've been craving eggs." Grace leaned forward with eager looks.

"No, you can't eat them," Che stepped in between to discourage her, "We're gonna hatch them."

"Baby turkeys?" Sly smiled, "Bet they'll be cute."

"If all four survive that gives us seven chances out of eight." Adam looked pleased.

"Chances? What do you mean?" Sly was puzzled.

"He means to get at least one boy and one girl," Grace explained, "to keep reproducing turkeys."

"That's not all," Adam continued, "Show her the bag, Che."

"What's in there?" Sly looked closely, "It's moving. A snake? Uggh!"

"A rooster and a hen we found in the barn," Che said, "They traveled well."

"Open it up." Adam ordered, "Let them out."

Che opened the bag. A hen emerged then a rooster.

"And, we found that Border Collie. We call him Toby. He's with the two new horses. And Pandi. She moved over to keep them company."

"My Lord, you've been busy." Grace was impressed.

They stopped talking for a moment and listened to the howling wind.

"Soon's this blizzard's over, don't you think we can move?" Sly asked Che and Adam, "Out of here?"

"Adam, we're just sitting pigeons," Che urged, "We gotta get outta here before someone comes."

"No one's coming here for some time."

"Adam, you were wrong before about them coming back. We were almost done for."

"Alright, so what do you want to do?"

"Move! They'll come back soon and we'll be trapped."

"If we move close by and they come back, then what?"

"We'll fight! Adam, we need to make a stand sooner or later. Why not now?"

"Alright, where do you want to move to?"

Che didn't have a ready answer to this but Sly jumped in.

"When I was out there, I saw an old house far from the river, and a huge barn further away to keep all these animals, and a very lonely bull. And a couple of pigs. All we need now is a stallion."

CHAPTER EIGHTEEN

Moving

Late Winter, 7 AP

After Sly commented that they needed a stallion, and after he stopped laughing, Che thought he should educate her gently on the subject.

"Honey, look more closely at those two horses." Sly did a double take, but then Grace responded to Che's point.

"Che's right. We should move all right. Far from here. Before we have more visitors."

"Quiet," Sly whispered and they froze. "I thought I heard a noise. Like a voice calling out far away."

"It's just the wind," said Adam, "Couldn't be anyone out in this storm. You're imagining it."

"I heard the voice too," said Sam, "far away."

"I've got to take the horses to the shed," Che moved toward the tunnel, "They'll be good company for old Bessy, and our mare Mollie. I'll check on the voice."

"I'll go with you," said Sam, "If it's alright. I'll take a rifle."

He nodded agreement, and they each grabbed a rifle.

"Sure. Give me a hand with this guy. Now we'll have four in our cemetery."

Che and Sam dragged him into the tunnel and took him away.

"Notice how thin he is," Adam observed, "They're starving. That makes them desperate."

"Sarah," Grace asked, "how did all this start? What happened?"

She took the "pork" and began to chop it up while she listened to Sarah's story.

"We belonged to a community group that survived the plague. We lived on the coast one hundred miles south of the river. Sam and I grew up together. I'm 17, she's 19." She stopped for a moment to remember.

"I mean what made you go on the run?"

"We got one day off a week so we saved our days to go on a long camping trip together. Just as we were leaving, a big ship came in to our community. As it was trying to land at our harbor, it was chased by a small ship that fired on it then turned away. The big ship then landed."

"A pirate ship," interrupted Adam, "What did it look like?"

"Sam can tell you better than I."

"What happened after that?" Adam asked.

"The big ship carried the plague, but we didn't know it until we came back after a week. The people in our community said 'stay away until we fetch you'. People were very sick. The commune was quarantined. No one in or out."

Sarah started weeping and Sly tried to console her.

"Sarah, it's alright. Take your time."

Sarah paused to control herself and finally continued.

"We stayed away. No one came to fetch us. Two weeks went by and we'd had very little food. We went back and everyone was dead or dying. We left and never went back."

"It must've been a really bad strain of one of the pandemic viruses." Grace came closer to Sarah and put a hand on her shoulder.

"I guess so. We wandered north to the river. We went up river for twenty miles, found a boat and got across to the north shore. We ate roots and berries but got very weak."

"Poor things. It must've seemed hopeless."

"Winter came. We were desperate. Sam found a transmitter and generator to call for help."

"Sam's quite resourceful," said Grace.

"And then what happened?" asked Sly.

"When we heard from you, we started up the river. Then we realized we didn't know anything about you. We were afraid of being killed or captured or …"

"Or worse," Sly answered for her, "We understand."

"And you had no guns, or any way to defend yourselves." Grace said.

"Then the snow came down hard so we holed up in a shed."

"It was amazing that we found them at all. We stopped in the shed and there they were. They were freezing and starving. Nearly dead."

"They came up with guns. We thought it was over, but they put them away, and Adam gave us milk."

Sarah stopped for a moment to slurp some milk.

"They drank every drop we had," said Adam.

"Then we rode slowly back through the snow, two to a horse."

"The snow. Was it bad?" asked Sly.

"Blinding," Adam answered, "Bitter cold. Worse every hour."

There were intermittent sounds of strong wind and snow blowing, which reminded them of the storm outside.

"We're in for one of the worst blizzards ever," he continued. "Keep that fire going."

Adam started the radio and ran through various frequencies.

"Adam, what are you doing now?" Grace asked sharply.

"Looking for other people. We need to increase the population."

"We pioneer women know how to do that." Sly smiled.

"After we finish eating, we'll show you," added Grace, "You don't need the radio."

He stopped turning the dial and frowned at her.

There was slight static from the radio that was left on.

Sam slid down the tunnel in a hurry without Che. She held Pandi in her arms and dropped her in front of Sly.

"You're back. With Pandi. Still snowing?" asked Sly. "Where's Che?"

The wind and snow continued blowing and rattling the barn slats steadily and never let up. Pandi ran away and into the hay.

"Up above. Adam, Che wants you."

"Something wrong?"

"Go. Quickly."

Adam left in a hurry up the tunnel. Sam turned to Sly.

"You were right about the voice."

"I thought so. Who was it?"

"Don't know. At first, we didn't see anything. A total whiteout."

"Where was he?" Sly asked.

"We heard him a mile west. Down along the river."

"How'd you know it was a person?"

"We took the horses north to the shed and when we got back here, we saw him. A scout."

"That's down near where the farmers used to live," interjected Grace, "What do you mean 'a scout'?"

"He stopped calling. I watched through the scope. He looked around."

"Did he see you?"

"I doubt it but he did stare our way. Then Che sent me to get Adam."

There were Morse signals from Che and Adam above, signaling that they were returning. Sly acknowledged. Che and Adam rushed down. Che reached for a rifle.

"He didn't leave. Looks as if he has backup. Sam, Sarah, come with me."

Sam grabbed a rifle and handed another one to Sarah as well. "We'll need these."

"We don't have much time. Sam, take the north side, Sarah the south side of the barn."

"We'll split them up." Sarah understood the plan.

Che led them up the tunnel followed by Sarah, then Sam.

"Be careful," Grace cautioned, "They outnumber you."

The others listened to the sounds above as they split up with Sarah moving to the south side of the barn and Sam going to the north side. There was a distant rifle shot, as they were seen, but then there were four shots in rapid succession at close range from various sides of the barn: first the south side, then the north, then the south, and finally the north again. One distant shot was barely heard after the first shot fired by

Sarah. They all returned: Sarah, then Sam, then Che, in that order. Che was smiling.

"I didn't get off a shot. They were awesome. That takes care of that."

"Not so fast," said Adam, "They lost four men, rifles and horses before. Now this. There'll be more."

"When we were talking to Sam in Morse, they must have listened in to our plans, spotted us, and followed us back," Che growled, "We're targeted. They won't give up."

There was a mighty roar of the blizzard as if it was driven by the very heavens above.

"I'm absolutely sure," Adam said quietly. He had an epiphany. He took charge. "They want to find us, take our food and kill us. This blizzard only stalls them so much. We've very little time. Here's what we're going to do."

"We're listening," said Che.

"Che and Sam, move all the animals to that barn. Toby will help. It's a mile or so, so no one can hear noises from here. I'll harness Mollie to that wagon near the shed."

"What about the three of us?" Grace asked.

"You and Sly collect all the food and supplies. Sarah, stand guard just in case others come."

"What do we do with it after we gather it up?"

"We'll move it to the big house and then move two loads of hay from here for the animals."

"What about all the tracks? Won't they see them?"

"If this blizzard lasts another day, the snow and wind will cover all the tracks. Questions?"

The heavenly roar of the blizzard continued, incessantly.

"What then?" Sly asked. "We'll find a big boat and sail away with all the animals?"

"Yes, we'll find one. While you keep an eye out, Che, Sam and I'll head down river to that big marina on the south side. We'll look for a large schooner we can sail."

"And the rest of us?" Grace asked.

"You'll work in shifts and I hope Sarah won't need to test her rapid-fire skills. The house is about one thousand yards away. Toby will warn you if there are any people. There could be many more."

"If I see them first it'll take me ten seconds to get them." Sarah stated emphatically.

"You can't go down this side of the river," Grace cautioned, "They'll be expecting you and you'll run into a trap."

"We have the advantage now. We'll ford the horses upstream, go down the south side, and look for a schooner. I'll take the small boat so we can scout both sides at night."

"You don't know where they are. Won't you run into them by mistake?"

"Even if we do, they won't be expecting us. When we sail down with the schooner, we'll never get past the mouth of the river and that pirate ship if we don't know where they are. We might have to take them out first. Or maybe I should say Sam will."

"How big is this schooner?" Sly asked, "We have lots of animals."

"About one hundred and fifty feet. Maybe more. Lots of cargo space below for animals and hay and the rest."

"Yes. Adam's Ark, we'll call it," Grace said, "He can sail anything. Can't you, Adam?"

The radio started crackling. The sounds gradually became clear. It was definitely Morse code coming through on the radio. Dash dot dash dot, dash dash dot dash. CQ – Calling anyone. Over and over.

"Adam, listen," Che yelled, "It's the radio, the call signal. There's someone else out there!"

HAL: CQ CQ CQ DE HAL SOS FUJI MM DOWN QTL N QUG HAL AR.

In the background, there was the sound of loose rigging, sails flapping, and a small engine stuttering.

"It's a FUJI ketch and the mainmast is gone," Adam said, "That's what they say. Their call name is HAL They say they were heading north and were forced to land. It sounded like loose rigging and slapping sails, and the engine sounds as if it's in trouble."

"A FUJI's thirty-five feet," Sam said, "There can't be too many people on board."

HAL: CQ QTH S STR RIV CURR = NO FUL = NO FUD HAL AR.

The background noise now sounded as if the engine was dying, and the sails and rigging were under duress.

"The engine's dead," Adam translated, "They're south of the strong river current. Out of fuel and food."

"They're still calling with CQ," Che said, "No one else has answered."

"I know where they are," Sam said, "I was there."

"We should answer," Sarah urged, "You helped us. We should help them."

"Hold on a minute," Grace cautioned, "It could be a trap. They could have the plague. Could be more of those pirates."

"And it could be a couple of people like us," Sly argued, "We need to take a chance. Answer them."

HAL: SOS SOS SK. Then the transmissions stopped altogether.

"Too late," Adam said, "They're off the air."

"There's someone out there," Che, Sam, Sly, and Sarah all yelled together, "We've got to go help them!"

"Hold on," Adam stopped them, "Something's wrong. Too much information. They don't want a response."

"What do they want then?" Sarah asks.

"This time Grace is right. It's a trap. Sam, tell me about that pirate ship you saw."

"There was a turret gun mounted on the bow."

"The ship itself. Length? Power boat or sailboat?"

"30 to 40 feet long. Two masts, forward one taller."

"That was the pirate ship. But they won't be on the south bank. They'll be on the north."

"There goes my island in the north." Grace was almost weeping.

"Doesn't change a thing," Adam said. "In fact, now we know where they are. Easier to get them."

"There're only three of you," Sly said. "What if there are 10 or 20 of them?"

"I doubt there are many. They're starving and desperate. With Sam at 800-1000 yards picking them off, and Che and I cutting off escape, I guarantee we'll wipe them out."

"What about the pirate ship with the turret gun?" Sarah asked.

"One exploding shell at the water line and it's sunk," Che clapped his hands, "I doubt they'll have time to launch."

"Everyone understand our plan?" Adam concluded.

"Yes, Captain," Grace saluted, and the others nodded yes.

"After we finish down river," Adam said, "we'll bring the schooner up river, load it up, and set sail north."

"I'd love to mount a turret gun amidships." Che said.

"It'd be in the way there but you can mount it on the bow."

"We can go to my island in the north?" Grace asked, "And have a nice safe home?" Adam nodded his head in approval.

"And we can take all the animals and have a real farm?" Sly asked. Again, he nodded his approval.

"And you can grow vegetables. and wheat, and.." Grace directed her question to Adam and he interrupted.

"And we can start raising a family." Grace opened her mouth in surprise and delight.

"Where everyone is equal regardless of what they look like?"

Sly added, "Including our children?"

"Just like how Adam described Tristanians?" said Che.

"Yes. A utopian world rising from the ashes of the dystopian world that no longer exists. Wouldn't that be wonderful?"

"Where honor, decency, respect, and truth prevail," spoke up Sly.

Grace added, "and hope, love, compassion, and caring."

"That's right. A new world. Well, let's get going. We have lots to do."

They each grabbed something from the "Burrow", and left, climbing up through the tunnel, with Adam first followed by Che. Sly and Grace were last.

Grace heard a meow coming from the hay.

"Sly, don't forget Pandi."

Sly went behind some hay and returned cradling a frightened Pandi.

"It's alright Pandi. We said all the animals. We can't forget you."

"If we each have 4 girls, they have 4, and so forth, there'll be 30000 in 100 years," Grace talked to herself softly. "We pioneer women know how to be fruitful, and multiply, and replenish the earth."

Sly climbed into the tunnel. Grace paused at the entrance to the tunnel before she left. She smiled.

"Goodbye, burrow. You've given us warmth, nourishment, some safety, and maybe the start of a family. I won't miss the hay, but I'll miss you." Grace left.

PART THREE

ADAM'S ARK

CHAPTER NINETEEN

Executing The Plan

Early Spring, 7 AP

Adam's plan was executed flawlessly. The team worked as a unit: they had a leader, they had a plan, they had a common set of goals, and each had a job to do. They were a small army of six dedicated souls.

Working at night to avoid being seen from afar, they worked from dusk to dawn. Adam hooked up the horse Mollie to the wagon they had found and kept near the shed where she was housed. Then they brought it to the barn entrance, so that Che and Sam could help him move all the animals to the barn a mile away. It was temporary but Adam thought it was the safest thing to do.

At first, they moved the goats, lambs, pigs, chickens, and newly hatched turkeys, ducks and geese. They had enough stalls for the horses, the cow, and the bull. It was pretty crowded but much better than what they expected on the schooner. Toby kept watch and listened for danger, with Pandi by his side. They had become the best of friends. Then the three of them moved some of the hay to that barn for the animals until they could get the schooner upstream.

Meanwhile Grace and Sly brought all the food to the barn entrance and they loaded up the wagon again and brought all of it to the house where they would stay until the schooner arrived. Adam made sure Grace took special care with his collection of seeds and bulbs for later planting. She did. Sarah guarded while all this was being accomplished.

Then they were ready for the next phase. Sam and Che and Adam headed to the hidden rowboat that Adam had used.to reach this part of the river. They launched it and hugged the south coast of the Columbia for two nights until they encountered the marina Adam had seen before. They searched for the rest of the night and finally found a schooner with two masts. It was about one hundred and fifty feet long with a draft of about ten feet. He knew it would be fast if that was needed. It seemed to be still in good shape. Adam checked it inside from bow to stern looking for leaks and found none. He found that the full set of sails was still there and in reasonably good condition.

They went below and Adam determined that they would be able to partition the boat into areas for different animals, for hay, and spaces for themselves. It would be cramped but Che and Sam agreed that it would be possible. In fact, they were eager to show Sly, Grace, and Sarah.

"That will have to wait," said Adam, "We have a journey ahead now."

They drifted down the river in the rowboat for several nights. It took the remainder of the week, traveling almost exclusively at night. They crossed to the north bank when they saw the remains of a high bridge ahead. They approached slowly until they saw a camp fire on the north bank close to shore and near the end of the once wonderful bridge. Adam anchored slightly upstream from the bridge and in thick reeds.

They climbed up a grassy knoll and saw in the distance a group of about twenty men gathered around the fire. They also saw the thirty-five-foot Fuji ketch Adam had expected to see. It was at anchor just off shore near the camp in a protected inlet. They rested a couple of hours until night arrived. Then they executed the next phase of their plan.

"Sam," he whispered, "take a position above the camp, east of it, and stay hidden until Che starts the firing. Che, drop me off close to shore up river from the camp, then drift down river from the camp. Start firing when you are ready."

Sam positioned herself behind a boulder. She waited for Adam and Che to begin the action. Che dropped off Adam behind a thick bush and then came ashore down river. Che started the fireworks by firing at the seated men, and Adam followed up. The group scattered from the crossfire and dropped to the ground for protection. At this point Sam began rapid fire, picking off men one by one. A few not sitting at the fire came out to see the action and were picked off by the three of them firing in a withering crossfire. Two men broke away and headed for the Fuji ketch.

Che saw them on top of the ketch trying to get the gun in action. Che loaded his special bullet designed to explode on impact and hit the boat near the waterline. He then aimed below the gun and knocked it off its support. Even then Che had dreams of his own special gun mounted on their own schooner. Sam saw what was happening and, with her expert sniper scope and skills, got the men. Soon, at the camp as well, there was no one left standing. Che and Adam came to the camp, checked around, and found no one alive.

Meanwhile upriver, Sarah kept watch with Toby by her side, and Sly relieved her now and then to allow her a short rest. The blinding snow and wind kept up during the day and the next night. Grace checked on the animals during the two weeks they waited, and a couple of times during the day when visibility was low. She cleaned up where she could and fed the animals a bit to keep them from starving from scraps they had accumulated from their own food. At about the same time Adam and the two others were attacking and decimating the camp downstream, all was quiet at the house and the barn full of animals. It continued this way for the remainder of the time, with decreasing snow and wind.

Adam and Che and Sam proceeded slowly up the river in the small boat, and after five days and nights of rowing, they reached the marina. Adam sought out the schooner that he had seen. The marina was lifeless. The three of them checked out the one-hundred-fifty-foot schooner again. It was a bit neglected but seemed to be seaworthy. *It must have been magnificent in its prime* thought Adam. Adam examined the gear, the sails and extra supplies, while Che started the engine. The engine took a bit to get working but it worked alright. Che checked the oil while Sam went in search of any gasoline and oil she could find. She found a hoard near the gasoline depot or what must have been some sort of office. It looked as if someone was about to leave but the plague must have stopped them. There were no bodies or corpses or bones. If there had been any they were picked clean by various birds that still hovered around the marina. These were mainly seagulls. Sam also found a feed store near there and broke in. It still had some bags of feed. Che helped her bring back the gasoline and feed to the schooner and loaded it all in. While they were at the marina and Adam was preparing to set sail, Che and Sam ventured out carrying rifles and found a small gun shop nearby, where they found a few boxes of ammunition hidden under counters. There were no guns left.

They prepared the sails on the schooner, checked the rigging, steering, and rudder, and sailed slowly up the big river with the rowboat stowed on deck. It took another three days to reach the smaller river and the barn. During the first two days, the weather was still windy and snow continued to blanket the surrounding landscape. The low visibility kept them on guard. However, during their last day of sailing upstream, the weather turned warmer, the snow turned to rain, and the wind grew stronger. The rain came down in sheets, and the visibility was even worse.

At about this time, with dawn approaching, Sarah was on guard with Toby by her side. She dozed briefly and woke up with Toby growling. She looked out in the dim light and saw four horsemen approaching the main barn that they had vacated. The horses came from the west or down river. The wind let up just enough for her to get a clear shot. She fired twice and took out two of the men. The other two horses bolted and she was able to get one of the men. The remaining horse was headed behind some bushes and Sarah reluctantly took the horse down before it escaped from view. The man stood up in the remaining snow and tried to run. Sarah took aim and got the last man. Sly came running and the three of them, Sarah, Sly and Toby ran out. Sly removed the gear from the three horses and let them run free. Sarah checked out the four men and was assured that they had all perished.

It was nearly dawn. Sly looked near the barn and saw Che making his way slowly through the torrential rain. She ran to hug him. They were all together again.

CHAPTER TWENTY

Loading The Ark

Late Spring, 7 AP

It rained continuously for a week. The snow up river melted and all along the tributaries, and the river level rose several feet. Adam and Che had initially anchored the schooner slightly off shore where the depth was greater, and secured it as well with ropes from the bow, starboard side and aft. As the rain filled the rivers and the water levels rose over the next few days, Adam felt it was time to load up the schooner.

"Che, we're lucky. Now we can bring the schooner in much closer to shore and figure out the best way to bring everything on board."

"Let's take stock of the layout then of the schooner," Che responded, "and have a plan before we start loading."

They walked through the one-hundred-fifty-foot-long schooner, and determined that they could manage to fit everything and everyone on board. The hold needed to be subdivided slightly to arrange stalls for the horses and cow and bull, and to separate pigs, goats, lambs, chickens, and baby turkeys, ducklings, and goslings. There was a small upper cabin astern of the cockpit and two other cabins in the bow section. Adam and Grace occupied the former, Che and Sly took one of the other cabins, and Sam and Sarah shared the third.

Toby had the run of the ship and took turns in each room but preferred Sly's cabin. Adam thought the presence of Pandi had something to do with it. They made room for hay in the middle of the hold, and also stacked hay in every nook and cranny, as well as the feed bags, silage, and other fodder. Silage was also put on the floor of the animal stalls, together with the hay strewn about. The kitchen was aft and the head was near the sail room in the bow. Extra fuel was also stashed in the bow. Sly thought it was almost overflowing and Che was confident it would be alright. As it turned out, in the beginning, they were both correct.

After several days of preparation, at night with a clear sky, the six of them moved all of the food, and gear, and supplies to the various places on the schooner. They had built a ramp from the bank to the deck of the schooner to make it easier to load it. Their 'gangplank' was wide enough for the horses and the bull. Their plan was to use only the nighttime just in case other men arrived. Sam and Sarah took turns guarding the area while the moving was going on. Adam had hooked up Mollie and the wagon to help move much of the food and gear. They also used the wagon to load up as much hay as they could, and fodder and grain for animals.

They stored it in many locations that they thought would be good places and not in the way.

They had just completed loading supplies and food and prepared to start loading animals when a storm settled in and it began to snow again. The wind picked up and their hearing was blocked. Toby, with Sarah and Sam taking turns, stood guard outside for two-hour shifts and saw no one. Finally, after a day and night, when they thought all was prepared, and the wind and snow had diminished, they began moving the small animals first, then the pigs and goats and lambs. Last of all, they moved the cow Bessy, the horse Mollie, the bull, and the stallion. They set sails and pushed off before dawn. The six of them and Toby sat in the cockpit as they moved into the big river. The engine was idling, and Adam and Che had hoisted only a jib and the mizzen. They toasted each other and the journey ahead, with milk. Even Toby joined Pandi in having some of the milk. He always let Pandi eat or drink first. Adam's Ark was on its way.

Grace, Sly, and Sarah went below, and Sam moved carefully to the bow. While Che stood by to handle the sails, Adam took the helm for the first night and relished the task ahead. Even though he was an expert at farming and growing food, he was really the most relaxed and at home on the sea. He felt the wind and mist in his face and looked at Che.

"I wish we'd sailed together to the south. It's exciting to be on the open ocean. You will love it."

"Adam, you'll get your wish. We'll be on the open sea soon. You'll get enough excitement then. Meanwhile, I hope we get where we're going before next winter. I wouldn't want to be out at sea with a major storm. Especially not with this load."

"My plan is to hug the coast going north. Even with stops, it should take no more than a couple of months. Maybe less. I've talked to Grace and we have a spot in mind that will be perfect for our community."

"First, we have to get this boat down the river and into the sea."

Adam responded, "No problem."

Now and then, Sam would spell Che and he would take the helm while Adam rested, then Adam would return and Che would rest. At this point it was easy traveling. After the initial period of unrest, the animals in the hold settled down and grew accustomed to the movement of the ship. They passed under one bridge that was partially destroyed and sections of it near both shores had fallen into the river. The river was a couple of miles wide at this point. After a couple of nights of drifting and sailing, they stopped on the south shore and dropped anchor. They cleaned out the boat from the droppings of the animals and continued on at dusk a day later.

The river headed north and they sailed slowly for another few days, and sailed under another bridge that was damaged but still largely intact. Che was at the helm while Adam took a break and Sam was at the bow. The others came up briefly and looked at the destruction on shore and the damaged bridge.

"We should be careful," said Grace one night, "that a bridge doesn't fall on us while we sail under it."

"As long as the wind is not strong," replied Che, "we are pretty safe. This has taken years to get to this state."

"Seven years to be exact," answered Sly.

"Call if you need help, Che," Grace yelled as she and Sly went down below just as Sam came back to the cockpit.

"Che, after we clean out the hold the next time, I'd like to take a rest. Alright?"

"No problem. We all will. After we rest up for a day or two, Adam can take the helm and I'll handle the sails until we reach the mouth of the river. I hope that turret gun is still there on the ketch. I'd like to take it if it is."

They stopped once again for a couple of days to clean out the hold, then sailed slowly along the south shore for another few nights. They saw that the river widened ahead to several miles across. They also saw a very long bridge in the distance.

"That's where the camp is," said Adam, "let's stop here for a couple of days and make sure we are prepared to sail into the open sea, which we will do soon after we go under that bridge."

They anchored early in the morning on the south shore where the current was not as strong.

"Look, Adam," pointed Che, "is that the remains of an old abandoned fort? It looks as if it's a couple of hundred years old."

"I think it's only a portion of the blockhouse they had here in the early 1800s, and probably a replica. All the other buildings here seem to be leveled or badly damages, so let's put the animals in there."

They were able to put down the gangplank to let all the animals go ashore. They also found some fenced areas for the horses and cattle, which they fixed and secured quickly before offloading the animals. They took this time to clean out the inside where the animals were kept, and sanitized the entire area. They did not want to leave them out at night and stay over one more day. As nighttime approached, they loaded them back into the clean hold. They set sail quietly and crossed the wide river to the north shore.

It had taken a week and a half traveling only at night to reach the mouth of the river. As they approached the location of the camp in the early part of the night, they saw the bridge remains, and then the wrecked Fuji, Adam approached very carefully and saw no life.

"Adam," Che asked, "I want to recover that turret gun if I can. I left it intact." Adam agreed.

They came alongside the ketch and Che, with the help of Sam, recovered the gun which had just fallen to the deck. They put it on the deck of the schooner and Adam pushed off. Then they heard a shot which just missed them. Sam saw two men about to fire at Adam and Che, grabbed her gun and fired twice, hitting each of them with deadly result.

"Let's get out of here," yelled Che, "before more show up. I thought we got all of them."

"It must be a group that is more widespread than I thought."

They sailed out toward the narrow neck of the river that opened out into the ocean. With the strong current propelling them rapidly into the high waves, Adam sailed slowly out through the gap in the mouth of the river past the abandoned fort to the south, and the sandy spit. The very fast and turbulent current caused the boat to rock back and forth and the bow rose and fell. The animals began to moo and bellow and every sort of noise came from the hold.

"That's the sandy spit I reached coming up from the south."

"Do you think," asked Sam, "that we'll see any ships at sea?"

"We might," said Adam.

"We must expect it," added Che.

After reaching the ocean waves, they tacked and Adam then sailed north around the point of the flat strip of land and along the narrow peninsula to the east that stretched north for many miles.

"I want to reach a large bay I know about," said Adam, "before dawn arrives. We can stop there briefly. Watch out for rocks."

Sarah came up to join Sam. They were trying to spot an indentation while Adam tried to stay away from crashing on rocks and had to tack back and forth with the help of Che. Sam spotted the mouth of an inlet at the end of the long spit going north that they had been following.

"Adam," yelled Sam, "it looks like the inlet you've been searching for, just beyond the end of the sandy spit."

Sarah spotted a sign with her binos that had fallen to the ground.

"That sign on the ground says Willapa Bay," she added.

"Coming about Che." Adam sailed into this deep bay out of the turmoil at sea. He sailed to an island in the mouth of the bay. "Get ready to drop anchor."

"Roger," Che said from the bow, "you got it."

Dawn was just arriving. They stayed anchored during the day and kept a fitful watch for any sign of life. There was none.

During the day they all did some work on sails and cleaned up inside the hold, but basically just relaxed. When the sun came out in the afternoon, Grace, Sly, Sarah and Sam snoozed on the deck. Che and Adam took turns as sentries. After feeding all the animals, they all gathered on deck in the late afternoon for a wonderful meal, and watched the gorgeous blazing sunset. They talked about the coming journey, hoping to reach Cascadia as soon as possible.

"We call it Cascadia," Sam said to Grace, "what does that mean to you?"

Grace thought for a moment and replied slowly. "It means living a healthy and safe life and being able to do the things we always wanted to do. I want to write, to record everything I know about the Great Pandemic and our journey to get to Cascadia, and of course I want to have children, lots of them."

"I can help with that," said Adam, "especially the second goal."

Everyone laughed.

"And what about you, Sly?" continued Sam. "What does Cascadia mean to you?"

Sly gave it some thought and answered. "Well, I guess the same as Grace about finding a safe home where I can feel comfortable about having children and having them grow up learning things I never did." She paused. "I also want to be on the sea and find oysters and clams and mussels and shrimp and crab and lobster."

"I'll help you with that, Sly," Che stepped in, "and help make a wonderful soup with those for all of us, and especially to help eat it. Now that's what I call Cascadia." They all laughed and agreed.

When dusk arrived and the sun had set, Sly asked if they could let some of the animals out again, this time for the night. Adam agreed and he and Che sailed closer to shore of the island where they could set out the gangplank. They led Mollie, Bessy, and the stallion out to graze first, but kept the bull on board. The lambs and goats were next. The pigs stayed on board. Toby kept watch and herded them back if they strayed. They grazed all night. During this period, five of them cleaned out the hold of the schooner while Sam and Sarah took turns standing guard with a rifle. Then and only then did they have a moment to eat and relax, and to celebrate the start of their voyage.

As dawn approached, Sly and Che and Toby herded the animals back on board. They took turns keeping watch during the day while others slept, and Adam set sail at dusk. He sailed for a few hours and came past a deep harbor that went in for many miles. Sam spotted a sign on the point of the opening which said Grays Harbor. It was too early to stop yet again so Adam carried on. After several hours of sailing north, the wind picked up, the seas began to grow, and soon they were encountering ten and then fifteen-foot waves. Grace came up and said that the rough seas were disturbing the animals.

"Can't we put in somewhere?" she asked.

"I don't think we have any choice since there is no harbor or bay. We must keep sailing until we find one."

"Adam," Che said softly, "this is too dangerous. We should turn back to that harbor. We won't lose too much time. It is better than capsizing with this load. We will lose everything, including our lives if we don't."

Reluctantly, Adam turned back and found the harbor entrance. He motored in to the relative calm of the harbor and dropped anchor. It was still pretty rough even in the protected harbor. The winds increased to sixty knots early in the morning and they hunkered down to wait for an end to the storm. By dusk it was calm again but Adam decided to wait an extra day before continuing on.

During the night, the wind increased again but then subsided during the day and Adam prepared to sail out again into the open sea. He was not as excited about the open sea at this point. Perhaps it was the heavy load, the major responsibility for the people and the animals. Last of all, he knew there was constant danger of encountering enemies on land or at sea. When dusk again approached, he got up his courage, prepared the team and the ship to sail once again into the open Pacific.

CHAPTER TWENTY ONE

The Open Sea

Summer, 7 AP

With the help of Adam, Che had used the time in the harbor to mount the large turret gun on the bow section. He'd found a box of shells for the gun in the cabin of the ketch and brought them along. Adam helped position the gun so as not to interfere with raising sails. Che had damaged the base when he had knocked the gun off of it but, together, they managed to mend it and mount it properly. Che was very fond of the turret gun. He had mixed feelings since he wanted to find a time to use it but that meant they would be under attack. In any event he was ready to use it if necessary.

Adam sailed out of the harbor at dusk and stayed about one mile off shore as they moved slowly up the coast. He dared not use running lights, so when it was very dark, he used either Sam or Sarah as a spotter on the bow. He sailed very slowly at first but gradually gained speed. He thought he could average five knots per hour if he did not run into bad weather or other danger.

Adam and Che reckoned it might be about one hundred twenty nautical miles to the Strait they were seeking. If they managed the five knots then they could cover about thirty knots at night without being seen at dusk and dawn. Therefore, it might take four nights under best conditions. But he still had several problems: he did not think he could hold to five knots per hour at night without running lights; if he ran into bad weather that would impact their schedule as well. In fact, they might even have to find a cove or river mouth for shelter and they were not that common along the shore. However, according to an old nautical map he found, there were some.

They had been sailing half the first night and they were beginning to feel comfortable on the sea. Suddenly the winds increased and the waves rose to ten feet or more. Once again, they had to seek shelter and Adam headed close to shore and followed it north for several miles. Sam and Sarah were trying to spot an indentation while Adam tried to stay away from crashing on rocks and had to tack back and forth with the help of Che. Sam spotted the mouth of a river and Adam thought they might be able to follow it briefly out of the roiling sea. On the shores of the river were the remains of a town called Taholah, according to a sign on a billboard that had fallen at an angle to the ground. They anchored in a calm inlet and stayed the rest of the night and the next day, keeping watch by turns.

With a calm sea once again, they set out sailing north. They covered about thirty more miles and sought shelter for the day. They were fortunate once again to find a river big enough to sail into and sufficient to anchor during the day. They sailed under a bridge, parts of which had fallen into the river. The roadway was hanging in places, dangling in the wind, looking as if it too was about to crash into the flowing river.

At dusk, they sailed out under a clear sky with light from stars showing the way. Unfortunately, this made for high visibility. They had been out for a couple of hours when the spotter at the time, who was Sam, saw two ships in the distance south of them and heading directly for them. They were each much smaller and had seen the big schooner before they had been spotted themselves. They were attempting to cut Adam off from sailing either direction but he outsmarted them by tacking sharply to port and heading out to sea before the outside ship could reach them.

However, the two ships were smaller and could maneuver better so they were closing on the schooner. Ordinarily the schooner could outdistance them but the huge load of the animals slowed them down. Adam and Che decided it was time to test the turret gun since they were not escaping. They were afraid that the two ships could begin firing on them from the stern and slowly cripple them.

"Ready, Che?" Adam suddenly yelled as he saw Che behind the turret gun which he had loaded. He had several shells ready to go.

"Alright, Adam. Come about."

As he did, they saw a flash and heard the sound of small arms firing at them but the shells landed harmlessly far from the schooner.

"Get ready, Che."

Adam came about and headed for the left ship which was approaching head-on. Che fired several shells at the ship and scored a direct hit. Fire broke out and the ship stopped. The other ship realized the danger and attempted to escape. Adam tacked and followed the second ship. Again, Che fired the turret gun several times and sank the ship. With both ships no longer a problem, they proceeded on their way past an island well out to sea, and stopped at dawn along shore where they found a small river entering the sea. The turret gun was a success and Adam and Che celebrated with Grace, Sly, Sam, and Sarah.

"Adam," Grace said when there was a pause, "we have a growing problem. We need to find a place to get these animals out for a little while. It is a mess down there and we can't keep up."

"Alright, I'll find a place. I think we might have a spot a few hours north."

Adam got the ship under way at dawn and tried to sail in the most direct line along the shore with minor tacks. Sam spotted a river in the middle of the night and Adam steered in to the entrance of the river. He found just enough draft to anchor and wait for dawn. Sam, Che, and Adam took the rowboat and searched both shores for a suitable place to offload the animals for a time. They realized they were in a part of what had been a national park, and searched for life. They found none, but did find a small grazing place. They dropped anchor, and tied ropes to several tree. They then set up the gangplank and began to offload animals. As before, they took Mollie and Bessy to the best grazing spot they could find. They took a chance and brought the stallion out. They had decided to name him Buck. They need not have worried. Buck stayed very close to Mollie. They wondered if they might be in store for a future colt or mare.

Then they brought the lambs out to graze near Bessy and Mollie, and the goats which they felt they should stake so as to keep them from wandering. They brought the pigs out to the shoreline close to the ship. They found some mud to roll in. The final issue concerned the bull. They decided to construct a makeshift corral and hoped it would constrain the bull. With some difficulty, the six of them managed to get the bull down the gangplank and into the corral. They were relieved to find the bull, that they had named Bubba, was more interested in the freedom and the grazing than he was in trying to wander or go after Bessy.

After all that, five of them began to clean out the hold, while either Sam or Sarah stood guard. They spent the entire day swabbing and disinfecting the animal areas, and then they foraged for straw and silage and found some good quality alfalfa as well as hay still rolled up and loaded all of it on board. Last of all, they searched the area for root crops and anything edible to sustain themselves until they reached their destination. They loaded the animals back on board at the end of the day rather than leave them out. They were afraid they might be visited by cougars or wild dogs and wanted to keep all the animals from being attacked.

They took this time to have another wonderful dinner on deck. They watched the sun set over the ocean producing a rich complex beautiful sunset of reds and oranges and yellows and pastel blues and pinks.

"We never heard from Adam about his dreams and wishes when we reach our Cascadia." Sam turned to him. "Well, Adam, what does Cascadia mean to you? What are you hoping for?"

"Grace and Sly, remember our conversation about wine. Besides all the planting of crops, vegetables and fruit trees, I have wanted to make wine. Perhaps I can find some grape vines that are still viable and start the process of making wine."

"I remember that there were some vineyards on the island that I hope we get to," replied Grace, "and also there was another really good winery that made excellent wine. It was on another island east of where we are going."

"We will find them Adam," Che replied, "you can count on it."

"That would be one of the many things I will look forward to."

"And what about the cheese and bread to go with the wine?" said Grace, "I can help with the bread but I don't know much about cheese."

"I can help make cheese," replied Che, "I learned something about that before the pandemic hit."

"Don't forget Bessy," Sly jumped in, "I like her milk but she will need to contribute some of her milk to make cheese."

"We have goats now," Sam said, "I have heard that goat cheese is wonderful."

"That settles it," smiled Adam, "we are all in this together. We will finally get our wine and cheese and bread. Does that answer your question, Sam?"

Sam smiled and nodded. "It sure does. I am looking forward to seeing how you make bread. I love fresh bread. Right out of the oven. I can't wait."

"It won't be long." Che got up off the deck. "Meanwhile, I'm getting a little sleep."

They all rested for the remainder of the night and most of the next day. As they watched another beautiful sunset, they discussed their plan. Adam and Che felt the weather was mild enough to resume sailing. Even the barometer was high. The sky had been clear during the latter part of the day. At dusk, they set sail out into the ocean and north along the coast. Adam had calculated that they had about sixty to seventy miles to go before reaching the northwest point of the former nation and the opening into the Strait of Juan de Fuca. This would take them two nights of sailing if weather permitted. They made good time the first night and accomplished about half of the journey to the Strait. Adam sailed into a river and anchored. There was a strong current as the river coursed into the sea but they were able to drop anchor to hold the ship, and then tied ropes to stout trees on the south side of the river.

They searched the surrounding area and found only abandoned buildings and cabins. Che saw a sign that read "La Push". Sam found some gravestones clustered together.

"I think those on the Reservation probably got hit hard and early," said Grace, "I don't think they had immunity to many of the virions. Sad."

"We might find a lot more of these gravesites over time." Adam added.

They collected some cans of food that seemed in good order still, and they also found some dried foods protected from predators in cabinets. After resting a bit during the day, they set sail while it was still daylight. Adam hoped to reach the opening of the Strait by dawn or early morning. All went well until the sky became overcast, the rain came down in torrents, and the wind began to hit gale force. They had covered more than half the distance, Adam thought, and could no longer turn back. He could not find a cove or river in which to anchor and ride out the storm, so they were forced to press on. To avoid being hit broadside by the huge fifteen-foot waves, he was forced to tack out to sea and head into the incoming waves, and then come about and run before the wind and waves until they again headed to shore. It was very dangerous and tricky to come about and head back out into the waves to avoid crashing ashore. The animals were mooing and neighing and baaing as the boat rocked back and forth and up and down at the bow.

Once they were nearly swamped when a giant wave crashed over the bow and filled the cockpit. Fortunately, all of the hatches were closed at the time. They had stowed all the mainsails and ran just with a jib and mizzen. Sam and Sarah helped Che with the sails and Grace helped Adam now and then at the tiller. Sly stayed below to try and calm the animals, and became seasick from the rocking. They were all becoming exhausted when Adam and Che spotted Cape Flattery, the north westernmost point of the forty-eight states. Adam nearly crashed on the rocky island off the point but managed to sail into the Strait and into Neah Bay. Sam spotted a sign that had fallen down identifying their location. They had somehow managed to reach the safety of the Strait and the Bay, still alive. They were grateful and exhausted. It was midday. They anchored out of the direct wind and took turns standing watch while the others rested. The animals gradually calmed down.

The ship hold was a mess with hay, silage, other fodder, and tools scattered about. The mainsail was tattered and part of the rigging was loose but they had made it. After a few hours of rest, they cleaned up and set the gangplank out to let the larger animals out to forage. All except for the bull were brought ashore. This time they let them stay out over the night, posting a guard at all times to protect against any predators. In the morning all was shipshape, the animals were content again, the sails and rigging were fixed, and they prepared to sail inland through the Strait and to the protected location where Adam and Grace hoped they could settle. They had high hopes that they were finally about to find their longed for 'safe haven'.

CHAPTER TWENTY TWO

Entering The Strait

Late Summer, 7 AP

Adam was concerned about the strong winds coming from the ocean creating a storm surge east into the Strait, but he was also concerned about staying too long in Neah Bay. If the wind shifted to a northwest wind, it would blast them and cause damage. He waited until a few hours after daylight when the tide was coming in and set sail directly east, along the south shore of the strait. The winds were still very strong as dusk was approaching. They sailed past a point and then turned southwest into a small cove which gave them sufficient protection from the wind which now shifted coming from the northwest.

The wind died down just before daybreak. Early in the morning after feeding all the animals, they set sail directly northeast across the strait. They hugged the coast, passing several bays and inlets, until they sailed past the eastern tip of the big land mass or island to the north of them and headed northeast into the Haro Strait. They crossed the open water of the Strait and followed the western shore of the island to the east, but stayed out about a mile from shore to avoid shelves and rocks.

Adam sailed with only two sails since the wind was now more than twenty knots aft coming in from the Strait. He slowly made his way up the coast until he encountered a huge island dead ahead and a channel on the starboard. He anchored at the entrance to the channel and sent Che and Sam with the rowboat into the Pass with a plumb line. They scouted the way ahead through the narrow channel with the rowboat and returned several hours later with grim news.

"We don't think it's wise to try and enter the pass," said Che. "The currents are tricky and rocks are everywhere." He continued, "Furthermore, I feel, that with a draft of ten feet for the schooner, we will surely run aground and probably sink."

Sam added, "By the way it says Mosquito Pass and I was bitten by some."

They anchored for the night inside the Bay east of them, and in daylight Che and Sam took the two horses down the gangplank into shallow water and rode them ashore. They each carried a rifle just in case they encountered danger of any sort. They rode east for a distance on an overgrown road and then north until they came to an abandoned marina with a few wrecked boats. They found what they were looking for. A place to dock the schooner with sufficient draft and docks to allow them to unload the animals. They returned to the schooner and Che swam aboard while Sam tethered the two horses to a tree. Sarah swam ashore to join Sam, and Che explained what to look for ahead.

Adam raised the anchor, sailed out into the Strait, around the long island, and came to an entrance into the harbor and marina with just enough draft to get through. Sarah and Sam greeted them from the docks and waved. Che and Sly were on either side of the schooner with plumb lines just to make sure they could get through without getting grounded. They pulled up to an outer dock and tied up. Sam and Sarah then rode the horses in a different direction, east of the one they had used to reach the docks, to continue a survey of the area. Each carried a rifle. While they were gone, Adam and Che scouted the nearby places and found no sign of life. Sam and Sarah returned with the horses in a couple of hours and reported the same result. Since it was late in the day, the group stayed aboard one last night, and relaxed and celebrated their success at finally reaching their destination.

After feeding the animals one last time on board the schooner, they gathered together on deck to watch the glorious sunset and ate a delicious dinner.

"Now Che," Sarah asked, "now that we finally got here, it's your turn to tell us your dreams and wishes about Cascadia. What do you want to do?"

Che thought for a moment and then answered, "I no longer want to build a guerrilla group, but we still need to be on guard. I want to live in peace, to have a family, to build a wonderful society where we all work together. I want to restore the good aspects of our old society. I feel sad about the loss of so many good people, good friends, but we need to look ahead now. I want to educate our many children that we will have. I also want to sail with Adam after we settle here and just explore the world. We will need to restore a few more ships. I am so excited about finally getting here and anxious to get started in the morning."

Everyone applauded Che for his fine speech, for he was often a man of few words, preferring action to talk. They watched the last glimmer of the sunset and turned in. Adam, Che, Sam, and Sarah took turns on deck keeping watch.

They rose early in the morning. Che and Sly searched for a temporary place nearby to keep the animals, while Sam and Adam rode the horses to seek out a farm inland with buildings that would be just right for housing the animals and grazing areas for all. Adam also thought it imperative to find land for planting vegetables and fruit trees, and finding a house that could be their own home. Adam felt he owed it to Grace to find her that 'safe haven' she always dreamed about. On this first foray, they could not find a farm that met their goals.

There were many buildings around the marina so Adam and the team decided to distribute the animals as best they could until they found and prepared their farm. They brought the horses from the schooner to the largest building they could find, an empty hotel, and then brought Bessy and Bubba there as well, lodged in separate areas. Finding a place for the goats, lambs and pigs was easy and placing the chickens, ducklings, goslings, and turkeys was the easiest of all. They set them up with straw, alfalfa and other silage for some and feed for others, and the animals were content after the tumultuous voyage.

Adam and Che and Grace started the process of finding a place to live in, for all of them.

The first thing Adam and Che did was to ride the horses along the eastern side of the island slowly looking for any signs of life. Adam was delighted to come across an overgrown vineyard.

"Che, as soon as we get settled, I want to come down here and start pruning these grape vines and get them back to a viable state."

"It will take some time before we get wine, won't it?"

"Yes, but it depends upon the type of grapes. I can't really tell now what kind we have here. And we need to find equipment and bottles and all sorts of things. This is a long process and we'll need some trial and error before we get really good wine. When we have time after we take care of other things, we can look through the buildings to see if there is any literature left about that. But finding these vines is a wonderful start. Now, we need to get going and get back."

"Grace also mentioned another island that she remembered that was well known locally for making good wines."

"Yes, I heard that. That's just another place to explore after we get everything settled."

They then moved slowly up the middle of the island. They heard no sounds of life and found no one. They trotted along one road in the middle of the island, heavily overgrown and in disrepair. They rode to the south end of the island and saw the many buildings, and another marina. Then they rode carefully up the overgrown road on the west side of the island, overlooking the wide strait they had sailed through, and also found no signs of human activity. They returned to report what they saw to Grace and the others.

"I'll start thinking about the bread," said Grace, "there must be some wheat fields around here. We used to have fabulous bread on these islands."

"Don't forget the cheese," said Sly, "that takes some time to make, doesn't it?"

"I think so. I've been thinking about that. They used to make wonderful cheese on these islands. This one and the one with the good wine."

"I know something about cheese," said Sarah, "when I was growing up, my mother made some. It does take time but not as long as wine."

"There are also several abandoned stores. Most of them have been looted but there might still be some old cheese that would tell us something about where they made cheese on different islands. We should check them when we get a chance."

"Alright, alright," said Adam, "let's not get the cart before the cow. Right now, let's search for a suitable place to move in to."

"Not just suitable, Adam," Grace cried out, "we must find a really nice spot where we could expand, and where we could build a community that will prosper and thrive."

The three of them took the two horses while Sly, Sam, and Sarah watched the animals, cleaned the schooner, and moved their own gear and food to two small buildings. Che rode one horse and Adam rode the other with Grace sitting behind him. They searched south for about five miles until they found a wonderful farm area with plenty of fields with fences and perfect for grazing. The decided this was the perfect spot. It had had grazing animals before. There was a barn, sheds and open shelters for all the animals. It had a wonderful house, a large barn and several out buildings.

They went back to the schooner and told the others about it. They were overjoyed. Sly especially was ecstatic. She helped Grace and Che and Adam move Bessy to the fenced grazing area. They then moved the lambs, goats, and pigs to a separate area. Each had access to the huge barn for shelter at night. The ducks and geese and chickens and turkeys were given their own area with a pond for the ducks and geese. Che and Adam built a reinforced area for Bubba away from the others and finally left the two horses in a grazing area. Buck was content to keep guard for Mollie and also for Bessy. Finally, the six of them took a wagon they found near the farm and returned to the schooner. They loaded up the wagon with all their gear, food, tools, guns, and the most special of all: Adam's cache of bulbs and seeds.

They had brought Mollie back to haul the wagon and walked behind with joy and hope. They settled into the wonderful house. They spent the next several weeks repairing and restoring buildings and sheds, without Adam during this time. Adam was happily planting bulbs and sowing some of the seeds for fall and winter crops.

CHAPTER TWENTY THREE

The Blizzard

Early Winter, 7 AP

Adam harvested as many crops as he could from his late summer plantings: many root crops that grew rapidly, even squash that matured before winter, and even a few peas. He covered the remaining root crops with straw, and planted other root crops such as potatoes, beets, turnips, rutabagas, carrots, radishes, parsnips, and onions that would survive under a protected ground. They had harvested what hay they could find in a nearby area. They did the best they could to prepare for winter. They were surprised by an early cold snap and early snow.

"It could be a long cold winter," he told the group. "We need to be prepared."

They spent much of their time repairing and shoring up buildings and sheds. Sly woke up shivering in the cold of the winter night. The wind whistled around the corners of the house and rattled the windows. It was dark in the upstairs bedroom but she was glad her night vision allowed her to see even in the darkest of nights. The clicking of the wind driving the snow against the windowpanes seemed like music to Sly with a rhythm of its own. She imagined what the countryside looked like at night, and pictured the windswept pastures with snow piled against the fences, the sides of the barn, and the farmhouse. The tops of shrubs and bushes would be barely visible under the high drifts. She hoped the horses Mollie and Buck, the bull Bubba and Bessy the cow, the lambs, the goats, the pigs, the chickens, ducks and geese, were all nice and warm in the barn, in their separate areas.

She pictured the barn owl huddled in the rafters, and visualized the many pastures and corn fields and barns for miles around, bleak and barren in the dim light from the moon, and the stars trying to break through the clouds. Her mind wandered to the nearby orchards they had found, and the fruit they would see in the spring. She pictured the woods behind their house and the woods at the far end of the pasture, and the frozen ponds down the hill. She pictured the great horned owl hunkered down on a branch looking for a meal. And then she stopped dreaming and snuggled close to Che. She wondered when her first child would be born.

Sly was not the only one dreaming of the next year. Grace was also cuddled up listening to the roaring wind and pelting snow against the window panes. She felt that she was on the way to executing her part of the plan. She hoped it was going to be the first daughter of the four she planned. They both were thinking of the ideas they had together in the fall.

It seemed as if Bessy was constantly looking in the direction of Bubba and mooing. They decided to give it a try and put her in with him. It worked. A few days later they returned her to her pasture and she then seemed content. Buck continued his close attention to Mollie and one day she returned his affection of sorts and they too began the next step in their job of increasing the calf population. The ducks in their space, the geese in theirs, the hen and rooster, the goats and sheep, all stayed warm in the barn and began the slow process that Sly and Grace had planned. The wind swirled the snow into giant drifts covering the landscape, covering bushes and smaller buildings with a thick blanket of white. It snowed steadily for two nights and a day. Che and Sly managed to get out with Toby to check on the animals and to feed them. Sly thought it was glorious and wanted to walk to the marina. Sam and Sarah went along.

"Che," Sam said as they pushed through the deep drifts, "do you think Sarah and I could fix up one of the smaller sloops and sail it around the islands in the spring?"

"I don't see why not."

"I think it would be a wonderful idea," added Sly, "I'll envy you but it would be important to see what it looks like around our archipelago. As time goes on, perhaps we'll want to use other islands to grow food."

"I'll check with Adam," Che added, "to see what he thinks."

When they reached the marina, Sam and Sarah selected a twenty-four-foot sloop they thought would be perfect. They thought it would be easy to sail. It had a small cabin if they needed to anchor for the night, and it even had a rudimentary galley. Sarah thought it was perfect.

When they returned, Adam was very enthusiastic about it as well. He thought it would be a great idea to search the islands for fruit trees, berry bushes, and any other edible plants. As the weather improved, Sarah and Sam spent time now and then fixing up the boat, checking and fixing and cleaning the sails. It had a small outboard motor on board and Che helped check it out and find some gasoline in the marina. They started the engine one day and it worked. They waited for warmer weather to start their adventure but they were ready.

Toward the end of winter, they discovered a dozen new chicks and helped set them up in a warm spot and provide them with lots of water and fine food. Sly took it upon herself to mother the chicks. In short order, there were more baby ducklings and goslings all needing attention. Early spring brought baby goats and lambs and piglets. Then Mollie produced a colt and Bessy a calf. Sly gradually slowed down as her pregnancy progressed, and Grace did the same. Sam and Sarah were called upon to help, and Che was needed specially to help with the larger animals. Adam spent much of his time planting new crops, harvesting the winter crops, and finding cool storage for root crops. The six of them were somewhat exhausted at first but soon became good farmers. They rose early and developed a routine of feeding the animals, cleaning stalls, tending to the new babies, and helping Adam to harvest winter crops. They worked until late in the day and then sat down to a wonderful meal, mainly prepared by Grace late in the afternoon, but everyone stepped in to help prepare meals, and clean up afterward. However, Grace was the primary "boss" of the kitchen and menu.

One warm spring evening, they were sitting outside enjoying their dinner, watching another glorious sunset when Adam spoke quietly.

"Che and I are going to take a couple of days and start preparing the grapevines so that we can have wine in a couple of years. When we finish with the ones on this island we will go across the strait on the east side and do the same to the vines over there."

"I went into that little store on the marina," Che said, "and found one bottle of wine from the other island and some old cheese as well. They made good cheese out of goat's milk. We can now enjoy a variety of cheeses from our cow's milk as well as our goat's milk."

"To go with our wine and bread," said Grace. "It seems I've heard that said before."

She looked at Adam and he laughed. Sly smiled and Che looked puzzled. Sly whispered in his ear and he smiled.

"And while we are talking about our dreams," said Sly, "any ideas about mine?"

"You mean about the oysters and clams and mussels and shrimp and crab and lobster? And being on the sea?" responded Che. She nodded. Che continued, "Well, we are definitely on the sea. And I said I would help with that, and make a soup with those. I've seen some crab pots at the marina. That takes care of one of them."

"We had wonderful Dungeness crabs right here in this marina. And there is a place close to here," said Grace, "where there used to be fabulous oysters. And some mudflats down south where we can get clams."

"Getting mussels on the shore," added Adam, "that should be easy."

"What about the shrimp?" asked Che.

"I remember a delicacy called 'spotted prawns' that we used to catch," answered Grace.

"How is that for a good start Sly?" Che summarized. "We can think about the lobster for the second time. I'll put that in my plan for the near future."

"Oh, that would be absolutely wonderful Che." Sly threw her arms around Che and hugged him.

They all raised their glasses of milk in a toast and all blessed their bounty and good fortune and looked to the day ahead.

CHAPTER TWENTY FOUR

Reaping and Sowing

Early Spring, 8 AP

Reaping and sowing, sowing and reaping, Adam spent the bulk of his time on his favorite pastime: planting and expanding the produce on their growing farm. He left the care of the animals mainly to Sly and Grace and Sam and Sarah. Sam and Sarah, with some reluctance, postponed their sailing adventure until the young animals grew old enough and did not require as much care. They also realized they needed to wait until the birth of the two babies and all was in control, and they could be spared. Adam said that as soon as he had planted all the new crops for the summer, he would have time to spare to help, and that would be just about the date when the babies would be born.

Meanwhile, he searched the island and found young apple trees, peach trees, and pear trees that he could transplant. He also located blueberry, strawberry, raspberry, and blackberry bushes, as well as wild berries such as salmonberry. On one of his forays on the west of the island, he came across a small charming cabin that was in good shape. It needed just a couple of windows to be replaced and the roof to be cleaned. It was perched high on the mountainside and had a spectacular view of the strait that they had sailed up on the way to the north end of the island.

He came back home and told Che and Grace about it. If they fixed it up it could sleep up to four people. He thought it would be a wonderful place for a retreat, where one could contemplate and think and plan and dream.

"And celebrate some events," said Grace.

They thought it would be a great idea. They all could use a short break now and then. Che offered to furnish it, to make it comfortable. It had a lovely stone fireplace and a deck facing the water.

"But for now, I have lots of work to do. We all do."

Adam harvested the winter crops of potatoes, carrots, turnips, rutabagas, onions, leeks, parsnips, beets, radishes, and garlic. He replanted those crops for the spring and summer, plus peas, beans, corn, squash, lettuce, cabbage, broccoli, Brussel sprouts, and even kohlrabi. He gradually expanded the area that he used to grow crops and realized he needed to have a plan for expansion. Adam was ecstatic over the possibilities and had waited a long time to develop such a bountiful and diverse set of foods. He had so much produce that he was able to give the pigs and other animals some variety in their diet. If their plan of expanding their community came to fruition, they would need to develop considerable food production to sustain it. For now, he was delighted at his progress.

As soon as he had the summer crops all planted, he turned his attention to helping Sly and the others care for the growing population of animals. He and Che also took time to improve the fencing, build a large henhouse that could also hold the ducks and geese and turkeys, and expand the grazing areas. Outside of these areas they grew hay and alfalfa. They also built sheds in various places as shelter for grazing animals when the spring downpours dumped considerable rain on the fields. Toby was on constant guard day and night.

One night, Toby heard some danger outside. He had heard foxes before and was not concerned but this was a pack of wild dogs. Fortunately, all the animals were inside the barn but they were being disturbed. Sly woke Adam, Che, Sam and Sarah, who immediately grabbed rifles and went outside in the dark. With the scopes, they spotted the pack trying to get into the henhouse and they took aim. They downed four of them but the others scattered quickly.

"They will be back one day," Adam said, "perhaps in the daytime when the animals are grazing. Now that they know there are chickens and ducks and turkeys, they will be back. The geese can take care of themselves but the others are fair game."

"I wish we had more like Toby," Sly said.

"Perhaps Sam and Sarah can find a dog that is not so wild when they explore the islands," Che offered. "I think it is time for them to sail away."

Sam and Sarah had been listening and were overjoyed. At last, they could start their adventure. They stocked up on food and ammunition. They realized that there was always the possibility of danger in this land, and that they should always be prepared. Adam had found some charts on one of the abandoned boats and went over the plan with the two of them. Grace joined them and suggested they head north to an island that she remembered as being very private and an isolated agrarian society. The people there did not like visitors and actively discouraged them. She wondered if there were any people alive, and if not, what had happened to the animals. There was a small dock they could moor to, if it was still there. She cautioned them to proceed slowly and carefully. Sam said she understood.

"Would it be alright to take Toby with us, just for a couple of days? If we want to stay out longer, we'll return and drop off Toby."

Grace agreed.

Sam and Sarah prepared the boat and gave everyone a hug. They sailed through the channel to the east and headed north by northeast. They hugged the coast of the large island to the east and found the small harbor which was quite exposed to winds but the dock was still suitable for landing. There was no sign of life but Grace had said that was almost always the case. The residents were inland and did not expect to welcome visitors. They tied up to the dock, took their rifles with them, and walked up the dirt road and inland for a mile.

There was still no sign of life. They turned left and walked further down a dirt road. They encountered a farm which was overgrown and unoccupied. They went further down the road and saw more of the same. After seeing several more overgrown modest homes, they approached another small building. Suddenly Toby ran ahead and a dog much like Toby ran up and wagged its tail. Since Toby was a male, they realized the other dog must be female, and understood. When Sam looked up and saw two young men approaching, she raised her rifle as a reflex. The shorter of the two called to them.

"Who are you?" he yelled. "We have nothing unless you want some food. We live in peace here and do not have guns. Take anything you want if you must."

Sam lowered her rifle as Sarah pushed it away.

"We also live peacefully. We have run into some evil people and this was just a reflex. We are sorry to have disturbed you. We will leave you alone. Toby, come."

"Please, do not leave. You are the only ones we have seen for a long time. What are your names? We are Ben and Harry. I am Ben."

The tall one stepped forward. Sam and Sarah shook hands cautiously and introduced themselves.

"My name is Sam," she said, "this is Sarah. We came from an island south west of here."

"Would you like to come inside for tea?" offered Harry, "we live a simple life but we have still managed to find some tea on a nearby island which has a store, now dilapidated."

They followed Ben and Harry to their small cottage. They remained very cautious for some time, on the alert for a trap, but gradually realized that the two men were genuinely interested in them and very peaceful. Ben explained how they had survived when the various virions decimated their local population. They did so by isolating themselves.

Harry laughed. "If you knew this island, you would know this was not unusual. People generally keep to themselves so we just stayed here. We are pretty self-sufficient. We have a cow still and grow many vegetables and have chickens for eggs and meat. We even have a cat to keep the rodent population down."

"What is the cat's name?" asked Sam.

"We call him Duke," answered Harry, "he's a charmer."

"I hope Duke can charm Pandi," Sam turned to Sarah.

"Who's Pandi?" asked Ben.

"Our only cat. We could use more of them," Sam answered. She turned back to Ben. "Is there no one else left besides the two of you?"

Ben shook his head.

"We have been considering leaving for some time and looking for others, but we have been concerned about running into diseases and wild people. Also, we do not have anything but a rowboat."

"But you do not look very wild," Harry said with a smile.

"Looks are deceiving," Sam said, "we are actually pretty tough." She laughed and they all did.

Sam and Sarah invited them to return with them to meet the others in their group.

"Then we will bring you back," Sarah said, "but they won't believe us unless they see you with their own eyes. What is the name of your dog, by the way?"

"Sally," they answered in unison, "if she can come, we will join you."

The four of them, together with Sally and Duke, sailed back to their dock. Toby jumped out and Sally ran after him as he ran down the road. Harry held Duke tightly in his arms, wrapped up. The four of them walked the distance back to the farm, and when they arrived, Adam, Che, Sly, and Grace were all waiting.

"When we saw Toby's friend," Che said, "we knew something was up."

Sam and Sarah introduced Ben and Harry to Adam, Che, Sly and Grace, and explained the circumstances of their meeting and visit. Ben and Harry stayed for several days and were treated to the wonderful produce from Adam's garden. They were astounded at his success and said they really struggled to grow things over on their island. They were given a room in the big farmhouse and Sally followed Toby everywhere. It was as if Toby was showing her around his magnificent spread and trying to impress her. Furthermore, she followed him around and seemed to be interested in doing so. Duke ran and hid but eventually he and Pandi found each other.

After getting to know each other over a period of days, Adam decided they were on the level and would be a good addition to their community, if they would choose to join them. He offered and they said they would talk it over and think about it. Ben said perhaps they could continue growing on their farmland and just combine into one community.

That is exactly what happened. After thinking it over, Ben and Harry decided to move to join the growing group. They were peace loving men but realized a combined larger group would be much safer. Sally and Toby were delighted. At one point, Sam offered to sail Ben back to gather up clothes and food and supplies as he saw fit to bring back. Harry stayed behind and learned a great deal about animal husbandry from Sarah and Sly. After a couple of other trips, sometimes with Sarah and Harry doing the sailing, they had moved permanently. They spent several weeks learning everything they could about all the animals so that they could be full partners in the venture.

"The one thing we do not want to learn," Harry said one day, "is how to handle guns. We have never wanted to have guns around."

"No need to worry," said Sarah, "Sam and I will take care of that."

CHAPTER TWENTY FIVE

New Life

Summer, 8 AP

The spring drifted by, filled with many days of rain. The group had developed a well-organized routine of getting up early and taking care of the animals, harvesting produce during the day, and doing odd chores including working on fences and expanding some buildings. Ben and Harry surprised everyone with some talents that were not readily seen. Ben was an excellent carpenter and Harry was a blacksmith.

Adam and Che had found a well-stocked lumber yard at the south end of the island. Adam and Ben hauled lumber to the north and worked together to provide professional additions to the barn for the younger animals to be separate from the older ones. The lambs and kids and piglets had their own little areas. Adam and Ben planned for the future growth of the animal population by starting to build additional structures. They used what was useful from the abandoned lumber places, but also prepared other wood. This involved cutting, drying, and trimming wood, laying out a plan, and preparing all the construction material before they began. They planned to have several buildings added over the following two years.

Harry turned old scrap metal into nails and spikes and joints and other necessary metal parts. He also worked with Che to create two additional wagons that they needed to bring in hay and sometimes to haul timber and other material to the farm.

But Ben and Harry each had an additional talent: they could play musical instruments. After the day's work was done and a wonderful meal was consumed, they sat around a fire while Ben and Harry played a fiddle and a guitar. They all gradually remembered old songs and Ben and Harry taught them some. This was a part of the day they all looked forward to. Sam and Sarah were especially delighted when this part of the day arrived. They laughed and sang and even danced a bit.

And then the good news. There was new life to go with the abundance of new life all around. Grace was the first to have her baby. It was a boy that they named Paul. He had dark hair and was a big robust baby with a bellowing voice. Sly was the next to have her baby. It was a girl that they named Jasmine. She had golden hair and a radiant smile. She was petite and made a face every time she heard Paul bellowing, but never seemed to cry. The most they ever heard from her was a little grumble when she was uncomfortable or hungry.

After Pandi and Duke got to know each other, they were always running and playing and hiding together. One day Pandi disappeared for a few days and emerged with six kittens. She was fiercely protective of them. Like a tiger, said Sly one day, a Bengal tiger.

Paul and Jasmine grew rapidly and often nursed side by side next to the fire as the days grew shorter and fall harvest approached. Pandi found a spot nearby Sly and nursed her litter. Everyone, including Grace and Sly, pitched in to bring in the root crops and squash and other crops that would last the winter. They picked the lettuce and tomatoes and cucumbers and beans and peppers on a daily basis while they were fresh.

"If only we had avocadoes," Grace said one day, "it would make a wonderful salad. I'll miss the fresh food when fall and winter arrive."

"Why don't I build a greenhouse to grow these during the winter?" said Ben. Adam thought that was a terrific idea and wondered how he had forgotten that. Harry and Che helped, and by end of fall they had constructed a thirty-foot long greenhouse. They had found glass at a nearby area that was unbroken and placed it facing the southern sky. Adam quickly planted tomatoes, lettuce, cucumbers, and peppers. He had quietly nursed along a couple of small avocado trees for a year which he had started with pits he found in more temperate climates. He planted them in larger pots and put them into the greenhouse. He also put in his winter crop of potatoes and beets and other root crops. Che also found time to fix up the retreat cabin overlooking the Strait.

One day while Adam and Che were occupied with all their activities, Ben and Sam sailed over to Ben's island to check on their garden. They loaded the boat with a bounty of crops to bring back. A sudden early winter storm blew across the island with strong winds and heavy rain. The squalls were so strong that they stayed overnight on the boat, making sure it didn't get blown off its mooring. When they returned the next day, they were met by Adam and Che who were worried that they had capsized or run into trouble. They were about to sail out in another sloop to search when Sam and Ben sailed into harbor.

"What happened?" Adam asked, "we were about to search for you."

"Don't worry," Sam smiled, "we were just fine." Ben had a sheepish grin on his face as well. Adam and Che said nothing more.

While they were gone, Sarah and Harry had hooked up the wagon with Mollie and brought in the fruit from the apple trees, peach trees, pear trees, plum trees, and also some crabapple trees they found. Sarah knew Mollie and Buck loved them. Under Grace's guidance, they had made plum jam and peach jam and learned how to preserve it. They also made applesauce for a special treat for Jasmine and Paul. With so many varieties of fruit saved for the winter they settled down to wait out the winter. The rains had come in together with strong winds. One morning they awoke to the soft silence of snow. It blanketed every building and shed and bush and many small trees. The winds continued and piled up the snow in drifts against fences and the sides of the barn and hen house and the greenhouse. Adam moved Bessy and her calf, named Lizzie, into the greenhouse to keep it warm and to keep the snow from accumulating on the roof.

The winter storm persisted for several days but they all stayed warm inside the various buildings. One night, Che again heard the yowling and barking of wild dogs nearby. They were thankful all the animals were inside. Sam, Sarah, and Che went outside and managed to pick off a couple but the pack was growing and this raised some concern. A really big pack could be a major problem. They obviously had food to survive this long, probably from rabbits and foxes and any other small creatures still surviving.

With some reluctance, Adam suggested they had to do some culling before the pack got out of hand. It could destroy half of their farm animal stock in no time at all. Che and Adam took the first round with Mollie and Buck and tracked them to a den like location in the middle of the island. They picked off several of them but the others scattered. Sam and Sarah took the next attempt, and tracked them to a different location. They hid and waited some distance away so as not to be discovered, and tethered the horses even farther away. They waited until the pack came out, and began picking them off with rapid fire until all visible lay dead in the snow. They feared that some escaped or were out hunting or in a den, and the pack would eventually recover. They returned with their report, and were somewhat subdued at having to kill off the pack as they did. Che and Sly tried to cheer them up.

"It wasn't the same as shooting those evil men before. These animals were only trying to survive." Sam said.

"At our expense eventually," said Adam, "we had to do it."

The winter storms continued for many weeks and eventually spring arrived, and with it, the spring crops of peas, and cabbage, broccoli, Brussel sprouts, and leeks, onions, and kohlrabi. The spring also brought the arrival of new baby chicks, ducklings, goslings, as well as lambs, goat kids, and piglets. The pond was getting full of ducks and geese and Che and Adam had to create another one from a small impression that already had the beginnings of a pond. They also needed to expand their henhouse, and started to put an addition on the barn.

The spring also saw the announcement of another baby, by Sly. Then Grace added her news, and finally Sam and Ben announced they were expecting their first. All heads turned to Sarah. She smiled and shook her head negatively. Sly whispered to Sam.

"But it looks as if she is working on it. I would not be surprised one day."

CHAPTER TWENTY SIX

The Growing Community

Summer, 10 AP

Nearly three years passed since they had first arrived by schooner. Grace had a girl, which they named Hannah, and was now expecting her third. Sly had another girl, named Rose, and was expecting her third child as well. Sam and Ben have had a boy, named Joe, and were expecting a second child in the fall, and Sarah and Harry have had a girl, named Shelly, and were expecting their second in early winter.

Meanwhile there were over one hundred chickens and chicks, a couple of dozen ducks, a dozen geese, many pigs and sheep and goats. They were overflowing their fields and ponds and barns. Adam and Che and Ben and Harry, with the consultation of all the women, used all the surrounding land that leant itself to pasture or arable land for growing. They also repaired houses and fences and viable barns and sheds and any building worth repairing.

Sam and Ben and their son Joe moved to a small cottage half a mile away from Grace and Adam, who stayed in the big farmhouse. Sarah and Harry and their daughter Shelly moved a bit further than Sam to a charming small cottage, and Sly and Che moved further south yet to another farm with barns and other buildings needing repair.

The entire group worked together over the course of a year and a half to fix and prepare each dwelling. Sly and Che were the first to have work done since they were soon expecting their child. All worked together repairing the damaged roof and windows of the house, then repaired fences and out buildings. They had large fields, and after the fences were repaired and the barn fixed as well, the group moved some of the sheep and goats and pigs, and most of the geese to a pond on the property.

Toby and Sally had had pups the previous fall so two of the pups went with Sly. She adored the little black and white female that looked much like Toby and a larger black male. They had learned to growl at any sign of intruders or other danger.

Pandi and Duke had two more litters of kittens which were distributed across the four households and farms. As a result, there were very few shrews and moles and voles and mice and rats in the buildings they occupied.

The next expecting a child received the next priority and that was Sam. The group fixed the house first. It only had a roof problem. Then they reinforced the stout fences surrounding the nearby field and fixed the open shed at one end. This became the home of Bubba the bull. Once a year he was visited by Bessy. Everyone felt as if Bubba kept Bessy young and full of energy. They were not sure how long this would last.

Sarah and Harry had a large field growing hay and alfalfa. They often grazed Buck there and he was content as long as he visited Mollie now and then. By this time Bessy had a calf and a heifer, and Mollie had a filly and colt. All of the chickens stayed with Grace and Adam, but they kept expanding the henhouse. Many of the roosters were caponized, a technique Adam had learned when younger.

Che and Adam had worked on the vast fields of grapevines the previous fall and winter and awaited their first crop of grapes in the coming fall. With the help of Ben and Harry they had done the same with the vineyards on the neighboring island. They knew it would be a few years before they would have the first bottles of wine but they located all the barrels and bottles they would need to create their first vintages and even longer to make truly wonderful wine.

However, that did not stop the making of bread and cheese by the entire group. Initially they made bread with an outdoor woodburning oven which was time consuming and they had so many other things to work on. The making of bread turned out to be relatively easy once they found an abandoned bakery and put an oven in good shape. They used a small generator at first but their love of bread soon reached the limit of production and they had to seek a larger one.

The making of cheese was a slow process. All eight of them had some degree of knowledge but the making of both cow and goat cheeses was done by trial and error. They had located a farm on the neighboring island that had literature they used to teach others to make cheese. They soon discovered there were many ways to make cheese but one thing was certain: it all started with milk and fermentation.

Che and Adam also had a big challenge. They had located a very large freezer near the marina but they were not sure if it still operated until Che hooked it up to a generator. They had brought the one they used in the barn but it was not sufficient to create enough electricity to drive this huge freezer. They searched and finally found another one, big enough to contain all the food needing to be frozen. There was still gasoline in the storage tank and they siphoned it out whenever they needed it to operate the generator.

"Adam," Che said one day, "we'll soon have a big problem. We cannot rely on gas. We have to think about an alternative way to generate electricity here."

"What about solar energy?" he responded, "or wind? Over time I think we should consider both, don't you think?"

"Absolutely," Che said, "in fact, I've seen many abandoned solar panels on the island. I'll start by checking to see which have not been damaged, and then start figuring out how to hook them up and how they save electricity. Long term I think wind energy would be better. We have some tall mountains here. By the way, I discovered Ben knows quite a bit about electricity. I'll ask his help."

"Great. Meanwhile let's use the gas sparingly." Adam concluded.

This large freezer was able to hold frozen capons, lamb, pork, and beef, which they used to feed themselves over the winter when there was not fresh meat. They met the deadline of preparing and moving each family and the animals before winter set in and just as Sarah's second child was born.

They also used the older smaller generator on a limited basis for other purposes. Che had found some old DVDs in the abandoned library and a television set and DVD player in one of the homes that showed the least damage from years of neglect and storms. He tested them on the generator and they still worked. They used the generator on a rare occasion for a special playing of a movie. Many of the DVDs they found also discussed the history of the world, and other historical events. Much to the delight of Grace, they also found operas, ballet, and a wide variety of music from classical to folk songs, rock, rap, rhythm and blues, and many others. Over the years, as the children grew up, they were treated to these movies.

"My grandfather loved folk songs," Adam said one day.

"Mine loved opera, especially Aida, Showboat and Porgy and Bess," said Grace. "We can teach all about this in our school when the children grow up."

At the end of the year, Grace and Sly each had two girls and a boy, and Sam and Sarah each had a boy and girl: Grace's children Paul and Hannah had a younger sister named Iris; Sly's children Jasmine and Rose had a younger brother named Tom; Sam's son Joe had a sister named Fawn; and Sarah's daughter Shelly had a brother named Charlie.

"I am half way home," Grace said quietly to Sly one day, "my promised goal was having four girls."

"Oh, I remember what you said. Well then, so am I. What prize is offered to the one that gets there first?" Sly did not expect an answer. She was content enough with the challenge. She had always wanted her own little nest and now she had it. She was on top of the world.

During the previous year and a half, they had had only one big scare. It happened in the spring. When Sarah was early in her pregnancy, she and Harry sailed north over to his island to check on the crops growing there. There were also fruit trees they wanted to prune and a few winter crops to harvest. It was early spring and the weather seemed to be holding up. They tied up the small sloop at the dock and walked to the small farm that Harry and Ben had created. While they were harvesting and pruning and checking on other crops, a storm suddenly came in from the north. When they returned to the dock the sloop had broken its mooring and was drifting about off shore. They had planned to stay only one night and when they did not return, Adam and Che became concerned. They had fixed up another small sloop for just such an occasion and decided to brave the storm to find Sarah and Harry.

Meanwhile Sarah and Harry had found shelter from the storm for the night, but in the morning, they attempted to go out in a small rowboat to try to find the drifting sloop but turned back in the heavy waves. They had just reached the dock when they looked out in the open strait and saw Adam and Che towing their sloop. They were relieved but their joy was short lived when Adam admonished them for being so careless and making such an amateur mistake.

"Ben and Sam were very worried about the two of you," he said, "and even prayed for you." He hid a small smile.

They did manage to load their produce on the two sloops and sailed back together in the heavy seas. Adam eventually stopped scowling and was glad they were alright. Harry vowed not to make that mistake again.

As winter approached and the temperature dropped, the group spent quite a bit of time in the big house with a roaring fire, and talked about their good fortune, and their plans ahead. Sly brought up the subject of a school.

"Our children are getting older. They should be starting to go to some sort of preschool and we don't have one. How about using that building above the marina? It's empty but it has a few chairs, and a fireplace at one end. It even has a kitchen of sorts at the other end. With Sarah's new baby boy, we have ten children and who knows how many more to come. We can each take turns teaching something we know. Grace especially knows a lot. Weren't you a teacher once, Grace?"

"I was and I would certainly give some thought to it. I think it's an excellent idea. It will give them a place to go, to play, and to get to know each other. I'm in."

During the cold winter months, they took time to set up a preschool. They collected toys from the downtown stores at the other end of the island, and created a plan for the day. At first it was just a couple of hours in the morning and was largely devoted to constructive play. In fact, it was really a daycare center. But it did free the other parents for chores, looking after animals, feeding them, cleaning, even minor repairs, and fixing fences outside. In this way, they learned to use their limited time in the most productive way. When it was blizzard conditions, which happened often, they would all assemble in the big house for warmth and safety and food.

On one such evening, Sly noticed there was no sign of Adam.

"Where's Adam?" she asked. "Is he alright?"

"He's fine," said Grace, looking at Che.

"Adam just wanted to get away for a night," replied Che. "He went to the retreat cabin to think I guess."

"He'll be back tomorrow," added Grace.

The next night, all were together. The wind was blowing hard and the snow was pelting the windows, and Ben and Harry were playing music and singing. When they paused for a moment, Adam suddenly announced that he would like to take a long sea voyage one day before he became too old. Everyone stopped talking. There was silence.

"Where do you want to go?" asked Ben.

"To an island I visited once in the middle of the South Atlantic." He then proceeded to tell them of his voyage to Tristan da Cunha on the trawler during the pandemic, and how he met a member of the Glass family. He said he really wanted to return to see if they were still thriving in spite of the pandemic. He said it did not seem to reach them in their isolated island but they were cut off from trade as well as diseases.

"When do you want to go?"

"Well, I don't think I can go for a few years. Perhaps when Paul and some of the other boys are old enough. Ten years from now."

Grace breathed a sigh of relief. His announcement had been a shock to her.

Che changed the subject.

"When I was at the south end of the island, I went through one of the abandoned schools there. If our population continues to grow, perhaps we can refurbish that school."

"How many children do you think we will have in ten years or twenty years?" asked Ben.

Sly jumped in. "Well, I can tell you the math of the ambitious plan that Grace has for us to repopulate the world. If we each have four daughters over a period of ten or twelve years, and they each have four daughters, then in another fifteen or twenty years, we will have over a hundred kids of various ages. That should be enough for us to think about, not only for schools, but also about houses and food and clothes and everything else."

"And in another fifteen to twenty years we could have over five hundred kids. Is that right/" summarized Sam.

"It is." Grace spoke softly. "But we have time. Let's get to work."

"On having the children or getting the schools and houses ready?" asked Harry. Everyone laughed.

"Both." They stopped laughing and went back to music and singing.

The winter wore on and soon turned to spring and the cycle started all over again.

CHAPTER TWENTY SEVEN

Major Projects

Summer, 15 AP

Another five years passed by since they had discussed the need for school facilities and supplies, and the greater requirement for electricity. Che led the project to build both solar and wind sources of energy. Harry and Sam assisted him. Grace led the drive to create school facilities. Ben and Sly helped her. Sarah volunteered to organize the preschool and run it with the help of everyone else taking turns looking after the children. Adam was involved in all the projects as they progressed.

He felt the need to organize the growing community so as not to overload any particular person. All of them were so dedicated and often took on too much until they approached exhaustion. Adam kept track of all the food sources and asked each of the others now and then to help harvest food as it reached maturity, and to find cool places to store winter squash and potatoes and other root crops that stored for a period of time. He also determined what crops, such as blueberries, would freeze well. The large freezer had various meat products, but it was soon joined by various fruits and vegetables.

Working with Grace, Adam helped create menus for meals based on what was available or would be available at a given time. She planned the meals but there was a rotating schedule of others to help prepare and cook meals, and to clean up. As the children grew older, they were included in clearing up after meals, and some were interested in learning to cook. Exceptions were made if someone was in the latter stages of pregnancy, or occupied in a critical stage of a community project, but it was rare for anyone to be exempt from responsibility of this daily requirement.

Adam also drew up schedules and requirements for every other project they embarked on. He was the de facto leader of the community, settled any dispute which was rare, and often was the one that others turned to for advice on most subjects. His authority was never in doubt, and was in fact welcomed by all.

Adam paid particular attention to the energy projects. He suggested they tackle the solar energy project first and Che agreed. They found existing solar energy panels at various places on the island. Most of them were damaged but many were still viable. They also sailed to other islands and found numerous solar panels, most of which looked as if they were still useable. Che and Harry each had some knowledge of solar energy and how it was stored. The major challenge consisted of finding the best locations to gather energy, and then how to transport electricity to the growing number of uses. Initially, it was easy since they just wanted to use it for the large freezer and the other freezers they wanted to use, but eventually they envisaged it to be used for homes and the school.

The building of the wind energy complex was a much bigger project than the solar energy project, which was well along after a couple of years. But Adam felt that the wind energy project would take many years, given all the other needs to be considered. They had lots of wind and many good places to put the wind turbines, or "windmills" as they called them, but there were no existing ones on the island, damaged or otherwise. From his recollections, Harry recalled seeing on another island a small wind turbine, and one day he and Che and Sam set sail around the islands to places where Harry thought he saw it. They did not find any on their first venture, but on their second, Sam spotted a small wind turbine they used as a model. It was neglected but only slightly damaged from the storms that ravished the islands. They made drawings before disassembling it and brought it back to their island.

Once they figured out how to hook it up to a generator and create electricity, they spent more than two years searching for others that were in good enough shape to bring home. Eventually they found a total of ten but they could only work on them in their spare time and they had little of that at this time.

Meanwhile, Grace, with assistance from Sly and Ben, chose the school that appeared to be in the best shape. Ben fixed a variety of broken doors and damage to the roof and other parts of the outside, put in new windows using glass he found at a place that had been the islands glass business.

Over a period of two years, working on this project along with their other responsibilities, they had the school itself in fine shape. Then they began the process of finding supplies. They searched the school buildings but found only a few books remaining that were useable, and these were for much older children and would eventually be part of education as the children grew older. Then they went to the library which was damaged in several places but most of the books and DVDs were still there. They also searched some of the homes that were abandoned years before, and found numerous collections of books and DVDs that were still intact.

At the end of five years from the time they started these projects, only a few of the children were old enough to leave preschool and go to an elementary type school. The growing population of children were in preschool which was now getting overcrowded.

Also, after five years the solar project was operable and gradually replaced the dwindling supply of gasoline. The wind turbine project was barely started. They had installed solar panels in several places near homes, and near the school, which generated large amounts of electricity.

In fact, Adam estimated they could generate enough electricity from the existing network of solar panels to support a population ten times the existing number of people. It was the future growth they had to prepare for, so this would be a continuous project.

The bright side to the use of the increased amount of electricity was the ability of families to gather in the evenings after dinner and watch one of the many movies available from DVDs they had acquired from various abandoned homes.

"I found a DVD with Sesame Street on it," said Grace, "I watched that when I was very young. I loved seeing all the different puppets, and people. I was very impressionable then. I think our children would love it."

Sly replied, "we also have old movies like Cars, and Finding Nemo, and Ratatouille. And Disney films. Do you think they'd like those?

"Maybe."

Early in the evening and sometimes during preschool the children were able to watch movies or DVDs for children. If it was in the evening, they usually fell asleep early and the adults turned to their movie. But since they all had to rise very early to attend to animals, they also went to bed on the early side. In the winters, when the days were very short, and it was cold and often windy and raining or snowing, they generally stayed in their own cottages rather than gathering in the big house of Grace and Adam.

One day in the fall when the weather was lovely Adam invited the adults to gather at the retreat cabin for a special event. Sarah had an idea of what it was about and offered to look after the children while they all traveled over to the west side and high on the mountain overlooking the strait. There was a beautiful sunset of blue and gray and red and orange stripes reaching high into the sky. They sat on the deck in the warm air with a slight breeze while Adam produced several bottles of wine. Grace brought out wine glasses and a variety of cheeses and delicious fresh bread and other snacks she had accumulated.

"Most of these are still quite young but I couldn't wait any longer. They will continue to age for many years. The Chardonnay is rich and full-bodied and will last for some years, and all the reds will also."

"How do you know this?" asked Sam.

"The winemaker is entitled to taste a bit now and then to see how things are progressing." Everyone laughed.

"What are all of these?" asked Harry.

"Besides the Chardonnay, we have Pinot Noir, Merlot, and Cabernet Sauvignon. We also have Syrah and some other full-bodied blends."

"How many bottles do you have and where do you keep them?" asked Sam. "I wondered what you were doing some times."

"Che has been helping me most of the time. These are the oldest and come from the grapes we harvested nearly five years ago. They all aged in the barrel until last fall when we bottled forty cases and a few more for periodic tasting like this, about five hundred bottles altogether. We still have lots of wine still aging in the barrels. There are caves near the marina that we use to keep them at the right temperature. I hope you like them."

"Alright, that's enough talk," interrupted Che, "let's get on with it. I'm thirsty." They all laughed again.

"Can I try the Chardonnay?" asked Sly.

"Absolutely," said Che. He poured a glass for her. Sam wanted the Merlot, as did Grace. Harry wanted the Cabernet Sauvignon, as did Ben. Che poured a glass of Pinot Noir for Adam and another for himself. They started to raise their glasses high.

"Wait just a moment," said Che. He went back into the kitchen area and brought back a huge pot. Grace helped with bowls and spoons. He raised the lid and the steam rose up. "It's my version of Cioppino. It will go well with the Chardonnay that Sly is about to drink and maybe the Pinot Noir. This is one of Sly's dreams."

"Oh Che," cried Sly, "I thought you had forgotten." She hugged him.

"Here's to Cascadia and Adam's dream," said Che, "and Sly's."

They drank a toast to Adam and Sly and Cascadia and watched the sunset disappear and nibbled on the cheese and bread, and ate cioppino and drank wine until it was dark. They headed back to the community center where Sarah was feeding children and reading to them. They brought the wine and cheese and bread and cioppino with them and continued to celebrate, with Sarah included, well into the evening.

The growth of their community was rapid. The introduction to greater education was a wonderful addition to their society which previously depended upon the telling of stories similar to the many native American societies in the past. Now they had the use of some of the technology from the recent civilization which now was destroyed.

"Grace," Adam said one day in private, "I hope that, as the size of our community continues to grow, we create a society that consists of many of the good aspects, and little of the corrupt and evil aspects, as it was in the past. After all, I believe the majority of people were well-meaning, looked after others, and not just their own self-interests. There were many good people. It was such a shame that so many great and wonderful people died, along with most of the evil and corrupt ones. We seem to have some of the latter kind still on the planet. Do you think we can keep building a good community without the corruption and evil creeping in?"

"I think we will." Grace replied, "I hope we will. We must."

PART FOUR

THE EXPANDING WORLD

CHAPTER TWENTY EIGHT

The Great Sailing Adventure

Early Spring, 22 AP

Sly's summary of Grace's plan was pretty accurate. The oldest child, Paul, was now fourteen. There were sixteen daughters all together and fifteen sons in the four families. Sarah was about to have her eighth child in a few weeks. The school was filled to the brim with over thirty children. All of the four mothers vowed that they were finished having children, and that the next generation would have to take their turn in five or ten years.

The farmhouse occupied by Grace and Adam was filled to capacity. Sly and Che had found a bigger farmhouse several miles south of Grace, and Sam and Ben had done the same. Also, Sarah and Harry had moved to the center of the island. Each had a pair of horses and a wagon to travel to visit each other and their families. Bessy had passed on but left many of her progeny behind. The same was true of Molly, but Bubba and Buck were still in the same place, just getting older. Pandi was still living with Sly but Duke and Toby and Sally had also passed on. Each family had at least one dog, one cat, many chickens, and various other animals. Ben and Harry still traveled over to their old place to collect fruit and crops but concentrated more and more of their time building and repairing fences and out buildings on their own new properties.

Two years earlier, Adam had decided that the time had come for him to realize his other dream. He had been repairing sails, stocking the schooner, teaching Paul and other children about sailing, and generally preparing to depart on his long journey. Che was restless and wanted to join him, along with six children between the ages of ten and twelve. He had taken a test run with the six oldest ones and came to two reluctant conclusions: perhaps the schooner was too big for a crew of only eight, six of whom were still children; and the children were just not old enough and strong enough. He realized that he had to find a somewhat smaller ship, repair it, prepare rigging and sails, provision it properly for a long sea voyage, and spend more time teaching the young children, and doing test runs. One day Che sat down with Adam and spoke softly and slowly.

"Adam, do you realize how far this trip is? It's almost as if you were sailing around the world. It's over ten thousand nautical miles just to the dangerous Horn and much further to Tristan. You will be sailing with an inexperienced young crew and not very many of them at that. At ten knots per hour and ten hours sailing per day that will be one hundred days just to the Horn. Think about it before you go."

Adam had assured Grace and Sly they would return before winter. Grace was not convinced but said nothing. She knew how important it was to Adam to take this voyage now. He had waited a long time. But when he announced that they would wait another two years until the children were stronger, she and Sly were relieved. Sam and Sarah were also happier that their two oldest children, Joe and Shelly respectively, would be better prepared for the voyage. Paul, Jasmine, Joe, and Shelly, were joined by Grace's oldest daughter, Hannah, and Sly's second oldest, Rose. The six of them were fourteen and thirteen and much stronger than they were two years earlier.

Once Adam realized he had more time to prepare, he searched the marina for a smaller ship, and found a sixty-foot ketch in good shape. It was slower at sea than the schooner but would be much safer in heavy seas. He and Che looked at all the sails and repaired some and created some backup sails from other sails on other craft. Che started to mount the turret gun on the bow, similar to the way it was mounted on the ketch that he had sunk when they had wiped out the enemy nest. It was also much like the mount on the schooner.

Che had another conversation with Adam after all the work they had put in on the ketch.

"Adam, I have been thinking about this quite a lot. Even though the ketch might be a bit safer, it is after all much smaller and quite a bit slower. With so many miles to cover it would be wiser to change back to the schooner. Remember how important speed is if you encounter bandits."

Adam agreed but asked Che, "but what about the crew? To handle the schooner, we will need more hands, won't we?"

This conversation created a crisis of sorts. Adam assembled Grace and Sly, as well as Sam and Ben, and Sarah and Harry. He explained the situation, the fast but bigger schooner versus the smaller ketch, the necessity of a sufficient crew which would be mostly teenagers.

"I have come to the conclusion that it is too much to ask. We would be gone for possibly a year and we would be putting a burden on those of you left behind in running the farm. I would probably need to take at least the ten oldest, twelve to fourteen years old, and possibly two adults besides myself. Perhaps in another several years I can try it."

There was silence for a few minutes until Grace spoke.

"Adam, I think you should go. Don't forget, we are pioneer women. We are not having any more children to slow us down. The oldest children are just the right age. And I think you should take the schooner. You will get there sooner and get home sooner."

"And I think Che and Ben should go with you," added Sly, "Harry and the four of us and the other children can look after things while you are gone. It is important to find out if any other people exist on islands or isolated spots."

"No time like the present, Adam," Sam put in. "Joe has been looking forward to it. Don't disappoint the teenagers. If you take four others as I think you should, Joe's sister Fawn and the others will be ecstatic."

"Go for it, Adam," cheered Sarah.

It was agreed.

Adam and Che spent many hours on the Strait with the ten teenagers teaching them about tacking and raising and lowering sails, and setting anchor, and even handling the tiller. Hannah and Rose were the most interested in learning about handling the duties of the cockpit. Joe and Shelly were particularly interested in navigation. Adam had collected as many charts as he could find from abandoned ships and taught them how to read charts, and how to create a sailing plan. Paul and Jasmine took charge of all aspects of sail handling, rolling up sails and stowing them below so that they could be rapidly deployed when it was necessary to change sails. Joe and Shelly also learned, as part of navigation, about detecting changing weather.

The four other children, Grace's third child named Iris, Sly's third named Tom, Joe's sister Fawn, and Shelly's brother Charlie, were assigned as backup to the older ones and told to learn everything just in case they needed to fill in for someone injured or ill.

Che came to Adam one day in the early winter just prior to the planned sailing in the spring and said he thought they were as prepared as they could be. He was now convinced the four women and Harry could handle everything for a year. Harry not only was a good blacksmith but could fix about anything. He laughed when he said that Sam and Sarah could handle any firearm requirements.

"Grace and Sly can handle the running of the farm, with the children helping out. They can keep going to school and help with food and the many chores in our growing community. I can fix engines and sails but with Ben, we have someone that is not only a carpenter, but he has skills to fix just about anything. It may well be a longer voyage than you believe, and this way at least you should be prepared for one."

Adam agreed. Che and Ben fixed up the cabin in the rear behind the cockpit to accommodate themselves and Adam. The six girls used the space in the bow as a sort of camping area with sleeping bags laid out around the edges. There were three small cabins inside. One cabin was taken up by Paul and Joe, another by Tom and Charlie, and the third served as a joint community cabin and chart room.

Adam and Ben and the ten teenagers took a trial run in early spring when the blustery winds and high waves gave them a challenge. They developed their sea legs during this sail around the neighboring two large islands and learned to lower and raise sails in high winds and rolling seas. Adam thought they were just about ready so they began to load water and dry foods aboard. Sam and Sarah had taught Joe and Shelly how to shoot almost as well as themselves, so Adam felt comfortable with bringing along four of their rifles, as well as the ammunition for the turret gun, which Jasmine had learned to operate from her father. Che was understandably very proud of her but that was true of all the parents.

On a beautiful spring day, they prepared to sail out of the harbor into the Strait. The parents and siblings of all of them came to the dock to wish them bon voyage. Grace turned away to hide a tear. They sailed out around the island to the west and south down through the Haro Strait into the Strait of Juan de Fuca. They were in the open Pacific within three hours. Adam's great adventure had begun.

CHAPTER TWENTY NINE

Sailing Around the Horn

Spring, 22 AP

Adam and Che set up a schedule that involved sailing for ten hours a day, just as Che had suggested. Che said the best plan would be to arrive at the Horn at the beginning of summer in the southern hemisphere. If they took one hundred sailing days and laid over at strategic points along the way, they would cover the ten thousand miles or so by fall or early winter. Then they could round the Horn up to Tristan and back by the end of the southern summer and sail back home by the end of the northern summer. The total time would be a year and several months but they would miss much of the bad weather around the Horn.

They took their time for the first twelve days while the young crew became accustomed to their duties of tacking, sometimes replacing a small jib with a bigger one, and keeping watch for other ships, whales, and dangerous objects in the water. They stayed out to sea about twenty miles off shore and reached San Francisco Bay in just over twelve days. They sailed south of the Bay a hundred miles and found an unoccupied isolated marina on the coast and moored for the night. The teenagers were exhilarated from the experience of being at sea, the wind and mist in their faces, and the sights of birds and a few gray whales going north.

"Look, out there," cried Iris one blustery day, "small dinosaurs."

Paul followed her gaze and where she pointed. "Those are pelicans. See how they fly in line and close to the water? They are amazing creatures and I think they are descended from dinosaurs."

They anchored off shore outside of the kelp beds in the deep bay, and the children marveled at the sea otters playing in the kelp. The children were becoming adept in the galley, putting together meals that included root crops and squash, together sometimes with potatoes or pasta or even rice upon occasion. The children were ravenous most of the time so the galley was one of their favorite spots.

The crew laid over a few days and took a rowboat into the kelp and further into shore but discovered no one. Che had acquired a zodiac from a local marine store before they left and an outboard motor together with a few cans of gasoline. He felt from his knowledge of various places where they might attempt to land that they would not be able to land easily in a rowboat from the distance of the off shore anchorage, and the zodiac would eventually come in handy.

For the next leg of their journey, they attempted to reach Baja by sailing day and night, for a week, covering about a thousand miles. Che and

Adam took turns at the tiller for eight-hour shifts. The children were on call also for eight-hour shifts, five at a time while the others slept. The children found it to be exciting, sitting at the bow, always with a safety line attached. Sometimes they sat at the stern as the magnificent schooner sailed on, making excellent time. As they approached Baja, they saw gray whales, most of whom had calves. They saw more pelicans flying low in line above the water. Fawn and Iris kept journals and even drew pictures of birds and mammals they saw at sea. Part of the responsibility of those on watch was to keep the galley active, providing small meals and drinks, usually water, as needed.

They arrived at the entrance to the bay inside Baja and anchored within the protection of the peninsula. So far, they had enjoyed beautiful weather, but Che observed storm clouds ahead.

"I think we should lay over until those storm clouds are gone," Che suggested. They stayed two days and nights and the weather cleared. Their next leg was about two thousand miles out to sea until they reached the Galapagos Islands. They planned to stay there for some time until the winter storms that usually occurred around the Horn faded away. They would resume at the outset of spring in the south, or fall in the north.

This leg would take about three weeks and they needed to take on some water from Baja before they left. Che and Ben took the four oldest in his zodiac to fill cans of water at a spring they hoped to find on shore. They landed on the tip of the peninsula and found no sign of life. After wandering around the area, they came across a spring and filled all their containers and departed. It was sad, Che thought, to see such a beautiful place empty and devoid of all life, other than a couple of starved dogs.

They hauled in the anchor and departed at dawn, sailing on a direct course toward the Galapagos Islands. They had wonderful weather and fair winds for four days but during the next night the winds came up and the winds created ten-foot waves. They were far out to sea on their direct course and had no chance of finding shelter. Adam and Che lowered the mainsail and reefed the jib to lessen the exposure to wind. This helped stabilize the schooner in the heavy winds. The children learned rapidly and helped with sail adjustments. They also tied down anything loose in the galley and cabins, and they all came out to see the giant waves, excited and not at all afraid. The waves grew to twenty feet swells and the wind rose to fifty knots an hour. Adam kept the bow headed into the waves and they rose up and down into the valleys. Two of the children, Iris and Charlie, became seasick for a couple of hours but Ben gave them some hardtack to suck on and eat and they gradually got over it.

The wind finally let up and the swells dropped to four to eight feet, so they raised the sails to full capacity, and the speed picked up to ten knots or more. Two weeks later, as they approached the north end of the

Galapagos, they began to see frigates, red-footed boobies, and swallow-tailed gulls. They anchored off the shore of the largest island and saw Galapagos penguins, marine iguanas, flightless cormorants, Sally Lightfoot crabs, as well as finches, hawks, and doves. Noddy terns, tropic birds, and storm petrels were also in abundance. All ten children went ashore with Che in the zodiac, while Adam and Ben stayed on board. Adam ate some food on his empty stomach and slept for several hours after the long sea journey.

Adam and Che decided to lay over for several days and let the children enjoy the island life. The four youngest had brought drawing pads and were sketching any animal or bird they saw. They told Ben they were being like Charles Darwin and recording all the unique wildlife. They said Grace had made this a school assignment if they landed on these islands. Always with one adult present, they wandered over most of the island surface looking for any creature that was unique. They came up over a ridge and looked down into a bay and saw a wrecked ship that had crashed into a huge rock and was partially sunk. Ben was with them and told them to stay low until he determined if there was any person on the ship or the shore. There was no sign of life as they expected but Ben would take no chances. He reported the sighting to Che and Adam.

They spent a few more days enjoying the weather on the equator until Che said it would be a good time to head for the Horn. He calculated that it would take another two months to cover the five thousand miles or so, and he suggested they stop at an archipelago in the pacific about three thousand miles from where they were before attempting the Horn. The children went aboard with some reluctance since they were having such a wonderful time ashore, but they soon settled in to the tasks of sailing.

They had a good start, but several days out of the Galapagos, they were becalmed. They put up the largest sails they had, including a topsail but only inched along. They even tried a beautiful spinnaker but that made no difference. Suddenly the winds came up from the southeast, along with a steady drizzly rain. They now had a slight headwind so the children had considerable experience with tacking and even a couple of sail changes which were the most exciting, since they had to drop a sail into the hatch and attach and raise another sail in a short time with wind blowing and rain pelting them. Che explained that, at this time of year, this is what they would expect and it was better than having no wind at all. They made steady but slow progress for two months and established a regular routine of sleeping for several hours, taking their turns on duty, handling tacking when needed, and managing the steady flow of food required in the galley. Toward the end of the leg, they did have a few days with very little wind, but still managed to reach the archipelago in just over two months.

They stayed over several days, found water to stock up with for the next couple of months, and prepared for the always dangerous trip of rounding the Horn. Che explained to the children that they could encounter high waves, stormy rainy weather, and strong winds ahead, so the children were prepared with warm clothes and rain slickers and made sure they were always attached to a tether when on the slippery deck. They would plan on stopping at the Falkland Islands briefly before continuing on to Tristan.

Rounding the Horn went according to expectations: they encountered high seas of twenty feet and strong winds of forty knots but Adam explained that this was mild compared to what they could encounter. He described waves of as much as forty feet where they would drop precipitously into the troughs and rise up again. They did encounter some of these conditions where the wave would break over the bow and fill the cockpit temporarily but the children were always careful to hang on to rails and tethers and to keep from falling in the wind and rolling deck.

They finally reached the islands and rocks at the tip of the continent and encountered heavy fog. The poor visibility called for lookouts at the bow. The children took turns keeping a lookout. They loved the feeling of the wind and the waves washing over them, but after an hour or two at the post, they grew cold and were relieved by another pair of teenagers. They would go below and get warm, eat a bit and sleep for a time and be ready to go again for their shift. They always had a partner with them. They paired off with Paul and Jasmine as one pair, Joe and Shelly as another, Hannah and Rose, Fawn and Charlie, and Iris and Tom as the others. They rotated shifts on deck, preparing food for themselves and either Adam, Che or Ben. The three adults always had two on deck as a precaution. They would rotate one off and one on every eight hours as a general rule.

After safely rounding the Horn, they headed for the Falklands. As they approached, Fawn, who was on lookout with Charlie, was the first to spot a ship, the first they had seen since leaving. Adam approached cautiously and Che noted it was adrift and there were no signs of life. They came alongside and discovered two people on board. They were both dead and the sails were shredded and the boat barely afloat. Adam cautioned that they must stay away since the people could be recent casualties of the pandemic. They could be contagious. They left and sailed on with heavy hearts.

CHAPTER THIRTY

Visiting Tristan

Late Fall, 22 AP

"The sea will soon claim that ship and its occupants." Adam was very quiet as he spoke.

They carried on until the sloop approached the eastern main island of the Falkland Islands. They anchored off shore on the eastern side of the island in a long narrow bay, and again, all but Adam and Ben went ashore. They found a spring to replenish their water and found no sign of human life. They did find fascinating birds and animals, including the Striated Caracara, along with the fur seals and the southern elephant seal. There were no trees but lots of grazing space for sheep, which were abundant.

The children were running across the pastures when an accident occurred. Iris fell hard on a rocky surface and broke her left arm. Che took the children back to the boat and he and Ben built a splint to support her arm to allow it to heal. She was treated by the other children to special care, making meals for her, and offering to take her turns on duty. Her arm healed quickly and one night when they were sitting on board having a warm meal of pasta with a sauce that Ben made, Adam asked if any of the children had thought about what they wanted to learn as they grew up.

"We could use a couple of doctors in our community as you can imagine," he said.

At first there was no response and then Fawn spoke up.

"I'd like to be a naturalist, like Charles Darwin."

"So would I," said Iris, "but I'd also like to be a doctor."

"And, so would I," added Tom, "and then I could have operated on Iris."

"Not on your life," Iris complained, "I'd rather operate on myself. Remember that movie we saw once where the doctor did that. He was also a naturalist."

The others mentioned various things such as sea captain, and farmer, and artist, and musician. Later Ben talked to Iris and Tom and told them he would look for medical books and help them to learn about medicine and as much about being a doctor as he could.

"Then I could practice by operating on Tom," Iris said, "I wonder what is in his brain." He pretended to chase her and she giggled.

The next morning, they raised the anchor, set the sails, and sailed into the always unpredictable south Atlantic. Che calculated that they still had about a month to cover another twenty-five hundred miles to Tristan. They had currents and winds with them for many days and raced ahead. They sailed day and night and never saw another ship. Adam and Che took turns at the helm for eight-hour shifts, with Ben on call if needed. The children worked in pairs on six-hour shifts. Iris was exempt for the time being and Tom served as a spare backup if someone did not feel well.

They were making excellent time, well ahead of schedule, when the first signs of stormy weather appeared in the form of dark clouds and then strong headwinds buffeted them and created huge waves often as high as twenty feet. This lasted twenty-four hours and during that time, Tom had to spell two of them because of violent seasickness. Ben helped out covering for a third. In spite of the turbulent weather, they reached Tristan in twenty-five days.

As they approached, from several nautical miles away, they could see the mountain looming ahead of them. They sailed slowly off shore of the settlement and the stone jetty sticking out from the ramp leading up the cliff to the settlement above. They were fortunate that they arrived while the weather was mild and the wind and waves were light. They knew it was often very stormy around Tristan.

It was spring there, and when the Tristanians saw them drop anchor off shore, a dozen of them raced down to the jetty. The Tristanians waved and the three adults and ten children waved back. All had life jackets on and Ben and the ten kids boarded the zodiac and motored in to the small harbor which protected them from the sea. Adam and Che stayed on board. They were helped out of the zodiac and onto the jetty. The group included a member of the Glass family named James. When they were told Adam was on the schooner, one of them went with Ben to get him, and Ben stayed with Che on board the schooner.

The Tristanians remembered Adam, and he remembered them, even though many years had passed.

"It has been more than fifteen years since we last saw you or anyone else," said a venerable Tristanian named Norman that remembered Adam.

"How have you survived so long?" Adam asked.

"We are used to that. We are self-sufficient. But what about you? The plague did not get you?"

Adam explained the entire process of finding the few others when he returned on the trawler, having lost all crew members. Then he explained the schooner and sailing to the north to found a small community.

"I wish we had a suitable boat to come and visit you," said Norman, "but alas, we are marooned here."

Adam explained the long voyage he took and thought perhaps there was a way in the future to bring another large boat for their use.

"But where would we keep it?"

"You will need to expand your harbor protection so that at least one ship could dock safely inside the protective rocky barrier. I don't think it could stay off shore in the stormy weather you often have."

"We will do it if you promise to return."

"I cannot promise that I will but certainly some of these children will. That I can promise."

And so, the ten children had the run of the island community which covered an area of two miles by half a mile. They explored the gardens and learned how the Tristanians pollinated vegetables by hand since there were no bees or other natural pollinators as elsewhere. They saw the fields filled with sheep and the many Border Collies running around. They climbed the side of the volcano part way and heard about the evacuation from the year 1961. They even visited the graveyards where the original settlers were buried, including the original Chief Islanders William Glass and Peter Groen. They visited the homes made of stone of many Tristanians, the schools and churches, and made good friends.

During their visit to the school, they were given a lesson by the science teacher named Sarah about Tristan. She let them look at a couple of bird books from the Tristan library while she talked about the wildlife.

"Tristan is primarily known for its wildlife," Sarah told them. "The island has been identified as an important bird area because there are 13 known species of breeding seabirds on the island and two species of resident land birds. The seabirds include northern rockhopper penguins, Atlantic yellow-nosed albatrosses, sooty albatrosses, Atlantic petrels, great-winged petrels, soft-plumaged petrels, broad-billed prions, grey petrels, great shearwaters, sooty shearwaters, Tristan skuas, Antarctic terns and brown noddies."

Sarah went on to explain, "Tristan and Gough Islands are the only known breeding sites in the world for the Atlantic petrel. Inaccessible Island is also the only known breeding ground of the spectacled petrel. The Tristan albatross is known to breed only on Gough and Inaccessible Islands: all nest on Gough, except for one or two pairs which nest on Inaccessible Island."

The ten Cascadians were awestruck by this information but still managed to ask many questions and remarked that they did not have half as many species of birds back home.

"We saw a little bird," said Fawn, "that was rustling around and singing. It was dark brown. What was that?"

The teacher answered, "what you saw was the endemic Tristan thrush, also known as the "starchy", which occurs on all of the northern islands and each has its own subspecies, with Tristan birds being slightly smaller and duller than those on Nightingale and Inaccessible. The endemic Inaccessible Island rail, the smallest extant flightless bird in the world, is found only on Inaccessible Island. In 1956, eight Gough moorhens were released at Sandy Point on Tristan, and have subsequently colonized the island. No birds of prey breed on Tristan da Cunha, but the Amur falcon occasionally passes through the area on its migrations, thus putting it on the island's bird list."

Fawn continued, "we have seen many birds on islands as we traveled to get here. Some of us are interested in becoming naturalists and all of us have been excited about seeing all the different birds. We stopped at the Galapagos Islands and also saw some wonderful birds and other animals. We thank you very much for telling us about Tristan."

"I have never been there," Sarah said in a soft voice, "you are very lucky." She paused and continued, "would you like to take one of our books for the rest of your journey?"

"We will bring it back," Iris interjected, "at least one of us will return for sure."

"I am so glad to see such a group of young people that are very interested in wildlife. I hope to see most of you if not all when you return."

Adam learned that the population, which generally held steady at around 250, had gone down to just over 200 at the beginning of the pandemic, but had slowly rebounded in recent years, as a younger group of Tristanians grew up. The ten children from Cascadia sat around a table once a day and were told by Norman and others about the history of Tristan from 1816, and how the island gradually grew during the 1800s.

Norman told them about the nine family names Collins, Glass, Green, Hagan, Lavarello, Repetto, Rogers, Squibb, and Swain. Tristan was settled by men from military garrisons and ships, who married native women from Saint Helena and the Cape Colony during the 1800s. Its people are multi-racial, descended from European male founders and mixed-race (African, Asian and European) and African women founders.

"That explains why your people are so ethnically diverse," said Iris.

"And we are a very healthy group of people," said Norman, "we live a long time."

"Maybe the diversity has something to do with it?" asked Paul.

"Perhaps," was the reply. There was a moment of silence. Then Joe spoke up.

"I never thought about it too much, but we Cascadians are a pretty ethnically diverse group also, aren't we?" He looked around and the other nine children nodded their heads in agreement.

After a week, they were disturbed by a huge storm gathering to the north and decided to make a run for it before it was too late. They said their farewells and promised to return, took the zodiac out to the schooner and raised sails. They were able to outrun the storm which seemed to be moving south just a little slower than they were sailing. It was critical to outrun it to avoid the very high seas they expected. They were able to reach South Georgia and dropped anchor in the small bay of the whaling station of Grytviken. Adam and Che stayed on board while the others went ashore and explored briefly, as the storm swept over them.

They sailed slowly along the coast until they dropped anchor one last time before leaving South Georgia. They learned they had stopped in the Bay of Isles, off shore from Salisbury Plain. They went ashore and walked among the King Penguins, who were unafraid of them. Fawn and Iris especially loved the baby penguins with their fur coats. They also saw the skuas and petrels hovering around trying to snatch one of the babies but the adult penguins kept a close eye on them and chased them away. Many of the penguins followed them everywhere as if they were big penguins.

Later on, all ten of the young people took a zodiac with Che to nearby Albatross Island to see the beautiful wandering albatrosses and their lovely greeting ritual. By this time all ten of them had formed a "birder" group. Using the book from Sarah, they identified and kept track of all the birds they saw and remembered from elsewhere.

They recorded many birds of South Georgia: albatross, king penguins, macaroni penguins, petrels, prions, shags, skuas, gulls, terns, pipits and pintails. Che teased them about becoming "bird watchers" but soon stopped when he saw how devoted and serious most of them were about learning.

They found no people on any of the islands. When the wind and rain abated, they decided to continue on, but another storm front buffeted them within a day of sailing. They reached the Falkland Islands and sought shelter from the storm in a long bay. They felt very lucky to have reached shelter.

The storm swept over them with torrential rains and fifty knot winds. They would have had serious problems at sea with huge waves astern that could easily have swamped them. While they waited for the storm to abate, Che and Ben slaughtered one of the large lambs they found wandering, and carved up the meat for several dinners to follow. They also loaded up a large supply of water since they had a long voyage ahead before reaching the archipelago off the southwest part of South America.

Iris was completely well again as they left the Falklands and took her usual turn with Tom, shortening the length of each slot from six to five hours. Adam explained to the children that rounding the Horn from east to west would be different since the currents would be against them and so would the winds. It was summer in the south so they had somewhat better conditions than in the southern winter. The seas were very choppy, and it was slow going against the winds. Adan had to tack often to get around the Horn but eventually they did and headed north along the coast of South America. Once they headed north, they had the winds and rain behind them so they made good time running before the wind. Adam and Che even had the spinnaker raised with the children doing the work, but they soon brought it down since the winds were squirrely, as Jasmine remarked one time.

They approached the archipelago with relief. Even though they were seasoned pros by now they were all exhausted from the hard work and looked forward to a break. They dropped anchor in a protected inlet and had a wonderful meal sitting on the deck. The slight rain at this time did not bother them in the least. Their confidence had grown so much that they were not fazed by any weather conditions.

Adam explained that they would be in favorable conditions with rain and wind expected to be behind them. Also, they were moving from summer in the south to summer in the north. Once they reached the Galapagos and the equator, they would then be in the northern hemisphere and the approach of spring and summer. He calculated that they would reach home in early summer, if all went well. They sailed along with the light rain and wind blowing them north. They anchored in the same spot as they had done on the trip down. The children were delighted to return to the island where they had had so much fun. All the children were careful about running around and not falling and breaking any bones as Iris had done. They saw their favorite iguanas and frigates and boobies and watched the small turtles head for the water to escape the hungry frigate birds. Three of the children, Paul, Jasmine, and Joe, with Ben, went over the ridge where they had seen the wrecked ship. In just a few months, it had disappeared beneath the sea from the storms, and waves, and winds.

Iris and Tom and Fawn and Charlie did more drawing and sketching of all the various animals and birds and insects they saw. This second visit to the Galapagos was a memorable and exhilarating visit for the ten children. Che and Ben asked them all to keep some sort of record and journal to tell all the other children when they returned. Adam plotted out the return trip for all of them and said they should return in about two months, and it would be late summer at home. They will have been gone for nearly one and a half years, and all of the children will have changed quite a bit. But everyone will want to know everything about the trip so that is why they needed to keep records so as not to forget things. With so many exciting things on the trip it would be easy to forget.

After loading up on water and stowing all the gear they had brought out, they pulled anchor and sailed out into the sea with a course of northwest and planned to make two major stops: one at Baja, and the other where they had stopped on the way down, on the fringe of the kelp beds and the sea otters.

CHAPTER THIRTY ONE

Returning Home

Late Summer, 23 AP

Adam and the crew sailed on from the equator, now in the northern hemisphere, in a direct line for Baja. To do so, they had to stay far out to sea, and this produced a huge risk if and when they encountered a tropical storm. Unfortunately, this is exactly what did happen. There was no weather system anymore to give warning so they had to rely on visual observation of storm clouds and rapid dropping of the barometric readings. When the barometer began to drop dramatically, Adam became worried.

They took a direct course north in the hopes at least of getting closer to land in the event of a major storm. They were able to reach the coast just above Acapulco before the edge of the storm hit. The direction of the winds at this point was north from the rotating outer edge of the tropical storm and the wind speeds were up to forty knots. They calculated they had about a day and a night of sailing ahead of the winds before reaching the eastern side of the Baja.

The winds of the slow-moving storm increased to fifty knots as they sailed into a small bay on the inside of the Baja where they quickly dropped anchor, and stowed all the sails after tying up at a sturdy looking dock. The jib had taken a beating from the wind and was beginning to be tattered. Adam was relieved that he had had the foresight to stow two extra jibs. They tied the schooner to the dock with multiple ropes and waited for the worst of the storm to arrive. They did not have to wait long before the hurricane force winds roared across the Baja, rocking them mercilessly.

"At least we aren't out to sea in this storm," Paul mentioned to no one in particular. After a night of heavy seas tossing the dock and the schooner about, the winds gradually decreased until all was calm again. Che and Ben checked the schooner all over for leaks or broken spars or any damage to the rigging. They found a few loose halyards and a few small tears in the mizzen but otherwise the schooner was shipshape. Che also tested the engine which they had not needed to use. It was in fine shape.

They searched out sources of good water from springs, had a few good meals, and prepared to sail out into the pacific on their next leg to the area with the sea otters. The children were again excited in anticipation of watching the otters in the kelp. Che calculated it would take about two weeks under fair conditions, and that is just what they had. The children were once again taking turns sitting at the bow and feeling the salty spray in their faces. They were always in pairs and each checked the other to make sure they had a safety line attached.

Che was very strict about safety and watched them like a hawk. He only had one occasion when he had to admonish someone to get the safety line on more quickly when up on deck. It was his own daughter Jasmine who was chagrined at being scolded, but she forgot it quickly. They settled into their sailing routine of taking their five-hour watch, day or night, and taking time to eat properly and to get enough sleep. Time went by quickly and soon they approached the kelp beds and the sea otters, and anchored just outside of the kelp. Ben took eight of the ten on a slow tour in the zodiac through the kelp, often just paddling slowly so as not to disturb the otters. Iris and Tom stayed on board drawing the otters in various playful poses.

After a layover of three days, Adam once again hauled up the anchor, raised the full set of sails, and headed out into the pacific. It was a wonderful summer day.

"We should reach home in about a week and a half," Che announced after his usual calculations, "I hope you recognize your brothers and sisters," he called.

"I hope they recognize us," yelled back Paul.

He and all the other nine children realized, that in one and a half years, all of them had grown, and it might also be hard for the younger children to know them immediately. Paul, the oldest, was now fifteen and a half. They followed the coast line closely as each day went by looking for the opening into the Strait. With the lovely summer weather most of the way, they spent as much time as possible at the bow or along the starboard side watching whales migrating north. Suddenly the schooner sailed past the point marking the entrance to the Strait and Adam tacked directly east and then a short time later he tacked north heading for their familiar harbor.

Meanwhile the children on the island had begun a game of their own, guessing when the schooner would arrive. The older ones had learned to ride ponies and small mares and they took turns riding two at a time down the center of the island to the old abandoned camp which had a high lookout. They had found two pairs of binoculars in an abandoned store and scanned the seas west for any signs of a ship. One day the younger sisters of Joe and Shelly were on duty at the high point and looked out at an approaching object in the direction of the big mountain.

"It's them. It's them," yelled Becky, Joe's sister.

"Are you sure?" called Jenny, Shelly's sister.

"It's a big ship and it's coming closer. I'm sure," Becky was convinced.

"Let's go then."

They hopped on their ponies and rode as fast as they could to the community at the north end. They jumped off and spotted Sly in a field.

"They're coming. We saw them," yelled the two girls.

It was the middle of the day and the sun was shining. All of the children and adults rode or ran or walked to the dock. By the time they had all dropped their chores and gotten to the dock, the schooner sailed slowly into dock, and the crew tied up and jumped off. It took some time for the ten children to identify their twenty-two brothers and sisters and cousins but they eventually did and hugged each and every one of them. Then the mothers and Harry stepped in to embrace all of them.

It took over a week for all the stories to be told and the drawings to be shown and the excitement to slow down but it did. Ben joined Harry and several of the children to play music and teach new songs to the seasoned sailors. It took even longer for Paul and the others to learn about all the new animals that had arrived in their absence. There were many more chicks, some ducklings and goslings, a few goats and sheep and pigs, and even a couple of additional calves and colts or mares. There were no more children yet but one night Sly remarked to Grace that it might not be long before that changed.

"What do you mean?" asked Grace.

"Jasmine came to me yesterday and told me that she and Paul had gotten very close on the trip," Sly smiled.

"What do you mean?"

"I mean very, very, close. She is fifteen after all and a very mature fifteen at that."

"Like her mother?" queried Grace. She paused. "And?"

"Well, it seems she and Paul are expecting an addition to our community."

"I guess I am not too surprised. This will probably start more of that."

Grace and Sly did their best to talk about being parents and responsibilities but it seemed as if Jasmine and Paul did feel as if they knew everything they needed to know.

Grace was accurate, when she said that this would be the beginning of a new generation and that the community would grow. Jasmine and Paul were not quite correct about knowing all that they needed to know. However, they learned quickly and did call on their parents now and then for advice.

And so, the community was back together again and thriving. There were forty people now and they were well along to dealing with the development of their needs. They had learned how to store winter crops without spoiling them, how to slaughter some animals for meat, and used the large freezer with a generator to keep the meat for the future. After he returned Che spent a great deal of his time, together with several of the older children, searching for gasoline in abandoned ships and old cars. They siphoned it out and stored it in empty cans they had collected. Che did not think they needed much for the generator used for the freezer, or for the engine on the schooner or zodiac or the two other sloops they had repaired and kept for short trips but they would never find any more of it, so they needed to plan for a long future.

Their energy projects from eight years earlier were very successful. They had acquired hundreds of solar panels from all over the many islands. Most of them had survived the fierce storms during the early days of the pandemic and were put to good use. Small ones were used on individual homes, and the larger ones were used for major buildings such as the large barns, or the energy of one complex was distributed to a set of buildings all in the same general location. The school had its own significant set of solar panels providing energy. By then they had rebuilt a number of buildings in the town that had been destroyed during the early days of the pandemic.

They had made some progress on the plan for wind energy in preparing for the future needs of the community but it was low priority. Using the wind turbines of different sizes that they had found, Harry studied the design of them, and learned what materials he needed, and how the distribution of wind energy to generators worked, and then converted to electricity. Che and Sam had developed a plan as to where they thought wind turbines would be placed. They used the existing ones they found to see how they could weather the winds and storms that hit Cascadia often, while helping Harry find the materials he needed. They searched every hardware store or other industrial building and gradually built up a supply of metals needed. Harry built his first one, of modest size, during the period when Che and Adam and Ben were at sea. He and Sam set one up in an open field and it worked beautifully. He built another and they placed it on a hilltop. When they had strong winds one winter, they also were pleased to discover that it also worked. Then they needed to scour the islands for as many generators as they could locate.

That was just the beginning for Harry, although he had plenty of help from the many adults who felt they understood electricity. Che and Sam and Adam also had some knowledge of generators and electricity but Harry was the acknowledged leader in this area. Harry then had to find electrical wiring to connect the electricity to one or more homes and other buildings, just as he did for solar energy. He found some that he could use in the abandoned and damaged hardware stores still standing. It was a slow process but together the solar energy and wind energy provided an increasing amount of electricity to the burgeoning community.

After Ben returned, he joined Grace and Sly in the plan which they had sketched out before of having a good-sized school and a full curriculum, involving music and art and theatre, in addition to basic school subjects such as math, English and writing and reading, science, and history. Their trip to the Galapagos and the Falklands was a boon to developing interest in science for most of the children, and becoming naturalists for a few. The number of children ready for the elementary levels of learning had been growing steadily and they knew it would not be too long before the generations of children filled the existing school.

One of the delightful discoveries by Adam when he returned was that, while he and Che and Ben were gone, Harry and Sam found time to harvest the next batch of grapes from the beautiful fields of vines on the islands, and to prune the vines for the next round of grapes. They also had a bit of help from some of the children, who ate as much as they harvested. The glorious wine was fermenting and aging in the barrels and waiting for Adam and the others. When they arrived home, it was almost time to harvest the next batch of grapes.

And so, life went on and two things happened: the community began to grow and grow and grow; and discussion began about sailing again to Tristan as promised.

CHAPTER THIRTY TWO

Returning to Tristan

Spring, 32 AP

Over the next ten years, the community expanded as the children began to be friends and then became special friends and then parents. Grace's prediction and hope gradually became reality. The sixteen daughters of Grace, Sly, Sam, and Sarah, averaged four daughters each and about the same number of sons over this period and beyond. By this time, the community eventually reached about one hundred fifty people as the families grew and moved throughout the islands and established their own homes and farms.

During this period, which went on for this decade and beyond, the eldest of the children of Grace, Sly, Sam, and Sarah, now parents themselves, decided to put together a plan to return to Tristan on two ships and leave one of the ships there. The four young men, Paul, Joe, Charlie, and Tom, did most of the talking, but the eight young women, Jasmine, Shelly, Hannah, Rose, Fawn, Iris, Becky, and Jenny, often interjected comments. All twelve of them joined in to describe their plans to Adam and Che. After listening carefully, Adam approved the plan, and said Che and Ben would join the twelve of them.

However, Che insisted that they all spend several weeks learning all that was necessary about sailing a ketch.

"Adam and I will give all of you lessons on the water," Che said, "especially since some of you have never taken such a grueling voyage, and none of you have sailed a ketch under such conditions."

"Keep in mind," Adam added, "that you can encounter fierce conditions at sea, especially on the route you will take, and they will be different sailing a smaller ketch compared to the large schooner."

All of the younger people nodded their heads and said they understood.

They would take two smaller ships, both ketches, about sixty feet long, each carrying a crew of seven. Che's crew consisted of Paul, Jasmine, Hannah, Rose, Iris, and Tom. Joe, Shelly, Fawn, Charlie, Becky, and Jennie made up Ben's crew. The young people formed their own pairings, which were then approved by Che and Ben.

When they reached Tristan, they would leave one ketch in Tristan and return with a full crew now of fourteen. Che and Paul would lead the first ketch, and Ben and his son Joe would lead the other. Che took time to install the turret gun on the bow of the ketch he would command. They provisioned both ships with water and dry food and some fresh food to begin with, and prepared to sail in early spring of thirty-two AP.

All of the crew had prepared themselves with clothes for such a trip, including waterproof slickers in bright colors and hoods, waterproof boots that gripped the deck, waterproof gloves for handling sails and halyards and sheets and winches. They all had tethers on deck and never handled sheets and winches without one or more other members of the crew with them. They had extra pairs of clothes for every condition, since the weather could range from very cold to hot, from rain to snow to hail, and would often be extremely windy.

They said goodbye to all the families and departed with a small rain coming down and a slight wind. They were often able to set the sails and the ketch would hold to a direct course without need for action from the skipper. The one in the cockpit would have to be on duty in the event that the wind shifted or a small squall came up. They sailed at a pace of about seven knots per hour so it took one and a half times as long as the schooner to cover similar distances.

The first part of the journey to Baja was relatively uneventful. When they approached the wide mouth of the great river, Che was apprehensive, but they saw no signs of life where the bandit gang had once ruled. Nevertheless, he sailed silently across the open water, somewhat out to sea, and did not relax until they were far to the south. They went ashore several times to take on fresh water, and searched for edible root crops, berries, other fruit growing on trees and bushes, and wild salad greens.

They went ashore in parties of four or more, and carried guns as a precaution. Only once did they have an encounter with a dangerous animal. A very hungry cougar confronted them and stalked them but when they fired a gun in the air, the cougar turned and fled. So did the shore group, and they rushed back to the zodiac and the two ships. They saw no signs of life, but as a precaution, since the sound of the gun could be heard far away, Che and Ben set sail quickly.

At Baja, they were fortunate in their timing not to encounter the huge Gray Whales that stayed in the bay during the winter in the north. The fifty-foot whales could easily destroy the ketches if they felt their calves were in danger.

As they approached the Galapagos Islands, the excitement grew for the crew. Most of them had been there many years earlier on the trip to Tristan, but for a couple of the youngest crew members, Becky and Jennie, it was a new experience. Che and Ben searched carefully in the bays and found no ships. Che picked his favorite location to drop anchor and go ashore. When he felt it was safe, he allowed the crew to explore in small groups, always alert and not too far from the ships. After a few hours, with reluctance, they returned to the ships and set sail.

"I'm sorry that our stop was so short," Che said, "we'll try to spend more time on the return journey."

The crew tried not to show their disappointment, and said they understood.

They reached the Horn and rounded it just as the warm southern summer arrived and had relatively mild conditions. Nevertheless, the five to ten-foot waves were still quite a challenge for the sixty-foot ketches, and Che and Ben had a full crew of seven on deck managing the sails. When the weather turned a bit foggy, Che and Ben had the crew work hard to keep the two ketches close to each other, and also had set up a signaling system to allow the two ketches to communicate with each other, using Morse code if they could not see each other clearly enough. They were all relieved when they cleared the Horn, and headed for the Falklands. They dropped anchor in a protected cove with the two ketches very near each other, and began to relax for the first time in many days.

Ben stayed on board his ketch and sent his crew over to join the others for a brief time. Che noticed that all twelve of them were quite subdued, and realized how dangerous sailing could be under such conditions. They took this time to have a wonderful meal prepared by all of them together. Joe and Shelly took a meal over to Ben, and he smiled.

"I'm glad you are all together again," Ben said, "even if it is only for a short while. I enjoy just sitting on deck and relaxing. Sailing can be quite exhausting, can't it?" They nodded. After the meal was over, Che sent them ashore in groups of four to explore the island they had anchored near, but they found no one alive. They did take on water from fresh springs they found, and then set sail for South Georgia.

Che had the lead boat as usual, and sailed north around the western tip of South Georgia to Grytviken, and anchored in the cove off shore from the rusty buildings, and bones of the huge whales slaughtered many years earlier and still visible. There was no sign of life. They went ashore briefly and wandered around.

"This is one of the most depressing sights I have ever seen," Iris mumbled, "I don't want to stay here for a moment."

The others agreed and they soon set sail for Tristan. They wanted to arrive at Tristan as early as possible and return around the Horn before the southern winter arrived in force. The trip to Tristan was exciting because of all the birds they encountered, and the waves were mild.

CHAPTER THIRTY THREE

Tristan and Home

Spring in North, 33 AP

They sailed in to the new Tristan breakwater and were able to anchor both ketches in the new larger harbor that protected the ketches from stormy conditions. They were fortunate to have favorable conditions while they were there. They spent two weeks teaching the Tristanians how to sail the ketch that Ben had captained, but soon learned that they were much more knowledgeable about sailing than Che and Ben expected. The Cascadians and Tristanians renewed old friendships and made new ones. They were all given a tour of the island by one of the members of the Glass family, Felicity, who also showed them the ancient graveyard and explained the long history of the island, and the topography. Felicity also told them about the last volcanic eruption in 1961, and how her ancestors had to vacate Tristan for a few years.

Jasmine asked, "Is it possible that you could have another eruption of the volcano?"

"Yes," Felicity was very subdued as she responded, "it is not only possible but quite probable within a few years."

"What will you do?" asked Fawn. Felicity just shrugged.

During their stay on Tristan, they moved all of their personal gear and food from Ben's ketch to Che's, and sorted out who would sleep where on the return trip. Both the Tristanians and Cascadians had tears in their eyes, and said they hoped to see each other again one day soon. They boarded the one ketch, but just before they were about to sail away, the head of the Glass family, Norman, promised to sail around the Horn and visit them in a few years.

"It's a deal," said Che, "we'll be waiting."

The fourteen of them had stocked up on water as always and set sail for the Horn with just enough time to round the horn before the southern winter came on in force.

They made much better time sailing north than their trip south, since they had prevailing southeast winds pushing on through a slight misty rain. They raised their beautiful red spinnaker and flew north at over ten knots per hour. They stopped briefly at the islands in between the Horn and the Galapagos along the coast but pressed on to reach the equator as soon as possible. It was fall and the weather was warm. They anchored at their usual cove in the Galapagos and the crew had the most fun frolicking around and discovering all the unique and beautiful animals and birds.

They were about to raise the anchor and sail north but Che noticed there was no wind. He and Ben decided to stay over until they had some decent wind. Finally, the wind rose and they raised sails and headed north. Winter was approaching quickly and Ben was very concerned about hitting storms in the Pacific Northwest before they managed to cover the long distance north.

"Ben," Che said after making some calculations, "I think we will hit winter up north when we return. It is nearly six thousand miles to our Strait, and we will probably take nearly three months to cover it. We can try to sail more than ten hours a day to make up some of it but we will have to stop a couple of times. The more experience the kids can get in foul weather the better we will be prepared."

"You'll get your wish, Che. I expect we'll hit very stormy weather off of Baja just as we did on our last trip. It'll be a warmup for the heavy winds at home." They sailed under fair skies and slight wind for two weeks and made excellent progress with a direct course heading to Baja. With only a few days to go the skies darkened, and the barometer dropped and they recognized they were approaching the outer edges of a tropical storm. They monitored it for some time and determined it was moving very slowly east by northeast. At first the winds were from the west and gradually shifted to north so they sensed they were on the eastern edge of the slow-moving storm. They were within a day of the inside east side of Baja that they sought. The winds picked up to a category one hurricane and the children on the bow deck were hard pressed to stand up.

When Che asked them to reef the jib, they got it tangled up in the anchor gear and it flapped so vigorously it began to tear. They tried to tie it to the forward mast but could not avoid the tearing. He had Ben and the children lowered the main and just hung on with the mizzen helping to move forward with the ferocious winds. They recognized that they had entered the eye of the storm just as they entered the small protection of the inlet on the east side of Baja. They managed to dock in the roaring wind and the heavy rain and tied down the main and mizzen. The crew worked to remove the flapping and tearing jib and went below. They were cold and wet and hungry and exhausted. Che and Ben waited out the storm as it passed over, going east over land, and were thankful they did not sustain any more damage other than the sail.

All of them carefully went over all the rigging and did find two loose halyards which they tightened. Relieved that they were now safe from the storm, they ate voraciously and slept like logs. They awoke to a calm sea and slight wind. After they replenished their water supply, Che decided to move on. To make up time and because he only had one regular jib left, he had his able crew put on the Genoa jib in the modest winds. The crew loved this jib and soon discovered how to tack and handle its huge size. It was a beautiful blue and white and red color and they were amazed at how much wind that sail picked up and dumped back to the main if they had it positioned properly. They flew up the coast and reached the "otter" bay in a week and a half. They stopped briefly to rest and draw the otters at play and then continued on to the Strait.

It was very late in the year and within a few days they encountered a massive storm off of the coast heading directly into their Strait. It was the remains of a late season typhoon that came across the Pacific. They had put the smaller jib on, reefed it and the mainsail, and slowly moved along the coast in the heavy winds. They were drenched but protected by their huge waterproof slickers and boots that grasped the deck, and always made sure they and their designated partner were attached to safety lines. When they did not need help with tacking, the pairs on deck sat in the bow and enjoyed the spray and the waves hitting the bow, and were at home in the sea. After all those days at sea they could imagine nothing nicer than sailing along with the occasional dolphins and porpoises and flying fish landing on deck, and the whales in the distance. They became expert at identifying gray whales and humpbacks, and a rare blue whale. They often saw pilot whales cruising across the bow far ahead.

Finally, they passed the point of the northwestern most part of the old country and tacked to the east into the Strait, north up the Haro Strait, around the big island and into the harbor. This time they were not being tracked carefully so their arrival was a bit of a surprise. It was also a very rainy windy day in the beginning of winter. Two of the children ran down to find the others and surprised them. The entire community was then notified and they all came to the dock, hugged them, and welcomed them on their safe return.

There had been some changes in the time they had been gone, over one and a half years. There were some new young additions to families, new chicks and lambs and kids and piglets, and a couple of foals. But the community was as organized and thriving as always. Those arriving told the tales of the sea and those at home told them of the new school they were repairing and cleaning at the south end of the island. And then it began to snow, and snow, and snow.

It was the worst blizzard that the older generation had ever seen. The snow came down for three straight days and covered everything but the tallest trees and the biggest buildings. The bushes and sheds were covered over. Even the original henhouse was virtually covered except for the tip of the roof. The wind blew all day and night and created huge drifts up against the sides of the barns and houses. The ponds were frozen and covered with a thick layer of snow. The only exception was the big pond at the far end of the outer pasture which the geese kept open by creating a hole in the middle and splashing the water continuously to keep it from freezing. The storm took its toll on the wild dog packs that still existed and reduced them to a few emaciated dogs. The children that were old enough to work were put together with parents and even a few grandparents still fit to dig out doors to buildings and pathways from building to building. Some of the chickens and turkeys and ducks and pigs went hungry for a short time but they were happy when they were finally fed. After all the chores were done for the day and before dark set in, the children of all ages played in the snow, building snowmen and snowwomen, creating sliding ramps down hills and using any sliding object they could find to slide down the packed runways.

As with all things, it came to an end as the snow melted, and signs of spring appeared. Trees budded and fruit trees bloomed and winter crops were uncovered and harvested and school resumed and life went on. The years passed by and children became older and learned everything they could and grew up. Some married, often of a very young age, and the usual discussions occurred between daughters and mothers and sons and fathers about responsibilities and such and the young ones usually tried to convince their parents that they knew everything they needed to know then and learned the usual hard way, by trial and error, that they didn't.

And then one day a pair of teenage girls were riding ponies on the high hill at the south end of the island and saw a sail approaching from the Strait, making its way slowly looking for the proper place to dock. The girls waved and beckoned and pointed north up the side of the island, and began to spread the word. Soon the entire population knew of the approaching ship and ran to the dock that they hoped the visitors would find instead of running aground in one of the shallow bays.

What they did not know was that this crew was composed of excellent sailors and navigators and would not make that mistake. They also did not know, with the exception of Adam, who recognized his old ketch, that these were visitors from Tristan after the visit by Che and Ben and crews earlier. They did not know that these were Tristanians until the ketch landed at the dock and the visitors waved and greeted them and were recognized by the young crew who had last sailed to Tristan to deliver the ketch. They had kept their promise. There were twelve on board. They were greeted warmly and brought to the large farmhouse. And then the stories began.

CHAPTER THIRTY FOUR

Visitors from The Sea

Spring, 42 AP

The Tristanians had had an exciting trip around the Horn, following the course Adam had once laid out for them, up through the long stretch of the Pacific to the Strait they recognized. They marveled at the wildlife at the Falklands, which they had heard about from travelers many years earlier but had never seen. They liked the unique animals and birds at the Galapagos so much that they were reluctant to leave, and continue north.

The Tristanians stayed nearly two months. They were given a tour of the entire island over a course of many days and were shown the various barns and houses and the school and crops. Before they left Adam made sure they took seeds or bulbs of every possible food source. They were especially pleased with taking back seeds of squash and other food that they did not have on Tristan and that they were sure would grow there. They did not have ducks and geese and pigs so they took a pair of each with them. Ben and Harry took them in a small sloop to their island where they had various fruit trees growing and other root crops. They added seeds or pits of various fruit trees to plant back on Tristan.

There were a number of teenage boys and girls from Tristan as part of the twelve-person crew that gradually became friends with some of the teenagers in the community. They had two months to get to know each other and some got to know each other very, very well. Grace half expected her oldest granddaughter to come to her with news of her warm friendship with a young man in the Glass family. Her daughter Hannah, now a mother of eight, felt the same way as Grace. Instead, Sharon, the oldest, came to both of them and said she and several others promised the Tristanians that they would visit them in Tristan within a few years.

Bill, the leader of the Glass family, had many discussions with Adam, Che, and Ben, about the fact that they have never had a visit from any ship since the news of the pandemic arrived via a small ship many years before, even before Adam arrived on the trawler, and he expected that by now their community and that of Tristan were the only ones extant.

"Don't you think there might be some little communities out there still, surviving and thriving as we are?" posed Adam.

"Perhaps. I suppose it would take many, many, years for you to know and even longer for us, maybe even a hundred years or more. What are your plans for your community as it grows? We are limited by the small size of our area but you have many islands and land to develop and populate."

"Well, that is exactly what we are planning. We are growing rapidly. According to Grace, at the rate we are growing, we will have more than thirty thousand people after one hundred years. I am getting older and will not see that but we are almost halfway there. Grace and I already have more than thirty grandchildren and we hope to live to see most of our great-grandchildren and that could be well over one hundred," Adam said, "we have lots of land to grow food and raise animals on all these islands. Perhaps you should send some of your overflow here," he added.

"I think we might do that, but perhaps we will have a number of joint projects before long." They both smiled.

"What is the name of this island?" Bill asked.

"We call the archipelago of the many islands 'Cascadia'. We are gradually occupying all the islands around. It is working well. And you? Glass Island?"

"Yes, we are renaming it from Tristan to Glass Island." Bill said.

The Tristanians reluctantly set sail after many, many, hugs and a few tears. They were concerned about sailing around the Horn before their southern winter set in, and departed as soon as they calculated their sailing plan. They sailed south along the island with the young teenagers following them on ponies and horses to the south end of the island and the high point and watched the ketch and its crew sail out the Strait and into the Pacific.

Life returned to normal on the island. Over the next fifteen years, Adam and Grace had many great grandchildren, as did the other original settlers. The big school in the south of the island was refurbished, families grew rapidly and so did farms and livestock. Some families began to feel they would be better to move soon to another island. There were soon over one hundred people on each of the other two big islands and a few on other smaller ones. They too repaired farmhouses and farm buildings and sheds and then the small schools and other community buildings and those communities began to grow rapidly. Many of the smaller sloops and a few ketches were put in good working order and a thriving business grew up overnight of small sailing craft that could take people to other islands. At one point an enterprising pair of young men converted a barge, which had been neglected, into a sailing craft with masts and sails at each end. That allowed them to ferry large loads, including cattle and horses and wagons, back and forth between islands.

Life went on in a regular routine. For the children, it was chores and school and homework and helping to prepare dinners. For the older generations, they were still quite active, but the large families provided a special opportunity to read many of the books they found in the abandoned library. And of course, the adults had the bulk of work involving harvesting throughout the year, planting and caring for new crops, helping new born chicks and ducklings and goslings and piglets and foals and colts to be born successfully. Mowing the hay by hand with horses, and bundling it and hauling it in after it dried for winter use, created a steady diet of farming chores for adults and older children.

But there were a few older teenagers that talked and planned and plotted to sail to Tristan, now called Glass Island. The main ones were those girls that became friends with Tristan boys and boys with Tristan girls. They convinced their parents that they were ready to undertake this journey. The clever ones called it education. They planned a trip of one and a half years, and set sail one spring morning, with the blessings of parents and friends and the entire community. The crew consisted of eight that had made the trip before and four that had strong reasons to meet the Tristanians again. They were lead by Paul and Joe.

They had fair weather and were very fortunate to make excellent time all the way south and around the Horn. Then they had their first mishap. The mainsail was torn in such a way as to render it almost useless. When they were in the Falklands, they contrived a way to stitch the tears together with twine. They had another older mainsail but did not want to be on the open sea with only one main sail so they had to do their best to patch it. Once done they set out for Glass Island and reached it in record time. The inhabitants greeted them with open arms and the special friends of four of them were the most enthusiastic. They had brought another pair of lambs and a pair of kids and two piglets. There were several celebrations of their trip and then the pairs of children came to the elders and the result was two of the Tristanian girls were to sail back with the crew and two of the Cascadian girls would stay. The rest of the crew and all of Glass Island celebrated the four marriages, and after considerable preparation the new crew mix sailed away to return to Cascadia.

The trip was uneventful for more than half of the return trip. As they approached the Galapagos, a storm sprang up and high seas and strong winds buffeted the ketch. They again had tearing of the main sail but managed to reach a protected inlet in the Galapagos using just the jib and mizzen. Two of them were exploring the island on shore and crested a ridge to a stunning discovery. They saw another ship and it appeared to be in good shape. It was a very small sloop. At first, they saw no sign of life, but soon they saw two small figures near the bow of the boat looking at the small bowsprit, which seemed to be damaged.

The two returned to their ship and notified Paul, who was the captain of this trip.

"We should sail away and leave them," said one of the crew, "it could be the plague."

"After all these years," said another, "I don't think so."

"We can't just leave them," said a third, "they might need help. They probably do."

Then there was silence until Paul spoke.

"Many years ago, my father and mother, and Jasmine's as well, faced a similar decision and they decided to take a chance and it turned out some of your grandmothers were rescued by them." Paul paused. "We will wait until night and approach the boat to see what is going on."

At dusk, with two of them carrying the powerful rapid-fire rifles, they all approached the small sloop.

"Hello," yelled Paul, "we come as friends. Who is there? Can we help?"

There was a long silence, and then a figure appeared holding a shotgun.

"Don't come any closer," the man said, "what do you want? We have nothing but a little water and a little food. We have nothing to give you."

"We want nothing. We have food and water ourselves. Is it the plague?" Paul asked.

"The oldest plague of all. It is called starvation. We just lost one of us and we are not far from death ourselves," said the man.

"We want to help. We can bring food and water from our ship. In fact, we have some with us now."

There was another long silence. The man put up the gun.

"Come aboard. You can do no harm to us that will not happen soon."

Paul and one of his daughters came aboard and found an emaciated woman and the man, who was nearly a scarecrow. They gave them water and what food they had with them and then heard their harrowing story.

CHAPTER THIRTY FIVE

The Castaways

Late Summer, 43 AP

Paul and his young crew brought the man, whose name was Carlos, and the woman, named Marta, aboard their own ship, and fed them and gave them some clothes to replace the tattered ones they wore. Paul learned that the man was about his own age and the woman almost the same. They were what was left of a small group of ten that had fled many years before from the mainland of Ecuador. They had traveled north to an isolated and abandoned village to escape the death and destruction from their homeland. Carlos explained that the plague not only brought death but also war as tribes sought to exterminate each other to gain food and to avoid death themselves, which they blamed on other groups. The people that did not die from illness soon died from warfare, but the plague continued.

Carlos said eventually the plague stopped but the wars did not. He and five others including Marta fled with a little food and water to these islands before four of them soon died. He suspected everyone died from starvation. They were not thinking but just greedy and did nothing to grow food. They just looked out for themselves. But soon their group ran into a problem when they ran out of food. In attempting to land they crashed the bowsprit into a rock. They had been marooned for several months on this island but had difficulty finding enough food and water. They tried to fix the bowsprit and the mast as well which was damaged but became weak and could not complete the work. The others died one by one and they were going to bury the last one that died in the morning.

After a few days Carlos and Marta grew stronger and Paul asked if his crew could take them back to their homeland. They cried out together.

"No. Can we go with you? We have no home. We will work hard as we always have to do our share of work."

Paul agreed.

"We were surprised to find anyone else alive. We have found no one for many, many, years." Then he explained about Tristan and the people there. Carlos helped with the sails as they headed for Baja. He knew the weather and the area from voyages he took long ago. Marta was not very skilled in sailing but did her share of galley duty. She did not speak the language of the Cascadians as well as Carlos but managed well enough.

They sailed night and day for several weeks and found fair skies and balmy weather as they reached Baja. They stopped only briefly and continued on to the spot they called the Bay of Otters and then up the coast to the Strait. Winter was arriving in the Pacific Northwest but they managed to reach the Strait and sailed north up Haro Strait to their harbor with only slight breezes and misty rain. They were home.

At first Carlos and Marta were overwhelmed by the enthusiasm and friendliness of the Cascadians but soon blended in to the community. They even contributed their own songs to the times when they all stood around to music and singing. When they learned Carlos could play the guitar, they never let him put it down.

Carlos and Marta were given a tour of the island by Ben and Che, and noticed all the work the Cascadians had put in to restoring dilapidated and abandoned barns and other buildings. They also noticed the many others that were still in a dilapidated condition, in particular the several churches.

"We noticed the old rundown churches. Do you have any religion in this community?" asked Marta. There was a long pause.

"Some of us privately celebrate certain days," said Ben, "for example, I celebrate Hanukkah and other days. And Sly celebrates Chinese New Year with us."

"And I always celebrate Easter with many of the children," said Che, "and we do explain some of these things in school so that this part of culture is not forgotten."

Carlos was very subdued as he spoke.

"Many such things have been forgotten where we come from."

"But our biggest celebration," added Ben, "is our own version of giving thanks for the establishment of Cascadia. We also call it Thanksgiving and explain the original meaning of Thanksgiving to the children in school as they grow up."

"What is most important to us," concluded Che, "is that we wanted to create a society that is inclusive and not exclusive and where we all look after each other and work together in harmony. To answer your question directly, Marta, although we don't dwell on the past too much, there were some very good things about some of the religions in the past, but there were also some evil, corrupt, and destructive things about religions."

"Many wars were based on religion and hate," added Ben, "there were so many deaths in the name of religion. We may want to remember them but not celebrate them."

"We understand," said Marta, "and we are so thankful to be part of Cascadia and to celebrate with you."

Then winter arrived with a vengeance and the Cascadians hunkered down with good food and warm fires amidst the baaing and bleating and mooing of their many animals, and the music and singing that comforted them throughout the long winter, that consisted mostly of heavy winds and steady snow. One night, Che turned to Adam.

"This winter reminds me of when we decided to take a chance and rescued Sam and Sarah. Have you ever thought there might still be someone out there? If Carlos and Marta have survived, others could also."

"You read my mind. I think we should hookup the radio and transmitter again. I hope I can remember my Morse."

"I'll get the generator and gas," he paused, "what will Grace think?"

Adam laughed. "She'll be furious. Won't that be fun?"

They went to work and soon had the radio receiver working, but he decided to wait and listen for a few days before sending out a CQ. They took turns with the radio by their sides but heard nothing. Adam grew tired of trying to find something so put it in the corner, still on just in case.

Why would anyone be trying to use Morse after all these years? Adam asked himself. The answer he thought was that they wouldn't.

Adam and Che were now grandfathers of more than thirty each and soon would be great grandfathers of many more.

CHAPTER THIRTY SIX

Cascadia Achieved

Spring, 57 AP

Many years had passed since the arrival of Carlos and Marta, and the trip to Tristan. Adam was in his elder years. He and Grace had more than one hundred twenty great grandchildren and soon they would have many, great, great, grandchildren. The community had grown to more than two thousand people and soon they would pass the milestone of twenty-five hundred. The families had spread to other islands searching for more land for grazing and growing crops. Each island had a school for elementary level children and several had middle schools. There was one high school on the main island for many years until the population grew larger and larger and each of the other large islands added a high school.

One winter night when the snow was piling up, and the wind was whistling around the corners of the big farmhouse, Grace turned to Adam and whispered to him.

"Do you remember when we left the barn with the hay all around and I said we would have thirty thousand in our community in one hundred years?"

"I remember."

"We won't be here to see it but I think it will happen."

"I believe you are correct. You know I am embarrassed that I don't know the names of all our great grandchildren?"

"That's alright, Adam. They know you, so when they come up and say 'Hi, Grandpa' believe them and give them a hug. In fact, even if you are not sure whether they are or not, give them a hug anyway." He smiled.

Che and Adam had the radio receiver on most of the time. They had collected many batteries and did not need to use the generator and gas. However, no signals ever came in. Adam once said to Che that he did not know what they would do if they ever heard signals. The range was many hundreds of miles but did not cover much of the land.

The population continued to grow at a steady pace. They had settled over time more than thirty of the islands and had a network of boats to travel between them. The barge that had been fitted with sails did a thriving business ferrying cattle and horses and large loads between the islands. Fruit trees that had been neglected were restored to productivity, many of the buildings were repaired and restored, and many small ships were hauled out and cleaned and fixed. The islands were gradually restored to a thriving archipelago of commerce.

The elder population that had had training in medicine and other scientific disciplines helped set up a curriculum for developing doctors and veterinarians and other special skills. Children were educated in the arts as well as science. That included music, dancing, singing, painting and drawing, and crafts.

One evening when many of the elder generation were sitting around the fire in the main house discussing school activities and classes, Grace spoke up.

"I have been wanting to talk about this for some time but never got around to it. We have a wonderful set of classes in the schools for our children, and also some evening classes for adults as well, but we don't have language classes. These languages will be lost forever if we don't teach the ones we can. I remember some German I learned long ago. I will need help in finding any material left in the library and schools and bookstores. I am getting old and will also need help in teaching." Grace continued after a pause. "What about other languages?"

Che spoke up. "I learned Espanol, that is Spanish, long ago."

Marta spoke quietly. "That is my native language. I will teach it. You and Carlos can help me."

"I learned Japanese and Chinese Mandarin," said Sly, "I was quite young and the languages are difficult but I will try."

Sarah jumped in. "Count me in. I learned French when I was young but I could teach it if I find some books."

Harry said, "I didn't know that, Sarah. I also learned some French when I was young. I'll help teach it with you."

Sam spoke up, "and I learned Italian at about the same time Sarah was learning French. We each spent a year abroad then. When we came back to our community, we had something very special in common. That is how we became good friends."

"I will help you teach it, Sam." Ben said. "I know a little bit of a few languages and would be happy to help."

With the apparent knowledge each of them had of one or more languages, they all became very excited about doing some teaching of these languages. Adam was the last to speak.

"No one has mentioned Russian or Dutch. I learned both. It is a long story. I will tell you some time, but starting tomorrow let us build a curriculum that includes all of the languages you mentioned."

"And don't forget," Grace said, "when you teach language you also teach quite a bit about the culture and traditions. Any books we can find along those lines will help immensely. We can do our best to remember many of the languages and traditions of the past before we pass on. We are the only ones that remember some of that."

And so, the teaching of many of the world's languages was not forgotten in Cascadia. But, sadly, of the hundreds of languages and dialects and cultures and traditions that existed before the Great Pandemic, all but a few were lost.

Meanwhile Cascadia became a vigorous thriving community.

As the population continued to grow at a rapid pace, it also declined now and then. The first sad event was the loss of the venerable Grace. She did not live long enough to see the conclusion of her bold prediction of a community of thirty thousand people but it was well on its way. She was soon followed by the patriarch of the community, Adam. Che lived a few years more, but after he became ill with a strange malady that could not be diagnosed by the fledgling doctors, he passed on his knowledge and caretaking of the radio receiver to his daughter Jasmine and her husband Paul. After Che's passing, they redoubled their efforts to improve the knowledge and research of the growing medical establishment. They never did diagnose the cause of death of Che.

Sly and Sam and Sarah lived on for many years. Sarah had lived for many years on the island of Ben and Harry, but upon the death of Harry she returned to the main island to live out her days. Ben followed Harry into eternity, and soon they were followed by Sly and Sam. Sarah became the matriarch and last of the original settlers of Cascadia to pass on at the age of one hundred. The entire community mourned the passing of this generation.

One day Jasmine was sitting in her rocking chair and she heard a strange sound. She and Paul had left the radio on for a time and she heard: *Dash dot dash dot, dash dash dot dash. CQ.*

She yelled for Paul.

"It's that sound we were to listen for. Isn't that the CQ call?"

He came running in and listened. *Dash dot dash dot, dash dash dot dash. CQ.* "It is," was all he said.

EPILOGUE

The Unknown

Spring, 107 AP

Many years passed and the Cascadia population exceeded thirty thousand just as Grace had predicted. The people had spread across more than forty islands and had developed the land to an historic high level of productivity. They had developed a complex intricate system of communication within the islands and the population spread to the main land. Jasmine and Paul had tried to respond to the increasingly weak signals on the radio but the signals faded and stopped. They were not heard again.

The islands developed their medical knowledge but never did find out the cause of Che's death. But oddly every year or so another case popped up and again they could not figure out the cause. The descendants of Paul and Jasmine, who had both passed on, continued to push for research on this strange malady. They suspected a mutant virion that took a long time to develop and went from generation to generation over a long period of time. But their fledgling science had not yet developed back to a high level of expertise and they could not decipher the illness and cause. It behaved much like some known previous illnesses causing gradual decline in motor nerves until paralysis set in.

And then one day three of the young people sitting on the beach at the south end of the island saw a sail in the distance.

"It's the ketch," yelled Melissa.

"The one like ours that the Tristanians have," added Jessica.

"But look, the mainsail is flapping," said Gloria, looking through the one pair of old binoculars they had, "it's all torn up."

"Let's go tell them."

The three raced to their ponies and galloped as fast as they could to the north end of the island, where they hoped to find the man with the siren in the guardhouse. They did and he sounded the alarm. Dozens of islanders raced to the marina and heard the story of the approaching damaged ship.

"We were attacked on the way into the Strait," said the skipper, a young Tristanian named Norman, "they shot up our mainsail but we managed to escape with the strong winds behind us and they had to tack away because of the big rock at the point."

There were ten on board and they were shaken up. They were also exhausted and hungry, and thirsty.

"We ran into heavy winds just south of here," said a young crew member, "they tried to cut us off but the heavy winds and waves were in our favor. They got close enough to fire rifles but we managed to escape. I think they don't know where to go in here, but they are still out there."

Mark, a great grandson of Paul, took charge.

"Let's go," he ordered, "we have that turret gun still mounted. We can't let bandit ships out there. Let's get them before they go elsewhere."

He hastily assembled a crew of eight. They untied from the dock, pushed off, and headed into Haro Strait. They sailed out into the Strait of Juan de Fuca and into the sea. From what the Tristanians said, they guessed the ship came from the south and headed that way. They saw the ship in the distance along the coast. The crew of the approaching ship made the mistake of sailing toward them thinking they could capture them, but realized too late that they were the prey, and not the other way around. One of the crew named Sally took aim at the waterline of the approaching ship with the turret gun before the other ship knew what was happening, shot a hole in its side and the ship began to sink. They sailed up to it to try and rescue some of the crew but they were too late. It sank quickly with all-hands on deck.

They sailed slowly back to dock and related the end result of their chase. Then the Tristanians told of their journey and the adventures they had.

"We had a wonderful journey with fair weather all the way," said the skipper, "that is, until we encountered that ship. It is strange in that we have never seen another ship or person at Glass Island, or on the high seas, in all these many years since we last saw you."

"We were sure that you and our island were the only ones that survived," said Sally, "I guess we were wrong."

"You aren't the only ones that got it wrong," said Mark.

"There must be some people living south of here," said Sally, "and it doesn't seem that they are too friendly to others on the seas."

"Maybe there are still some descendants from the people that sailed inland on one of the rivers, landed there, and created a community." remarked Mark. "Do you remember the story we heard from our ancestors about the flotilla of boats that came from far away one hundred years ago? There must still be some people alive besides ourselves and the Tristanians."

"I think you may be correct," added Sally.

They went back to the big farmhouse where they still had the radio set up. They turned it on and monitored it day and night for several weeks to see if any CQs came in. None did.

The Tristanians then brought them up-to-date on the progress at Tristan in expanding the growing area in their small community beneath the volcano.

Then Norman dropped his voice and became somber.

"But we have had one ominous event," he said, "the volcano is becoming active and we are being forced to move, at least temporarily, to another island which is much smaller."

"Have you thought about moving here?" Mark asked. There was silence for a couple of minutes.

"How could we possibly do that?" said Norman, "there are three hundred of us."

"There is a way but it would take some planning. We have that one-hundred-fifty-foot schooner that got us up here with the horses and cattle and pigs and goats and sheep, and hay. If we put together a convoy of two or three large ships and sail to Tristan, we could carry back your entire community. I know you also have those many dogs that you love and some livestock, but I think it could be done."

There was a long silence while everyone there listening in to the conversation thought about it.

After some thought, Norman spoke.

"I think the elders might go for it, Mark. What choices do we have for ships?"

Together they went down to the south end of the island to the very big marina and searched for the biggest sailing ship they could find. They found another one about one hundred and fifty feet long, a schooner with two masts. Mark thought it could hold more than half the population of Tristan.

"If we help with two crews, you could sail our two one-hundred-fifty-foot schooners, along with the ketch for good measure. If the population doesn't want to move you can keep these ships. If you leave a couple of Tristanians behind here and we replace them with our eager and willing, and skilled, young folks, then they can help plan the relocation of your community. You can tell them of course that they can go back once the danger of the volcano is over."

"Even better, we will leave a few people on Tristan or Nightingale to sail here when the danger is past. I am only afraid many will stay here."

"They would always be welcome, but I believe 'once a Tristanian, always a Tristanian'."

And that in fact is what did happen. They provisioned the two schooners and the ketch, trained two crews, and prepared a sail plan. As it so happens, the Tristanians were quite skilled in sailing, as well as the Cascadians. The community had developed a series of sailing endeavors, such as solo sails around the main islands, even sailing in rough seas around the large island called Vancouver Island. The young generation was quite skilled, and very eager for this adventure.

While the two schooners were being prepared, the ketch sailed out alone to get an early start since it was a slower ship. They planned to rendezvous at the Galapagos. In late spring, the two schooners sailed out into the Pacific. The original one-hundred-fifty-foot schooner had the famous turret gun mounted on the bow. The two of them sailed at record speed and caught the ketch even before the Galapagos. They stayed only briefly and sailed on, reaching the Horn in late fall just as summer weather was arriving in the south. They cruised directly toward Tristan, stopping only briefly in the Falklands. When the two schooners arrived before the ketch, at first the Tristanians were astounded at the sight, but immediately began asking questions. They wanted to know what happened to the ketch.

Norman told them the whole story of being attacked and making it to Cascadia with shredded mainsail. Then he sat down with the elders and explained the reason for the two schooners. They had been gone for nearly three years and the volcano had shown no sign of being quiet. In fact, the community was just preparing to evacuate Tristan before a very big eruption occurred. The elders were very interested in the plan Norman presented but cautious about the long sea voyage. The younger generation, especially the ones that had sailed to and from Cascadia, were very vocal and urged the community to take up the offer. They finally did.

Each of the large schooners took about one hundred and fifty people and as much food as they could fit in every corner of the schooner. The Tristan dogs were distributed equally between the two schooners, and they were great company. Ten people stayed behind to monitor the volcano with the understanding that they would sail to Cascadia on the ketch when the threat of danger was over. Norman was captain of one schooner and spent much of his time reassuring many of the people that they would like it where they were going. He explained as best he could the open fields and many barns and farmhouses and assured them that they were finding some wonderful places for them to occupy. They stopped briefly in the Falklands and explored the land. Many of the Tristanians had never been to the Falklands and were delighted to see the various birds and animals. They began to relax and enjoy the wonders of this trip. They reached the Horn and encountered some rough weather and high seas. A few people became seasick but soon recovered, and they soon rounded the Horn without too many problems. They sailed up the coast to the north and finally reached the Galapagos. The Tristanians were amazed and astounded at the unique wildlife and many of the students sat and drew pictures of every insect and animal and bird they saw. It was the most amazing science lesson the young Tristanians ever had.

They sailed up the coast to Baja and stopped briefly to watch gray whales and their young in the safety of the bay. The two schooners continued on making terrific time as they sailed up the coast and into the Strait of Juan de Fuca. They sailed directly into the large marina at the south end and docked on the outer docks as the Cascadian population descended upon them. The Tristanians that had stayed behind had arranged for homes and farmhouses and a variety of dwellings within close proximity to each other. The new arrivals were delighted at the wide-open spaces and fields and the many opportunities for farming. The Tristan dogs had a fine time as well. There were so many animals and fields to explore. The Tristanians had arrived in late summer and enjoyed the food of fall, including the many types of squash.

The Cascadians and Tristanians had many celebrations for the next several weeks and then settled in for the long winter weather. One of the major celebrations that continued every year was that of Thanksgiving where every family or groups of families gathered together after harvest to enjoy the bounty from the land and the good company of each other.

Another one of the traditions that continued many times a year was the sharing of wine and cheese and bread in the hilltop retreat which had been steadily expanded over the years. Before he passed on, Adam continued to go there any time there was a new vintage of wine bottled and a sunset to watch. As time went on, and the population grew, it was often used to celebrate marriages and other significant events. Cascadia was a land where people worked hard most of the time but still took time to relax and celebrate their good fortune.

APPENDIX A

THE FOUR FAMILIES

Grace/Adam	**Sly/Che**	**Sam/Ben**	**Sarah/Harry**
Paul	Jasmine	Joe	Shelly
Hannah	Rose	Fawn	Charlie
Iris	Tom	Becky	Jenny

Jasmine/Paul

www.ingramcontent.com/pod-product-compliance
Lightning Source LLC
Chambersburg PA
CBHW032008170626
46807CB00006B/2702